A LESBIAN ROMANCE

by Clare Lydon

First Edition June 2016
Published by Custard Books
Copyright © 2016 Clare Lydon
ISBN: 978-1534626072

Cover Design: Rachel Lawston
Editor: Laura Kingsley
Proof-reader: Isabella Pickering
Typesetting: Adrian McLaughlin

Find out more at: www.clarelydon.co.uk
Follow me on Twitter: @clarelydon
Follow me on Instagram: @clarefic

Also by Clare Lydon

The London Series

London Calling (Book 1)

This London Love (Book 2)

The All I Want Series

All I Want For Christmas (Book 1)

All I Want For Valentine's (Book 2)

All I Want For Spring (Book 3)

All I Want Series Boxset, Books 1-3

Other novels

The Long Weekend

Coming in 2016

All I Want For Summer (July)

All I Want For Autumn (October)

New book in the **London** Series

ACKNOWLEDGEMENTS

First up, thank you to my early readers for their comments and feedback — your encouragement and honesty made this a better book, so thank you! Gratitude also to Hilary Sangster for her advice on emergency response to floods.

Tip of the hat to my editor, Laura Kingsley, for being a cheerleader while also delicately pointing out what needed to be changed; to Izzi for her on-point proofing; to Rachel Lawston for stepping in and providing the bang-up front cover; and to Adrian McLaughlin for his brilliant typesetting and London Book Fair wine drinking.

Love & thanks by the bucketload to my ever-patient wife, who puts up with my writing habit with style & grace. Yvonne, you're my everything. Well, you and Tottenham Hotspurs.

And finally, thanks to you for reading. I write because I have to, but it makes it a way more fun journey sharing my work and getting feedback. I love all of your comments, especially on the days when I doubt myself. You rock. Thanks for reading and supporting.

Connect with me:

Tweet: @clarelydon

Instagram: @clarefic

Email: mail@clarelydon.co.uk

Sign up for my mailing list at: www.clarelydon.co.uk

To everyone who's ever hit rock bottom.
I hope you find your Joy.

Chapter One

It was 4am when Scarlet woke up to the insistent banging on her blue wooden front door. It came in great, thumping thuds, making her eyelids spring open with fear. She rolled over and reached for her lamp. There was shouting now, too.

Scarlet's heart began to gallop as she flung back the duvet, grabbing her red dressing gown which was in a huddle on the floor. Who the heck was at her door at this time in the morning? Whoever it was, they wanted to tell her something urgently, and that thought made her hurry all the more. What if something had happened to her twin brothers, Fred and Clark?

Ice crackled in her veins.

Not after Mum and Dad.

Please don't let anything have happened to Fred or Clark.

The banging got louder.

"Okay, I'm coming!" Scarlet snapped on the hallway light and squinted as her eyes adjusted to the harsh glare. She'd been meaning to get a shade to house the bulb, but that task had got swamped on her never-ending to-do list.

She ran up the stairs as the shouting came into sharp focus in her ears.

"Hello! Police! Open up! Is anybody home?"

Scarlet fumbled with her door keys, goosebumps breaking out all over her skin. It was cold enough to snow in her flat, never mind outside. She took a deep breath, pulled her dressing gown tighter, and opened the door.

On the other side was a police officer, helmet under his arm. He looked about 12. Then again, as she was nearing 40, everyone was beginning to look young to Scarlet these days. His face was creased with concern and when he exhaled, she could see his breath all around him.

"Sorry to wake you, but they're about to open the flood barrier and I'm afraid you've got to get out." He paused, apparently searching for the next words. They eventually came. "Sorry to be the bearer of bad tidings, but the likelihood is your flat will be flooded, so take what you want with you. You've got half an hour."

Scarlet blinked at him. Fear bunched in the back of her throat, quickly followed by confusion and nausea.

What did he just say? *Flat. Get out. Half an hour. Flooded.*

Her brain couldn't compute any of the words, much less put them anywhere near each other. Not when it came to talking about her flat. This was her haven, the only safe place she had left in the whole wide, disastrous world.

What the fuck was he talking about?

"Sorry?" she said, her forehead scrunching as she tried to make sense of the situation. "I don't understand — wouldn't the flood barrier *stop* us being flooded?"

She'd been promised when she bought the flat that it hadn't flooded in over 60 years. "Even though you're right by the river, it's very unlikely," her estate agent had said at the time, handing over his red shiny pen. He'd been especially proud of that fact.

The police officer shrugged, his eyes apologetic, baring his yellow teeth in a pitying smile.

"I'm just the messenger, madam. The barrier's electrics have flooded and they can't risk it getting stuck and flooding more, so the environment agency has ordered it be opened to save as many homes as possible. They're trying to limit the damage to hundreds of homes and businesses, rather than thousands. Unfortunately, yours is one that might be sacrificed. We're preparing everyone for the worst case scenario."

Scarlet shook her head. There must be some mistake. This couldn't be happening. The estate agent had said so. Her body was frozen to the spot, her brain stalled. She'd thought her life couldn't get any worse than the previous weekend, but now this? If there was such a thing as a god, he or she was having a ruddy good laugh.

"So you're telling me I've got to get out now? Right now?" She pointed a finger to the floor.

He nodded again, turning to his right. She could hear one of his colleagues telling the same story to her neighbour, Ben, who had two dogs. He was going to be even less happy than her.

"Afraid so. Take what you want and get out. Get to the community hall and you'll be sorted out from there."

She gripped the doorframe to steady herself. Wooziness swamped her brain. "And there's no chance you could be wrong? You said this was just a possible scenario?"

He winced, then ran a hand over his stubbled chin. Scarlet reckoned there was at least three day's growth. "It's a worst possible scenario, but if they're opening the flood barrier and you're a basement flat by the river, I'd say the likelihood of you being affected is 100 per cent. If I were you, I'd take everything that's valuable or irreplaceable with me now." He paused, looking past her, his eyes kind and sympathetic. "Will you need help with children or animals?"

His words stung, even this early.

"No, it's just me." Scarlet didn't have a child or a pet; it was just her, like always. Unworthy, unloved, all alone. And even when her life had suddenly turned into a disaster movie, it was still being brought up to twist the knife that little bit further.

The police officer nodded, already turning away. "I'll be back in a bit to make sure you've left." His boots squeaked on the pavement as he turned. Then he glanced back. "And I really am sorry about this." He gave her a pained smile and ran along the road.

Scarlet peered out onto the street and held her hands up at her neighbour opposite, a balding man named

Mark who always wore terrible animal-print fleeces. This morning was no exception, and he'd paired the fleece with some scruffy jeans and a bobble hat. In her two years living in the street, she'd spoken to him twice before.

"Can you believe this?" she said, rubbing her eyes.

Mark's movements were in slow motion. "It was the reason I moved here, to escape the flooding. And now they're opening the barrier. It's beyond words." He shook his head and walked back into his flat, kicking his doorframe as he did.

Scarlet stood on her front doorstep and glanced up and down the street, buzzing with flashing lights and shocked utterances as news spread. Every property's front light was blazing, but the air was still, just like it should be. There was no great feeling that something major was about to happen.

But apparently, it was.

She stepped back inside and closed her front door with a heavy thunk. Then she rested her forehead against the cool hallway wall and listened to her elevated heartbeat in her ears.

Ba-doom. Ba-doom. Ba-doom.

Half an hour.

Scarlet stood in her lounge, staring at her possessions. Did she want *any* of them, honestly?

Last weekend, she'd read an article on suicide and idly contemplated what it might be like. Kicking away a stool, hanging herself with a belt, overdosing on pills.

It'd turned out all of them required research, and she didn't have the energy for that, so she'd parked it. Now, she was thinking that had been a mistake. If she was dead, she wouldn't have to deal with this, would she?

She could just stay in the flat and wait for the water. Would anybody miss her? She doubted it. At work, they'd probably put her absence down to the flood; within weeks, she'd be forgotten, just somebody they used to know. And she hadn't been in touch with her brothers for a couple of months. How long until they noticed she was missing?

The only place where her absence would be keenly missed would be on the touchlines at Dulshaw FC, her beloved local football club. Matt and Eamonn would miss her swearing, that was for sure. Both of them were approaching 40 and both still amused a woman could swear just as much as them.

Scarlet grabbed a rucksack from her wardrobe and began putting her essentials in it: wallet, passport, phone, tablet, laptop. She walked through to the living room and stared at her shelves, full of books and CDs, the story of her life. She couldn't take them. The first stab of regret hit her, almost taking her breath away. She closed her eyes and waited for it to pass.

In her old life, in happier times, this had always been one of those questions her mates would ask after a few pints down the pub. Scarlet, Liv, Nancy, and Sarah, three pints in down The Golden Lion; crisps ripped open on the table to share, music blaring, cheeks red, senses dulled.

It'd been their Sunday routine for well over a year: lunch, followed by a few pints and slurred, slanted chats about their future together.

"Your house is about to burn down and you've got minutes to get out. What would you take?"

Liv had always gone for their dog, Alfie, jewellery, and her photos. Nancy always said her record collection — she had been a vinyl nut. Sarah never knew what she'd take, so they'd always surmised that Sarah would be burnt alive trying to make the decision. Scarlet had always been the one who said she'd just walk out and leave, not giving a thought to any of her possessions.

"It's only stuff," she'd said. "It's replaceable. By the time you've collected all your records, you're dead from smoke inhalation."

But now, standing in her lounge on a peaceful January morning, she wasn't so sure. She didn't want to lose her books and CDs. Or her photos. She might not like her life, but did she really want it all washed away, like it had never happened?

Urgency overtook her now. She flung open her largest suitcase and began stuffing it full of things. Clothes, shoes, photos, toiletries. She ran from bathroom to bedroom to lounge like someone on a gameshow, trying to fill a case as quick as they could. If anybody had been watching, they might have thought she was late for a plane and packing everything but the kitchen sink. It was exactly what she wanted to do, only she couldn't.

She ran to the kitchen — where was her mum's favourite Silver Jubilee mug? She couldn't leave without that; it was one of the only things she had left. She opened the cupboard above the kettle, moving mugs aside. Her gaze raked the shelf; she couldn't see it. Scarlet scanned the draining board — not there. She wrenched open the dishwasher and spotted it, still stained with tea from the previous day. She didn't have time to wash it up. She ran through to the bedroom and wrapped the mug in a jumper. Then Scarlet checked her watch — how long did she have? She bargained around ten minutes. Her case was nearly full, and in contrast, her mind was blank.

Real life didn't work like the pub game. Real life had decisions and consequences.

She'd give anything to be back in the pub in happier times.

When she brushed her teeth, tears pricked the back of her eyes. She swallowed down and nearly choked on her toothpaste. She spat, and eyeballed herself in her bathroom mirror she'd been meaning to clean for weeks.

It didn't matter now.

None of it mattered.

In the back of her mind, Scarlet had always known that.

She was proud of her flat, kept it spick and span. It was the one thing that was hers now, after everything. After the split with Liv. After the ripping apart of their carefully woven lives and her delicate heart.

Scarlet took a deep breath, sucking it right into her lungs. One of the last she'd ever take in this flat.

There were the tears again, threatening to bubble up and out of her.

Scarlet blew out a long breath. Yes, she was losing her haven, but she wasn't going to cry. She didn't have time.

She dressed quickly in jeans, T-shirt, and her favourite sweatshirt, then added her trainers and coat. She couldn't bring all her coats. She couldn't bring her mum's fake fur.

The tears sprung up again.

Fuck it.

Scarlet unzipped her case and crammed the fur in, sitting back on top of it to make sure it closed. It did. She was pretty sure a fur coat wasn't going to be needed in a flood, but it was one of the only things she'd taken from her parents' house after they'd died. That, and their crockery, but she wasn't about to start packing that up. She had the mug; that would have to suffice.

Then her eyes fell on her guitar. Should she leave it behind? Scarlet stood over it, gazing at the life it used to represent: a better, more in-tune life. She ran her finger through the layer of dust coating its surface. She couldn't leave it, even if she hadn't picked it up in over a year. Scarlet got on a chair and grabbed its case from the top of her wardrobe, laying the guitar down carefully and snapping the case shut.

Maybe the flood wouldn't be as bad as they were predicting. Then again, basement flats and water were the best of friends. She should anticipate the worst, she knew that. But the thought of never seeing her clock again that she'd bought in the flea market in Lisbon? But she'd also bought it with Liv. On second thoughts, maybe it was a blessing.

A banging on her door interrupted her thoughts. Scarlet wasn't startled this time.

She went from room to room, checking if she'd left anything important. It didn't feel any different than all those times she'd done the same thing when she was going away for a few days, checking she'd switched off lights, the oven, the iron. It didn't feel different at all.

But it was. Who knew what she'd come back to? She had no idea at all.

Her feet were suddenly dead weights, not wanting to move. Her television stood quietly, as it always did, no idea what was about to happen; her print on the wall, a shot of the surrounding hills, a shot she was proud of and had blown up.

She could get it done again.

She checked her bedroom. She'd tried to make it her sanctuary, but it hadn't quite worked, she'd just never been in the right frame of mind.

Her bathroom, with its double shower and mosaic tiles — of all the things in her flat, this was the room she loved the most. Her boutique hotel shower. She'd modelled it on one she remembered from a visit to Milan, back in the day. She exhaled.

Maybe it would survive.

Maybe.

There was more banging and shouting. Scarlet grabbed her suitcase, backpack, and guitar, then thudded slowly up her staircase, every step sealing her flat's doom. At the front door, she turned and cast a glance backwards. Her eggshell-blue hallway. Her old-fashioned wooden hat stand. Her metal light fitting she'd looked everywhere for. She didn't want to leave, but she had to.

When she opened the door, the police officer was there again, looking anxiously over his shoulder, then back to Scarlet.

"You ready?" he asked. "We've got a van if you want to put a suitcase in it. We'll drop the lot at the community hall. Anything else, you can carry."

Scarlet stared past his shoulder and saw a white transit van with doors open, and her neighbours filling it with suitcases in the chilled darkness. It was eerily silent, save for the bang of luggage and the slap of footsteps. Nobody was saying a word. Because really, what could you say? Scarlet nodded her head and handed him her case.

"That the lot?" said the PC. His tone and volume went up at the end. Scarlet got the feeling he'd asked that question a few times this morning.

She nodded again. "Yep." Her life, her claimed possessions, all in one hard black suitcase, subtle and unassuming. Much like Scarlet.

"Okay," he replied. "I need to see you're out, too. We

can't have anybody drowning." The policeman gave her a smile to go with his last comment.

Scarlet wasn't in the mood for humour. She took a deep breath, checked her pocket for her keys, shifted her rucksack up on her shoulder; then with a leaden heart, she picked up her guitar and pulled her front door shut with a final slam.

Bang.

Chapter Two

Scarlet had only ever been inside the community hall twice before. First, to vote in the general election, but she'd ended up on the losing side in that contest. Second, to vote in the local elections — on that occasion, she'd been a winner. The Labour party had won, and the council leader was a lovely guy named George who Scarlet had a lot of time for. What's more, the council had then voted in a female mayor, their youngest ever — younger than Scarlet, under 40. There had been much fanfare in the local papers about it: Joy Hudson was recently divorced, and not bad looking either, if you liked the blonde bombshell type. Scarlet normally went for brunettes.

However, even the mayor hadn't been seeing her promises through of late, reneging on her support for the local division two football team, Dulshaw FC, against some property developers who wanted to come in and bulldoze the ground to build yet more flats in a few years' time. The one thing Scarlet held dear in her life was her love for Dulshaw FC. She didn't get out much anymore with family or friends, but she went to watch Dulshaw every home game, rain or shine. Without the football team, sometimes she wasn't sure what there was to live for.

The community hall's walls were an off-yellow colour, like the surface of a curdled pint of milk. There were electric heaters dotted around in an attempt to throw out warmth, but they were also filling the air with a stench of burnt hair, mingled with hot bodies and school hall.

It was the smell that hit Scarlet first, and she wrinkled her nose as her stomach churned.

A row of camp beds had been erected down one side of the hall, and parents were tucking children into them, in the vain hope they might fall asleep. Scarlet didn't think there was much chance as the noise level was at fever pitch, with space and supplies being allocated, as well as strip lights blaring overhead. Elsewhere, adults and children milled about, dazed looks on their faces at what had just happened.

It was a surreal feeling knowing this could be it. That everything was gone. Or if she looked at it another way, a clean slate and the chance to start afresh. But she'd tried that once before and look how that had turned out. A blank page appealed to her on one level, but absolutely terrified her on another.

"You here on your own?" A woman appeared at Scarlet's side, all pink cheeks and frizzy hair that hadn't seen conditioner in quite a long time. When she smiled, her teeth were slanted at an array of angles.

Scarlet nodded. "Just me, my guitar, and my rucksack."

She jerked a thumb to her shoulder. In less than two hours, two strangers had verified the fact that yes, she was completely alone.

The woman nodded far too enthusiastically. "Right you are," she said. "You can give us a song later when we might all need cheering up. But nothing about water."

Scarlet's stomach churned. "Land-themed songs only, I promise."

The woman held out her hand. "I'm Sue. Grab a space where you can; there are some singles over there in the corner. If you can find a blanket, grab it."

Scarlet glanced over to the top left-hand corner of the hall where some men and women were sat, chatting.

A singles corner. She didn't think she'd ever heard a more depressing phrase. It might as well have been called 'the corner of doom', with them all wearing loser hats and one of them ringing a bell.

The woman winced in her direction. "Families are getting the beds, I'm afraid. But there's tea, coffee, and sandwiches in the kitchen area. And once you've got a drink, go and see Simon over by the far wall to register you're here."

Scarlet followed the line of Sue's arm to a kitchen on the right-hand side, ably staffed by the sort of women who always seemed to staff such efforts: stout, cardiganned, stoic. Even from the other side of the room, Scarlet was irritated by their irrational cheerfulness. If Scarlet was ever invited to appear on *Mastermind*, her specialist subject would have to be misanthropy.

By process of elimination, the unfortunate man with a clipboard and a queue of impatient people must have been Simon. He had a beard and was wearing one of those hessian jumpers that probably seemed like a good idea when he'd bought it on his travels, but now, back home in the north of England, just made him look like a chump.

"Got it," Scarlet said, but Sue was already turning away, greeting the next unfortunate through the door who Scarlet recognised from her local gym. Not that she was a regular there much anymore, not since her membership had lapsed and she'd given up on life.

Scarlet stepped over a pile of suitcases on the floor in front of her and made her way down the impromptu pathway that was already established, walled in place by shoes, bulging bags for life, coats, and tables. At the kitchen, she accepted a cup of tepid black coffee from an overly smiley woman whose hair didn't move when she turned her head. She'd clearly had more notice about the evacuation than Scarlet, time to administer great gales of hairspray.

Scarlet stepped to one side before the woman had time to strike up a conversation with her. She wasn't in the mood to deal with small talk this morning, not when her world had just been turned upside down.

Two women to Scarlet's left were in deep conversation, so she edged closer. Scarlet had always been nosy, and she could do with something to take her mind off her current situation.

"The mayor's house?" The woman who spoke had deep brown skin and a winning smile.

Her friend, who in stark contrast was as white as a ghost, nodded. "Just now. The mayor's opened her house up and someone just came in and selected people to go there. Daniel was one of them."

The first woman clicked her tongue and shook her head. "Typical. We get to spend the night on the floor of the community hall, while Daniel gets to live it up in the lap of luxury. That boy was born with the golden ticket, I tell you." The woman shook her head again.

Scarlet turned back to the room, processing the information in her head. She glanced at the 'singles' corner, already full, with no spare blankets on show.

The noise and the lights of the hall were jarring her brain already.

Some people had gone to the mayor's house. She'd met the mayor a couple of times at the football, when she'd promised to try her best to lean on the council about the ground development. Most importantly, Scarlet worked for the local council, so she knew where the mayor lived. A ten-minute walk away. Not far at all. What if Scarlet went to the mayor's house now and pretended she'd been sent there? Perhaps she'd take her in, too?

It took Scarlet precisely 30 seconds to make up her mind. She took a final gulp of her coffee, then strode back down the makeshift pathway, past Sue and her clipboard and out into the freezing early morning darkness, the streets humming with life. Right out of the community hall, left up Culverdale Avenue, then walk to the top of the hill. There was no danger the mayor's house was going to be flooded. Scarlet hitched her bag up her shoulder, gripped her guitar, and began the journey.

She was halfway there when she began to wonder if this was such a good plan. What if the mayor didn't recognise her? What if nobody answered? Should she have stayed and claimed her spot on the dusty community hall floor? Would Sue even let her back in? She couldn't dwell on these questions, though. Her decision was made when she left the hall.

Even though it was perilously cold, Scarlet didn't feel it. She was running on adrenaline, on pure nervous energy. She took the final steps in galloping strides, wanting to get inside before the flooding began. Would she even know when that was? One thing was for sure: she didn't want to be on the street, alone, to find out.

Scarlet arrived at the front door and knocked four times. Her knock was confident, sure-footed. It said she'd been sent here, no question. She tried to ignore the sweat dripping down her back, the heat at the base of her neck. She rubbed her fingers inside her gloves.

Nobody came.

She was just about to knock again when the door opened. It was the mayor herself; for some reason, Scarlet hadn't been expecting her to answer.

And now that she had, Scarlet was stumped. She just

stood on the doorstep, flicking through her vocabulary for appropriate words to say. She couldn't locate any at all.

The mayor glanced down at Scarlet's guitar, then back up at her face. She raised one eyebrow, then broke into a grin.

"Maria Von Trapp on my doorstep at 5am — this day just gets more surreal. You're missing the wide-brimmed hat, mind." The mayor stood back. "Come in, please." She beckoned Scarlet across the threshold with her hand, as if she was directing traffic. "But I must warn you, I'm not a fan of *The Sound of Music*."

"Me neither, so you're safe there," Scarlet replied as she stepped inside the hallway.

She'd cleared the first barrier; her plan was going to work. Relief soaked through her. If this was going to be one of the worst nights of her life, at least she was going to spend it somewhere warm and inviting. Scarlet's feet sunk into plush grey carpet, and the decor was rich olive green, as befitted a Victorian hallway. Abstract fine art prints draped the walls and the curtains were thick and lined. The hallway told Scarlet this was a home with similar taste to her own. She immediately felt at ease, even though she knew she should be seething at the mayor for her treatment of the town's football club. Still, that was a topic for another day.

"Baltic out there, isn't it?" the mayor added. "I thought we had the lot already, but you were clearly a straggler." Her face was warm, her teeth straight and white.

Scarlet had noticed that about her when they'd met at the football. Scarlet's own front teeth had been knocked out playing hockey at university and the replacements glowed neon under ultra-violet light. The mayor's teeth looked permanent, real.

She was far more casual than Scarlet had ever seen her before, too. Off-duty and in her own home, the mayor wore well-fitted jeans and a powder blue top that brought out her piercing blue eyes. Despite the early hour, the mayor was well put together.

"Yes, I was a bit late leaving," Scarlet said. "I ran as fast as I could."

The mayor nodded. "With a guitar, too? Well done. Although I've already allocated the spare bedrooms, but you're welcome to take the office sofabed." She paused. "First off, let me take your coat."

Scarlet put down her rucksack and guitar, then shrugged off her jacket, smoothing down her sweatshirt as she did.

"Sounds great," she replied. "Better than my flat, which will be a soggy mess when I get back, so the police told me."

The mayor glanced over her shoulder as she hung Scarlet's jacket on top of a pile of others. "Terrible shame, but it had to be done. It was either that, or flood many more. The environment agency had no choice after the pumping station was flooded and there was a risk of electrical failure." She put a hand on her hip. "Still, it doesn't make it any better for those affected. I've only just got back myself — we all had to get home before they activated their plans." She sighed. "It feels like we're in a disaster film, doesn't it?"

"Only it's very real," Scarlet replied, fixing the mayor with her gaze. "Horribly, life-changingly real."

The mayor nodded. "I know." She stepped forward, and then fixed Scarlet with a puzzled stare. "I've met you before, haven't I?" She paused. "Do you work for the council?"

Scarlet nodded. "I do, but we've met up at Dulshaw FC, too. I'm a big supporter there."

At the mention of the football ground, the mayor dipped her head. "Right," she mumbled, turning on her heel in the square hallway. "So you probably don't think very highly of me right now, am I right?"

Scarlet blushed, remembering her thoughts from earlier. If anything, the mayor was possibly her *favourite* person right at this second. "I think you're pretty okay, taking me in like this. Let's not worry about the football — it's not high on my list of priorities tonight."

The mayor looked Scarlet directly in the eye, then gave her a nod. "Probably best. But just know, I'm on your side still — it's the rest of the council that needs convincing." She paused. "Do you want to come through to the kitchen for a drink? The others are in there now, I can introduce you."

"Love to," Scarlet replied.

* * *

The others turned out to be the aforementioned, golden-ticketed Daniel and his boyfriend Harry, along with Joe and Daisy, a young couple who'd only owned their flat for three months on the next street over from Scarlet.

"Our sofa was only delivered last week," Daisy said, her face revealing she didn't quite believe she was even uttering that sentence. But she was.

After a cup of tea and biscuits, they all trooped off to their respective bedrooms, leaving Scarlet and the mayor alone. After a few seconds of silence, the mayor walked around the breakfast bar and nodded her head one way to Scarlet.

"You want me to show you to the office and get your bed made up?" she said, before pausing. "Or if you fancy going through to the lounge, we could have a drink first. Something stronger than tea? I think we might have earned it tonight."

Scarlet smiled a grim smile. "Something stronger than tea sounds good."

The mayor's house wasn't as big as Scarlet had envisioned, the lounge situated towards the back, leading off from the square downstairs hallway. The decor was modern, neutral, and although there were a few homely touches, there weren't as many as Scarlet might have imagined for someone who'd lived in the area all her life. Scarlet, at least, had an excuse — all the personal touches had been ripped from her life and she'd had to start again from scratch.

Now, it looked like she'd be doing it all over again.

The lounge had two large cream sofas facing each other, with the television cleverly concealed on a shelf in front of a dark wall panel. The rest of the walls were painted white and there was a cream rug thrown on the polished floorboards in front of a log burner. It looked like a show home, not one that was lived in much. Scarlet was almost afraid to sit down, for fear of making a mark.

"Please," the mayor said, indicating the first sofa. "And my name's Joy, just in case you were wondering. You don't have to call me mayor."

Scarlet had known, but had just avoided addressing her directly until now. "Thanks, Joy," she said, sitting down. Her body sunk into the plump cushions and she relaxed for the first time since she'd been woken up so abruptly. Scarlet sighed, allowing her muscles to relax, her spirit to unclench. Then she checked her watch. It was still before 6am. Only two hours since she'd been woken up, but it felt like she'd been up for hours, like this was her new reality.

"Single malt?" Joy's voice came from behind her, along with a slight squeak as something was opened.

Scarlet turned her head to see Joy standing beside a teak sideboard, the middle of which was now opened up to reveal a cocktail cabinet, complete with a lit, mirrored interior. She'd only ever seen such things in films, and got up to stand beside it.

"Single malt would be lovely," Scarlet said, her fingers

caressing the smooth curves of the cabinet door. "This is ace — like something from a Bond film."

"I can make you a dirty martini if you'd prefer: shaken, not stirred?" Joy said, a smile playing around her lips.

Scarlet shook her head, returning Joy's smile. "Single malt's fine."

Joy took a crystal tumbler from the shelf inside the cabinet, poured Scarlet a generous measure, and handed it to her.

Scarlet mumbled her thanks and retook her seat on the sofa. It wasn't lost on her how normal this situation felt, despite it being anything but. She was sat on the mayor's sofa drinking whisky, her whole life on hold, waiting to be drowned.

Joy took a seat on the opposite sofa, raising her glass to Scarlet. "Cheers," she said. "Here's to making the best of a horrible night."

Scarlet grimaced and raised her glass to Joy. "Cheers." She took a sip of the golden liquid, rolling it around her mouth before letting it slip down her throat. Its searing heat scorched its way down her system, landing in her empty stomach and lighting a fire there. She settled back again on Joy's sofa and allowed herself to be soothed by it, comforted.

They sat in silence for a few moments, sipping their drinks and mulling over the situation. This wasn't where Scarlet had expected to be this morning.

"Did you have plans for today?"

Scarlet blinked. What day was it? Saturday. "I normally go to the football." She paused. "Other than that, nothing much."

Her Saturday routine was football with Eamonn and Matt. It wasn't the best social life in the world, but it was the day she most looked forward to out of the whole week. Saturdays out of the football season were just as bleak as Sundays, if not bleaker because Scarlet knew what she was missing. And Sundays were the worst days ever. At least when she was at work, she was kept busy. For Scarlet, free time was the enemy, not to be trusted. The hours stretched into days, and the days went on forever.

A pained look crossed Joy's face. "Ah yes, the football. You know, when all this is done, we can chat. The issues are political when it comes to the ground, which I'm sure you've read about."

Scarlet nodded. "I have." The developers who wanted to build on the club's site had fingers in many pies at the council, hence the push-back on their plans hadn't been as swift or categoric as the fans had hoped for, despite Joy's support.

"But I'm still working on bending some ears, believe me," Joy added.

There was sincerity in her face, which Scarlet appreciated.

"What about your weekend plans?" Scarlet asked.

At that, Joy let out an enormous sigh. "Well, the office of mayor is only held for a year, so you have to be prepared to be pretty full-on for those 12 months," she said. "Weekends I normally have some engagements to attend, be it an opening, a mayoral visit, or an appearance somewhere."

"So you're not in charge of the response to the flood, I assume, seeing as you're sitting here?"

Joy shook her head. "The police, council leader, and emergency planners take care of all that — I'm the civic head, the public figure for the town. I oversee the council, but I'm not on any political side, although I can speak up on certain issues if I think it's right. My job is to turn up at events, unveil new wings of libraries, open school fairs. I thought it would be time-consuming, but you've no idea until you do it — the hours can really add up. My life hasn't been my own for the past nine months, and with a full-time life coaching business to run, too, it doesn't leave much time to spare. That's the only reason it's worked, because I run my own business and can be flexible." She smiled. "But I'm *not* complaining. And I will be putting in extra time this week to help out with stuff where I can."

"I'm drinking with a local celebrity," Scarlet said, taking another sip of her drink.

"You are," Joy laughed. "But give it three months and I'll be back to being a regular councillor again. When I explained the role to my gran, she told me it sounded like I was the town's bodyguard for a year, and she wasn't far off." Joy smiled. "It's been great, wearing the robes and doing all of the stuff, but I'll be glad to hand it all back, too. I don't get to sit on this couch half as much as I'd like."

"It's very kind of you to take us in tonight, too. I doubt the rest of the council are doing the same."

Joy waved her comment away, shaking her head. "I'm happy to help. I've got the room, so if people are homeless, it's stupid not to. I'm going to put an appeal out to the rest of the community to take people in, too. There are enough spare rooms around here for that to happen, nobody needs to be sleeping on the floor of the community hall. Times like this, everybody needs to pull together."

"Let's hope they come through for you."

If Scarlet had seen that appeal, she wouldn't have offered her spare room, which was shameful. If Joy had ignored it, she'd still be in the community hall. Would many people open up their homes? She doubted it. In Scarlet's world, people looked out for themselves and nobody else.

The mayor smiled at Scarlet, Joy's eyes caressing her. "They will. People are generally very giving. Everybody was checking on the old folks' home earlier, which I was thankful for. My gran lives there. Luckily, they're unaffected. I would hate to think of her and her friends coping with a flood. That really would be an all-out emergency."

"I hadn't thought of that," Scarlet replied. "At least everyone on my street could evacuate easily enough." She paused. "Has your gran lived there long?"

"Five years. It's a great place — I go and see her every week. Old folks' homes get a bad press, but that one is just great — fab facilities and staff. And I'm so glad they're up high because they've just built an amazing social hall there, too. It'd be a crying shame if that was ruined."

Scarlet nodded, running her finger around the rim of her whisky glass. Scarlet used to own crystal tumblers, too, but she'd lost them in the divorce, like most things. She really should have fought harder, but it turned out Liv was better at arguing than Scarlet, and in the end, she'd just walked away. She'd treated herself to two more tumblers this year, but had only ever had the need for one. Soon, they'd be floating down a nearby street.

"It's just you here, I take it?" Scarlet had no idea if Joy had a partner, but she guessed not. Otherwise, he'd probably be here, drinking whisky with them.

Joy stopped momentarily, before she nodded. "Yes, just me. Now Steve's gone, just me."

* * *

Why had that come out of her mouth? Three sips of whisky and Joy was blurting out Steve's name. She wasn't even married to him anymore, for goodness sake, and here she was, mentioning him like he was still a major part of her life.

Scarlet's face didn't change much. "Who's Steve?"

Joy just assumed everyone knew. "My ex-husband," she said, her voice coming out clearer than she imagined.

She sounded strong, in control. She raised an eyebrow at Scarlet. "You look surprised. I thought the subject of my love life was all over town. The local paper seems to slip it into every article they can — 'newly single mayor, Joy Hudson'." She put the last bit in air quotes and rolled her eyes.

Scarlet shrugged. "I don't get out much," she replied. "All I knew was you were divorced; I didn't know his name."

Scarlet didn't know the half of it, Joy thought. Like the real reason Joy had left her husband after ten years of marriage. The real reason she'd taken on the mayoral role; to fill up her life, to stop her fretting about how to be who she truly was. But Joy had a feeling that if Scarlet did know, she wouldn't be judgmental. No, Joy was pretty sure of that.

In the past year or so, Joy had still only shared the real reason she'd broken up her marriage with her ex and her gran. She knew it was stupid, but Joy was reticent to share it with the rest of the world. Did it really affect them and was it their business? No, it was not. Joy would share it when she was good and ready, and she didn't see that happening any time soon.

"So yes, just me here, and I quite like it. I'd never lived on my own before I left Steve, and nobody tells you how liberating it is. They just go on about being lonely and depressed, but honestly, I've never felt freer. I can do what I want, leave things where I want, and be who I want.

I should have done it years ago, instead of rushing into a marriage." Joy paused, assessing Scarlet. She swirled the whisky round her glass, and took a sip, the acrid smell hitting her nostrils before the liquid itself, making her recoil. "How about you? I assume you're not married?"

Scarlet sat up, clearing her throat. "Do I have that look about me?"

Joy laughed gently. "I just mean, you're here on your own, so I assume you don't have a partner waiting in the wings."

"You assume right; I'm divorced, too. I'm 40 in a couple of months, single, and now homeless." Scarlet let out a strangled laugh. "Not much of a catch, am I?"

Joy regarded Scarlet — she recognised a lost soul when she saw one. She'd been that her entire life, never quite cottoning on to the fact she was looking in the wrong place. It was only in the past year since she'd got her own home that she'd truly come into her own, claiming her life back while being her real self. Well, nearly all of her real self. As near as she dared at the moment. As soon as Joy's mayoral duties were over, she planned to come out to her family, friends, and the wider world, but for now, it could wait.

"I wouldn't say that," Joy replied. "You've got your health and you've got a glass of whisky in your hand, so the world isn't such a terrible place, now is it?" Joy jumped up. "Top up?"

Scarlet nodded. "Yes, please."

Joy went to take her glass from her. When she did, their fingers touched for a second and a frisson ran up Joy's hand and arm. The contact made her stop in her tracks and jolt a little.

Scarlet, looking past Joy, didn't seem to notice.

Joy cleared her throat and walked over to the drinks cabinet, biting her lip as she eased off the cork on the single malt — a Christmas present from Steve — and poured two fingers into each glass. The warmth inside her now wasn't just coming from drink, but she was trying ignore that fact. She smiled nervously at Scarlet as she handed her glass back, then sat back down on her sofa, happy for the space between them. Just because she was sat in the same room as an attractive woman didn't mean she had to come undone, now did it? Because Scarlet was an attractive woman, and Joy couldn't deny it: she was long and lean, with dark hair, polished like an onyx stone. Joy was intrigued — she wanted to get to know her visitor better.

When she glanced over at Scarlet, her visitor had a panicked look in her eye.

"I wonder how my flat's doing?" Scarlet's features were set to grim.

Joy shook her head. She'd hate to be in Scarlet's shoes, and she wanted to do as much as she could for her guest.

"I've no idea how you must be feeling," she said. "It's just awful. For you, for the whole town." She paused. "But like I said, I'm sure it'll bring everyone together, bring out the community spirit."

Scarlet harrumphed. "I'm not really one for community spirit — I haven't seen much evidence of it. The world isn't full of peace and love where I live."

"I think you'll be surprised."

Scarlet shrugged again and sipped her whisky. "We'll see." She paused, readjusting her body on her sofa. "Do you know if the flood's happened yet?" Scarlet shook her head. "And how odd is that sentence to say? It's so weird, like it's an organised disaster."

Joy put down her whisky. "It kind of is. Let me go and get my phone — there was a hashtag to follow on Twitter."

Joy came back a few moments later, jabbing her phone with her thumb. She clicked on a video, and the unmistakable sound of rushing water and shouting filled the air.

Joy's face dropped. She hesitated, took a sharp intake of breath, then gasped. "Shit." Joy couldn't fathom what she was seeing. She desperately wanted to protect Scarlet from it, but that was impossible. She couldn't protect her from it, no matter how hard she tried.

Scarlet put her drink on the floor and sprang up to stand beside Joy. "What is it?"

Joy glanced up and winced, before handing the phone to Scarlet.

When she saw the footage, Scarlet's face drained of colour, like the life was slowly seeping out of her.

Joy had just watched the video clip playing under the #dulshawflood newsfeed; she could hear the rushing water again, as if it was gushing right out of her phone. Looking at Scarlet watching it now felt like an intrusion, almost too personal — like Joy should look away.

"Oh my god," Scarlet said. But she didn't tear her eyes away from the phone. "My entire flat's under water." She paused. "Everything I own is gone." Beat. "*Every single thing.*"

Joy didn't know what to say. The flood was real now; 100 per cent real, and she had one of the victims in her lounge. All the platitudes of earlier had left her mind, because seeing it happen and knowing it was right on your doorstep were two completely different things. Joy's stomach was churning watching Scarlet's reaction, and she couldn't bear it.

Perhaps Scarlet was right and the world *was* a terrible place.

If everything Joy owned was currently under water, she knew she might feel that way.

* * *

Scarlet put a hand out, not quite sure of her bearings after what she'd just seen. She wasn't sure how it was possible her whole life had simply been washed away, but it had. Her hand eventually hit the sofa and she collapsed onto it, her body giving way, knowing there was nothing left to fight for. When she put her hand to her cheek, it was wet.

She was crying, and Scarlet *never* cried. She hadn't cried when Liv had left her; rather, she'd clicked into auto-pilot, shuffling from day to day, existing rather than living. Friends had visited, encouraged her to let it all out, but she'd been firm. She'd made a pact with herself that Liv wasn't going to destroy her, and that's what had happened. Liv hadn't won.

Scarlet hadn't cried when her dad died, either. He'd been ill for a while, even though he was taken far too soon, aged only 50. Her brothers had cried; her mum had been distraught. Scarlet had been the rock, the glue that held the family together. She hadn't cried. And she certainly hadn't cried when the glued-together family became unstuck years later after her mum died. What was the point? Would it get her anywhere, would it help her predicament?

So she'd held firm. Solid. Everyone always described Scarlet in those terms. Scarlet was a rock. She was dependable, would never dissolve in a crisis; Scarlet was a project manager, a problem-solver, unflappable.

Yet these were her tears, falling down her demi-curved cheeks, bringing hot, salty grief into her mouth. Because Scarlet had felt grief before — through death, through the loss of her relationship — she was well aware of the feeling. She knew what it felt like to drag a slug-covered wheelie bin into the street, alone, week after week; what it felt like to stand in front of the M&S meal-for-one stand and want to break down and sob. She knew what it felt like to look in the mirror and not even recognise your own reflection.

And this was grief. She'd just lost her entire life, washed away in the blink of an eye. Her whole body stuttered as that thought crashed over her brain, making every wire in her body short-circuit.

She had nowhere to go. She couldn't style this one out or bluff her way through, pretending to be tough. She was homeless and lifeless.

Yes, *lifeless.*

Scarlet didn't think she'd ever come up with a term quite so apt. Having become a self-styled hermit, her life took place within the four walls of her flat. And now, that option had been ripped from her hands. She wasn't sure why she'd felt so breezy, so casual about it all when she'd walked out. Perhaps, somewhere deep down, it had all seemed unreal, like they were bluffing.

Why would they open the flood defences? Surely that was the antithesis of what they were there for? But they had, and the water had arrived. Thick and sludge-like, swamping her life, making her look away.

Scarlet stuck out her tongue to catch the tears that were falling freely now. She was vaguely aware of some movement out of the corner of her eye, and then some tissues were being thrust under her nose. She took one gratefully and blew.

She cast her gaze downwards; she was still holding the phone, and the clip was playing, over and over again. She couldn't tear her eyes away. The moment when the river rushed down her street had been captured perfectly by someone up high. One minute, it was a normal street in the morning twilight, groggy and just wiping the sleep from its eyes. And then, all of a sudden, the harsh stampede of muddy brown water, rushing, slapping, slithering like a monster in a horror film. Within seconds, there was two or three feet of water cascading through her neighbourhood, whooping and screaming for all she knew, breezing into homes unwanted, like a cavalier force.

Her basement flat never stood a chance.

Scarlet couldn't watch anymore — she had to look away. She put the phone down on the sofa and buried her head in her hands. Her body was convulsing now, and her tears had turned to sobs. Pain was seeping out of every orifice she possessed, owning her completely. And somehow, even though she was sitting on a stranger's couch in an unfamiliar home, Scarlet didn't care.

She didn't have a reputation to uphold here: Joy hardly knew her. Joy didn't know this wasn't the normal Scarlet. And given the situation, Joy wasn't going to judge her. Scarlet was able to act and do as she pleased, and right now, she had no control at all over what that might be.

Right now, those actions were wet and wild.

* * *

Joy moved the offending phone, sat beside Scarlet, and took her in her arms. Yes, it had seemed like it would be a crass move a few minutes ago, but now, there was no other option — this situation screamed for barriers to be broken down. Scarlet had just watched her entire home being flooded, watched everything she worked hard for being washed away. Joy couldn't imagine how she was feeling. But she could see the physicality of it, the great, heaving sobs coming from her guest's body. To ignore that, to walk away, would have been plain mean.

Joy wasn't sure how Scarlet would respond. However, she gave in right away, collapsing into Joy's arms with more, uncontrollable sobbing. Joy got the feeling this wasn't normal behaviour for Scarlet, but she didn't blame her. These were hardly typical circumstances.

Joy was studiously ignoring how her body lit up with Scarlet in her arms.

After a few minutes and at least five more tissues, Scarlet stopped sobbing and was breathing normally. Her dark hair crowded her face, like it was trying to soothe her, reassure her.

Joy gave her another clean tissue.

Scarlet took it and blew her nose. "It's amazing how much snot there is, isn't it?"

"It is," Joy replied, giving Scarlet a sympathetic smile. "I'm really sorry about your flat." Adrenaline was pumping round Joy's body from everything that had happened, so she could only imagine what Scarlet was feeling. Out of her depth. Confused. Scared. Alone. But Joy wanted to make her feel like she wasn't alone. Because she wasn't; Joy was there for her and the community was there for her, no matter if Scarlet believed it or not.

Joy passed Scarlet her whisky, the amber liquid glinting in the light. Their fingers touched, and there it was again, hot and bright. *Boom!* A frisson right up Joy's arm. Joy steadied herself on the sofa, taking great, gulping breaths of air.

Scarlet was still beautifully unaware. And why wouldn't she be? She had bigger issues to consider.

Instead, Scarlet gulped whisky. One gulp, two gulps, three. The whole glass, all two fingers, down in one. She winced as it went down, before flopping back on the sofa, defeated.

"You want another?" Joy asked, indicating her empty glass. Scarlet's hands were smooth and delicate, at odds with her persona.

Scarlet shook her head. "Maybe in a minute." She exhaled heavily. "I just feel so fucking helpless, you know?" She paused, her eyes scanning the room. "I'm normally the one who solves things, clears up messes." She stopped. "Actually, more than that, I stop them happening in the first place. How did it even get to this stage? That's what I don't understand. Why were the basement flats dug out and sold when there was a chance this could happen?"

Scarlet sat forward and slammed her tumbler down, the sound of crystal on the glass-topped table shattering the air. She jumped, staring at the table. She cringed. "Shit, sorry. I haven't smashed it, have I?"

Joy sat forward beside her, picking up Scarlet's tumbler and shaking her head.

"It's fine, it always sounds worse than it is," she said, running a hand over the tabletop. "I keep meaning to get coasters, but I keep forgetting. I got it when I moved in here — my first act as a single person. Steve never wanted a glass-topped table." But Joy had fallen in love on first sight — glass tables were cool.

"I've got a glass coffee table, too." Scarlet paused. "*Had*. It's probably halfway to Manchester by now." Her voice cracked as she said the final words, and then she laughed. "It's just too fucking surreal, isn't it?"

Joy nodded; it really was, and there was nothing she could say to make it any less so. The flood had been eminently avoidable if the authorities had put the money in to keep the barrier maintained. But they hadn't; it'd failed, and this was the result.

"Yesterday, I got up and went to work, had a ridiculous meeting where I got into an argument with a guy from accounts about my budget for the month and how I should spend it. The discrepancy was less than £100, but he just wouldn't let it go. It wound me up all day, but last night, even though I was angry and upset, I didn't want to have a whisky in my lovely crystal glasses when I got home, because it's January, we're just coming off Christmas and I was trying to be good."

"Dry January is over-rated," Joy replied.

Scarlet snorted. "I agree. I should have had that whisky, shouldn't I? I should have used my lovely glasses, because I'm never going to see them again." She stared at her hands, twisting them one way, and then the other. "And yes, I know they're just things and they can be replaced, but it makes you wonder why we get things in the first place, when things can so easily be taken away, or stolen, or destroyed." She exhaled again. "What's the point of any of it, if one day, the river bursts and takes it all away?" Scarlet put her head in her hands again and Joy braced herself for another round of tears, getting the tissues ready in her head.

But this time, there were no tears. Instead, Scarlet started laughing, shaking her head from side to side. "I'm sorry, I'm really sorry."

Joy frowned. "What are you sorry about?"

Scarlet peeled her hands from her face and shrugged, her palms now facing upwards. "Being such a blubbering mess in your lounge. And nearly smashing your table." She paused, staring straight ahead. "It's a really lovely coffee table, by the way. Much better than mine."

Joy grinned: Scarlet loved her coffee table. Steve had never got it, had told her it was impractical. Scarlet got it, and she'd been in her house for less than two hours. That wasn't lost on Joy one bit. Scarlet got the point that furniture could bring pleasure, that it could be art.

Joy's ex had never understood that, along with many, *many* other things.

"It is lovely. But it's just a thing, like you said. Easily replaceable." She paused, fixing Scarlet with her gaze, hoping her guest wasn't too melancholy. She had every right to be, but Joy was trying to dilute her loss, sweeten the taste.

"And I think you're allowed to be a mess after the night you've had. The good thing is you're okay, and you can buy more stuff when the waters recede. Until then, you're welcome to stay here, honestly. I've got the room, and frankly, the company would be nice." A blush hit Joy's cheeks. "But I understand if you've got friends or family to stay with, don't feel obliged."

But Joy hoped she stayed. Putting everything else aside, she *liked* Scarlet. She wasn't being 'the mayor' around Scarlet, she was just being herself. And that was all too rare in Joy's life these days. Even Steve had started talking about local building projects he thought she might be able to influence when he came round.

Scarlet leaned her head back into the sofa again, before turning to Joy, her eyes glassy.

"Thank you. I'd love to stay if that's okay. I don't have anybody else." Then she cast her gaze downwards and let out a huge sigh. "Like I said before, I'm pretty much a solo package." She paused. "A solo package without insurance. So getting my flat back together might not be such an easy thing to do."

If Joy had been gulping air before, that statement made her gasp even more. "You don't have insurance?" *How could she not have insurance?*

Scarlet shook her head, her face telling Joy she couldn't quite believe it either.

"Buildings, yes. I mean, you have to have that, right? But my contents — I had it, but it lapsed just before Christmas. And what with one thing and another, I just haven't quite got around to renewing it. I meant to, I totally did, but I never quite got there. I was racing to get stuff done. And now… well, now it looks like I really should have prioritised doing that, doesn't it?" She let out a strangled laugh, low, whisper-like. "My dad, when he was alive, always told us to get this stuff done, do it on direct debit. He'd never have let his insurance lapse. And I wouldn't normally, either."

Scarlet shuffled on the sofa, and Joy's heart went out to her. She was shrinking visibly as she spoke, embarrassed and clearly befuddled about what had happened in the past few hours. It was as if Scarlet was trying to burrow into the sofa, trying to find a secret escape route via its cushions and disappear.

Joy stepped in. "Like I said, you can stay here as long as you need; I don't mind." She felt a connection to Scarlet and she wanted to help — and there was nothing she wanted in return. She'd opened her house up to the town tonight, as was her civic duty. But she was more than happy to find she might also have made a friend. "And I promise you this," Joy added. "When the time comes for you to move back into your flat, I will personally deliver your first bottle of whisky to drink and we'll have a toast in your new front room. Deal?" Joy held out a hand to shake on it.

Her speech brought a smile out of Scarlet. "Deal," Scarlet replied, squeezing Joy's hand as she shook it.

Chapter Three

She had no idea what she'd done to land up here and be so looked after, but Scarlet was filled with gratitude. To think, she could still be in the community hall, trying to sleep on musty blankets under striplights. Instead, Joy had taken her in, wanting nothing in return. Scarlet had almost forgotten such kindness existed in the world.

And now, she was tucked up on Joy's sofabed in her office, in a light blue duvet that smelt of freshness and promise. Straggly threads of sunshine were streaming in through the window, and pillars of dust particles danced in front of her, caught by the light. It was odd having so much natural light flooding the room after living in a basement flat.

Flooding. That word had taken on a new significance now. She could no longer use it casually in conversation or thought. It'd never be the same again.

A new day was dawning, but it wasn't going to be a day like any other. Today was the start of a whole new chapter of her life, the chapter marked *After The Flood.* Scarlet had no idea what it was going to hold, and she was both eager and afraid to find out. Would she be able to get back into her flat today? She doubted it.

She had no idea how it would look, what it would feel like, how it would smell. She'd only ever seen it on the telly, and you never truly understood it via a small screen. It always just looked like a lot of dour people and houses engulfed by grey water. Like they could just pull the plug and it would all drain away and everything would be exactly the same as before.

But that wasn't the reality she was facing now. Trouble was, when you watched it unfold on the TV, it was like a soap opera, unreal, almost cinematic. Water cascading and sadness had a narrative about it, after all. Scarlet had never before stopped to consider the lives disrupted by the floods, the homes ruined, the belongings drowned, the memories eroded. The human cost of such disasters were always covered, but she'd never truly paid attention.

She was paying attention now.

She'd checked her phone before sleeping, and the flood was headline news, the video she'd seen earlier getting thousands of plays around the nation. Flooding was endlessly fascinating to watch, whether it affected you or not. She should call her brother Clark and let him know what had happened — she'd woken up to a text from him this morning and texted back to let him know she was okay. She hadn't mentioned the flat. Scarlet would have to message her other brother Fred, too, although he lived in Australia, so was probably ignorant of what was going on.

They hadn't stayed up much longer after Scarlet's breakdown, both of them knowing they needed to get some sleep so they could face today. She'd managed just over four hours, and in retrospect probably felt worse than she had before. Whisky remnants were lacing her brain, giving it a dull ache, but Scarlet didn't mind. The whisky had been worth it. Scarlet could hear people up and about, and knew she should get up, too, and see what her life consisted of today. It wasn't a normal Saturday, that much she knew.

The sofabed creaked as she got out of it and got dressed in the same clothes she'd had on last night. She'd left a wardrobe full of clothes behind, including her little black dress — not that she'd had an occasion to wear it in the past couple of years. Her exercise bike. Her trainers. Her degree certificate. Her books, CDs, television, DVDs. All of them drowned and never to return. Regret bubbled up inside her, but she clamped it down and busied herself getting dressed. She didn't have time to dwell on what she'd lost, because it wouldn't do her any good. She was going to employ the same tactic here as when her dad died: head down, keep going. It was the only thing she could do if she didn't want to collapse in a heap. And she was determined not to do that again, especially in front of Joy.

Kind, reassuring Joy. She'd put her hand on Scarlet's knee and it had burned. It'd been a very long time since a woman had put a hand on her, and Scarlet had a strange feeling about Joy, that she might not be quite as straight as she thought she was. Or perhaps that was wishful thinking on Scarlet's part. Whatever, even though the brief contact wasn't sexual, Scarlet had still craved more, leaned in. When Joy had stroked her back, Scarlet had wanted to weep with relief.

Scarlet ran a brush through her hair and aired the duvet, smoothing it out on the bed. She didn't want Joy thinking she was an ungrateful or untidy guest. She was anything but.

Joy's office was messily ordered: clean, but she needed to sort out a better filing system. It was the sort of thing a project manager like Scarlet could do for her in a morning. She made a mental note to offer her services when things had died down a little. It was the least she could do after everything Joy had done for her.

Joy's walls were littered with self-help mantras: *Embody the change you want to see*; *Leap and the net will appear*; *It's never too late to learn, especially to do your best*. Whatever it was Joy did, she was big on positivity, that was clear.

Scarlet yanked open the pine office door, noting the shiny chrome handles, and nearly walked straight into Joy on the landing.

To stop them colliding, Joy had held out both hands and they were now in an awkward embrace, their faces inches from each other, both of them smiling awkward smiles.

Joy was the first to respond, breaking the hold and smoothing herself down, her gaze landing anywhere but on Scarlet. "Morning!" she said. "Did you manage any sleep?"

Scarlet nodded, the effect of Joy's hands on her still pulsing through her body in waves.

"I did, amazingly." Her thoughts momentarily scrambled, she quickly shuffled them back into order like a skilled croupier. Scarlet pointed over her shoulder with her thumb. "That sofabed is very comfortable, and I was out like a light, the whisky made sure of that. Although I still feel like death warmed up."

Joy smiled at her. "Some food will make you feel better. The others have just left to go and see the damage. I've got to get down to the community hall in an hour or so, but let me show you where everything is in the kitchen." Joy was already off down the stairs as she spoke, and Scarlet dutifully followed, like she'd been doing it every day of her life.

She was surprised at how at home she felt here, given her arrival less than seven hours ago. And Joy looked fresh-faced, like staying up half the night and putting up a load of strangers in her home was something she did every day. Perhaps it was all a part of the mayor's remit. Whatever, Scarlet was impressed.

Joy's kitchen was straight out of a magazine, all sleek white surfaces, sparkling cupboards, and chrome fixtures. It was an interesting mix of masculine and feminine, exactly the kind of space that Scarlet would have chosen, had her kitchen been more than the size of a postage stamp. From the little Scarlet knew of Joy, it seemed to fit her perfectly. Did this kitchen represent the two sides to her personality? Or was it a remnant from her previous marriage?

"Now please help yourself to tea, coffee, milk's in the fridge." Joy was pointing to a cream American-style fridge, taller than Scarlet and about three times as wide. "If you want anything stronger, I think you know where that is," she added with a grin.

"Bit early."

Joy shrugged. "These aren't normal times, are they?" She paused. "Bread's in the breadbin, there's bacon in the fridge, and cereal in this cupboard." She was pointing at the cupboard above her head. "TV and radio, help yourself." She stopped and assessed Scarlet. "Are you going to the community hall?"

Scarlet nodded, picking up the kettle and filling it with water. "Think so," she said, when the noise had died down. "Going to have to face the music at some point, aren't I? Plus, I need to see if my suitcase is there, otherwise I'll be wearing the same clothes for quite some time."

Joy nodded, now grim-faced. "I don't think you're going to get into your flat today, from what I've been told — the waters won't have subsided. I'll know more when I meet the police chief later — the council leader's asked me to be there so I'll be able to give you some concrete news."

Scarlet nodded. The thought of all her things underwater made her nauseous now. Was her flat like a weird dream, a freeze-frame of her life, underwater? She couldn't picture it, all her possessions, floating like they were in some time capsule, suspended in space.

"Did you have any other plans?" Joy's voice broke through Scarlet's thoughts.

She blinked, trying to gather her thoughts in a neat bundle, but it didn't work. Her thoughts were destined to be scattered today.

Scarlet cleared her throat. "If I can't get into my flat, I'll probably go to the football later, take my mind off things."

Joy's face dropped.

Scarlet clocked it and frowned. Expressions like that were never good news. "What's that face for?"

"I don't think the football will be on," Joy said, folding her arms across her chest. She winced before she continued. "The club's been hit hard. The pitch is under water and the stands are buried, too. I saw it on the feed this morning — the water was up to five foot. It's affected the surrounding houses, too. So if you can't get into your flat, maybe you could help out there? I'll try to get down there later after I've been to check on my grandma, then onto the community hall and the town hall. There's a lot to do."

Scarlet could feel the blood seeping out of her features. Besides work, football was the one constant in her life that kept her sane, never let her down. It was the one thing that had kept her afloat over the past three years.

Afloat. She really did have to stop using these water metaphors.

"They've just had all that new equipment installed in the gym and everything," Scarlet said. She sat down on one of the breakfast bar stools now, shaking her head.

"I know," Joy replied.

Scarlet simply couldn't take it in, it was too much. First the flat, now the football club. And what about Eamonn? He was due to get married there next week. She doubted that would happen now.

"It's just all too real, isn't it?" Scarlet said, her earlier optimism now drying up. "You cope with one setback, and then another comes your way. My home and my club?" She shook her head before getting up. "Still, keep calm and make tea, isn't that what they say?"

Joy nodded. "It's the British way."

When Scarlet turned away from Joy to re-boil the kettle, tears pricked the back of her eyes again. She took three deep breaths before turning back to her host.

"Do you want a tea or coffee, by the way?" Her eyes were watery, but she was determined not to cry. If this happened every time anything to do with the flood was mentioned today, she'd be spending a great chunk of her day underwater herself. She didn't want that. What was done was done. Now, she wanted to help fix it.

Because Scarlet was a fixer.

Joy flicked her eyes up to the clock on the wall, then back to Scarlet. "That'd be lovely. Mugs are here," she said, pointing to right. "And the dishwasher is hidden here when you're done." Joy opened what looked like a cupboard beside her, to reveal a dishwasher.

"Goddit," Scarlet replied, swallowing madly.

"My tea is white, one sugar," Joy added, sweeping out of the kitchen, before stopping in the doorway. "And I'm really sorry about the stadium," she added. "I know it's been a bone of contention for some time, but I think the football club is vital to the community."

Scarlet bit her top lip and swallowed down hard, nodding at Joy.

Keep it together, keep it together, keep it together.

"And you know what, this is the third cup of tea someone's made for me this morning. And I have to say, it's an upside to having people here. Living on your own, you forget how nice it is to have someone else make you a cup of tea, don't you?"

Scarlet smiled at that. "I know exactly what you mean, and I'm happy to make it for you. It's the least I can do," she said, her voice getting lodged in her throat. Yep, Scarlet was well aware of the kindness of small acts, especially when they never normally happened to you.

Joy gazed at Scarlet for a brief second. "Good," she said. "I'm going to jump in the shower and when I come back, I'll dig out some wellies for you. I've got a few sizes in the garage."

She flashed Scarlet a broad smile, before disappearing up the stairs.

Scarlet made the tea on auto-pilot, adding water, then milk, then slumping down on one of the breakfast bar stools. She wasn't hungry now, after all. This time yesterday, life had been shitty, but predictably shitty. Now, everything had been turned on its head, and Scarlet was reaching out for something to cling onto.

Joy had thrown her a lifeline, and for that, she was eternally grateful.

Chapter Four

Joy trotted up the steps to Grasspoint, the old folks' community her grandma had been part of for the past few years. It was a forward-thinking home, which Joy was grateful for, because the thought of leaving her grandma there had filled her with anxiety at the time. The thing was, her grandma didn't have dementia and she wasn't ancient, at 80. But her failing joints meant she had trouble getting around sometimes, and Grasspoint provided her with all the assistance she needed. Now, Joy's grandma still had a modicum of independence with her own bathroom and shared lounge area, and she got all her meals cooked for her. Plus, she'd made some great friends who she was sitting in the lounge with when J oy arrived.

Joy nodded to Fred, the handyman, as she crossed the sitting room to the circle of friends. There was Carol, who'd apparently dyed her hair a rasping shade of pink since last week; Annie, who liked to moan about anything and everything; and Robert, one of the few men in the home who lapped up the female attention with glee. Joy had a soft spot for them all, but none of them were her beloved grandma.

"Hey, shortie," Joy said, bending down to give her grandma a hug. Shortie was the affectionate nickname she'd given her over the past few years, as her grandma had slowly but surely begun to shrink into old age, literally.

Her gran gave her a grin as Joy pulled up a chair. "Wasn't sure if I was going to see you today, what with all the flooding," she said, sweeping her wispy grey hair off her smooth forehead.

It was one thing Joy hoped she inherited: her grandma's skin. Sure, she had some wrinkles, but people were constantly amazed she was 80 years old. Most people put her at least ten years younger.

Joy smiled. "I'll always come and see you, especially after the flooding, make sure you're okay."

Her grandma dismissed her comments with a wave of her hand. "We're fine, we've lived through worse, haven't we Robert?"

Robert furrowed his brow. "What's that, Clem?"

Joy's grandma was named Clementine, and Joy had spent her entire life wishing she'd been named after her grandma, instead of some wispy, difficult-to-pin-down emotion.

"I was just telling Joy, we've all lived through worse than this flood, haven't we?" Her grandma was shouting now.

Robert grinned when he heard, still fiddling with his

hearing aid. "World wars, Clem," he said. "And I've lost count how many floods I've lived in. Even London used to get flooded all the time. We're an island; people shouldn't be so surprised."

Joy laughed — whatever the crisis in her life, she could always count on being soothed when she visited Grasspoint. Grandma and her friends had a way of putting events into perspective.

"I can't stay long, though. I've got to get into town and see how people are doing." Joy rubbed her hands together as she spoke. Even though the lounge was baking, her hands were still acclimatising from the cold outside.

"People will be going bananas," Clementine replied. "You know that."

"Some people have lost their homes, so I'd say they have good reason. I've got some staying with me. One of them is a local woman who's lost everything — Scarlet. She had a basement flat and it's completely flooded." Joy smiled, picturing Scarlet this morning, her dark hair unruffled. "The devastation is shocking, even if you have seen it before."

Her grandma put a hand on her arm. "I never said it wasn't shocking, I just mean people will recover. It's how things work." She squeezed her arm, and Joy was taken back to all those times in her childhood where her grandma used to do exactly the same thing while Joy spilled her troubles at Clementine's kitchen table. They'd always been close, ever since Joy was young. Joy had a brother,

Michael, but it was Joy who was her grandma's favourite, a fact Clementine never tried to hide. Clementine even favoured Joy over her own son, Christopher, Joy's dad. And in return, Clementine was Joy's favourite grandma.

Her only grandma, but always her favourite.

"So this Scarlet — is she single?"

Joy's cheeks flushed red — she didn't need a mirror to know, she felt as though her whole face was a bright neon light blinking at her grandma. Joy looked out the window at the rolling hills, before glancing back.

"I'm not sure," she said, shaking her head, glossing over the fact. Trust her gran to arrow straight to the pertinent point. "But she's got nowhere else to go, so I've said she can stay." Joy shrugged, as if inviting a stranger into your home was the most natural thing in the world. "She's nice though, I like her. We get on, and I could use a new friend."

Clementine eyed her granddaughter, then gave her a nod. "You're not wrong there," she said. "It'll be nice for you to have some company. And if she's single and available, all the better." Her grandma followed up that comment with a knowing look. "And because I can see you're entertaining the idea, I take it she's gay, too?"

If Joy had been blushing fire-engine red before, she was pretty sure her cheeks had just burst into flames. Being in politics, she really should be used to dealing with tricky questions, but her grandma always had known which buttons to push. She guessed it was all a part of the whole *I've known you since you were in nappies* deal.

Joy glanced at her gran, then looked away. "I've no idea."

But if Joy were a betting woman, she'd be prepared to put a sizeable bet on the table to gamble that Scarlet was. Joy wasn't sure what it was, but she got an inkling from her, a notion. Yes, Scarlet had been married, but she hadn't said whether it was to a man or a woman. And Joy, of all people, knew that sexuality was a fluid thing and could easily change.

"But even if she was, it doesn't mean anything's going to happen. It's not like I'm going to fall for the first lesbian I meet in my daily life, is it? I need to feel an attraction, a connection." But even Joy knew she *was* protesting too much, that she *did* feel that attraction, that connection. She'd felt it from the moment Scarlet walked into her house last night.

Clementine lowered her reading glasses from her face, giving Joy a tender smile. "I never said any different, did I?" she said. "And I understand how dating and attraction works; I've been around a bit longer than you have." She gave Joy a wide smile. "But I also know when you're interested. And judging from your reaction, I'd say you are."

Joy went to respond, but they were interrupted by the home's warden, Celia, hovering over Joy's shoulder.

"Cup of tea, Joy?"

Joy swivelled her head. "That'd be lovely Celia, thanks."

Saved by the bell — Joy had always liked Celia.

Clementine was still watching her, but Joy wasn't giving her anything else, because there was nothing to give. For now, Joy was doing exactly what she'd told her grandma— helping out someone in need.

"Another round of tea here, too?" Celia asked, raising her voice to the group.

They all murmured their approval.

"And some of that cake that Maureen brought round earlier," added Clementine. She squeezed Joy's arm again, telling her, "It's your favourite, Guinness cake. She should go on that *Bake Off* programme, I keep telling her. And she'd get to meet that Peter Hollywood."

Joy smiled. Another slice of Maureen Armitage's Guinness cake. It was a good job she ran three times a week. "It's Paul, Gran," Joy said.

Clementine frowned at her. "Who's Paul?"

"Paul Hollywood, on the *Great British Bake Off*."

Clementine looked at Joy like she'd gone mad. "That's what I said, Paul Hollywood." She shook her head.

Joy let it go.

"Anyway, has your dad been in touch? I texted to let him know the whole town was drowning, but I doubt he cared that much." Clementine had been less than impressed about her son's decision to move away from his family to Spain after his retirement. Joy had always felt a little sorry for her dad; she got the impression her gran had been a harsh mother, but had softened into being a grandmother. Or at least, she had when it came to Joy.

Joy nodded. "Yeah, Mum called when she heard — I let her know we were all okay. More than I can say for Michael, though. He dropped me a text to check I was alive, but that's about it."

Clementine waved a hand through the air, dismissing Michael as she always did. "He gets it from your father, that boy. Plus, it's men — they're different creatures. Thank goodness for your lovely mother is all I can say. Although how she puts up with Christopher is beyond me. The woman's a saint."

* * *

Joy's phone had been non-stop all morning, being kept up to date of the multi-agency response to the flood. Co-ordinated by the police and the council's emergency planning officer, it involved a number of organisations including police, fire, army, council, mountain rescue, and ambulance. But there was one thing all of them had in common: nobody had good news. The flood warnings had proved correct, and the water had caused more damage than expected. Yes, the controlled flooding had meant less damage, but there were still hundreds of homes and businesses underwater, along with tons of allotments, the football club, and the town cinema. The main bridge over the river had collapsed under the strain of the water, too, leaving the town cut off at one end.

Joy stepped into the community hall and the noise level hit her, with kids screaming and voices elevated to be heard. The smell of bitter coffee and burnt toast wafted into her nostrils, and she struggled to see the floor as she stepped over makeshift beds, clothes, and discarded sleeping bags. An eating area had been set up near the kitchen in the far corner, with a couple of tables and a handful of scuffed red plastic chairs. It wasn't ideal, but it was the best that could be managed in the circumstances.

Despite this, everywhere Joy looked, she saw smiles. This was the community spirit she expected: everyone in the same boat, and they were going to sail on together. In one corner was a tower of bleach — bottles and bottles of the stuff. They'd been shipped in this morning by the council, and residents were helping themselves. By the time the clean-up was done, Joy was sure Dulshaw would be one of the most sterile towns in the UK.

"How's it going, Sue?" Joy was addressing a portly woman with a clipboard. Sue Janus was a regular at the council, at her happiest when clutching a clipboard with a pen on a string. This morning, she was positively beaming. The flood was manna from heaven for her.

"As well as can be expected," Sue replied, pursing her lips and nodding slowly.

"Sure you're making it better, though," Joy said. "Keep up the good work."

Joy felt someone draw up alongside her, and when she turned her head, it was Scarlet.

Joy gave her a grin; it was already automatic. "Didn't expect to see you here."

Scarlet didn't look happy — her face was set to scowl. She shrugged. "I went to the ground, but they're in disarray. They told me to come back in a bit when they'd pumped some of the water out, so I thought I'd come and get my suitcase, take it back to ours — I mean, yours — and then go back. There are some residents round there that need help, too."

"You brought a friend along?" Sue enquired, smiling at Scarlet, then at Joy, but the smile didn't reach her eyes.

"Scarlet, this is Sue Janus, one of our community heroes," Joy said. "Scarlet was one of those I put up last night after her flat was flooded."

Sue frowned. "That's right, I remember you now," she said. "I thought you came in after—"

"—Looks like you're doing a great job here," Scarlet said, interrupting Sue abruptly.

Sue stopped, thrown off course with whatever she was saying. "Yes, well, you have to pull together in times of need, don't you?" She raked her eyes up and down Scarlet. "There are food parcels being delivered later if you need them, and coffee over there." Sue clasped Scarlet's hand and shook her head from side to side. "It's a really tough time, but we're here for you."

Scarlet stiffened on contact, withdrawing her hand. "Thanks, I appreciate it."

Sue gave her a nod, assured her duty was done, and scuttled away.

Joy gave Scarlet a half-smile. "Sue Janus, community

hero and busybody," she said, in a whisper. "Still, she means well."

Scarlet nodded, wordless, scanning the room. "Listen, I just came to get my case," she said, indicating downwards with her head to where it was standing at her feet. "I was hoping to take it back to yours, like I said. Are you heading home or can you give me a key?"

Joy checked her watch. "I wasn't planning on it just yet." She fished in her bag and gave Scarlet her set of keys. "It's the blue one, or else I'd forget every day," she said, pointing at the key resting in Scarlet's outstretched palm. "And the gold key unlocks the deadlock. Can you drop it back here on your way to the ground?"

Scarlet nodded. "Of course." She paused. "Everything okay with your grandma?"

Joy nodded. "Luckily, they're up high, or that could have been a huge disaster. They're all talking about how they survived the war, so people will get through." She paused. "When we're old, we won't have stories of war to fall back on, will we?"

Scarlet smiled. "We'll just have to tell them about the great flood that nearly washed us all away."

"But we survived."

"Just about." Scarlet shifted, then picked up her case. "Thanks for this," she said, holding up the keys. "I'll be back within half an hour, so don't go anywhere."

And with that, she picked up her suitcase even though it was on wheels, and turned on her heel.

Joy wished there was more she could do, but there was nothing. She simply watched Scarlet rush out of the community hall, and then turned back to the hubbub in the hall. Now, all she saw were crying children, crumbs, and strained faces.

* * *

Scarlet slammed the door to Joy's house and ran down the road as fast as she could, the wind whistling in her ears. She had no idea why she was running, but it was something she needed to do. Expel the excess energy that had built up inside her body and try to make some sense of what had happened in the past 24 hours.

She'd just dropped off a suitcase containing her life to the temporary home she was sharing with a stranger. She needed to call her brother, to hear his voice. Not that she'd heard it much lately, having not returned his calls or emails. He'd probably given up on her, and she didn't blame him. She made a mental note to call him later.

The town looked eerily calm and normal from up high — you wouldn't be able to tell there was anything different. But when Scarlet turned the corner and got a view of the city centre again for the second time that day, her run came to a crunching halt. She struggled for breath, gasping as she put her hands on her thighs and leaned forward. If she'd eaten any food, she might have vomited, but she was running on empty.

She couldn't believe her eyes.

It was as if a section of the town had been erased, and the gaps coloured in sludge brown. The bridge had collapsed under the strain of the water, that much she knew. But the whole east side of the city had just been swallowed up, too, as if Mother Nature had been tremendously hungry the night before.

The cinema was half-submerged, as were all the streets near the river and beyond. Water was lapping at the bottom of the hill she was standing on, and she knew she was going no further in that direction. There was movement on some of the roads that were now impromptu rivers, with rescue boats ferrying people and belongings to safety. The army had been bussed in to help, too, along with countless mountain rescue teams.

But any hope Scarlet had of seeing how bad her flat might be were now confirmed. She'd guessed as much when she'd seen the damage to the football ground, near the smaller part of the river. The scene in front of her was one of devastation. Where there had been fields, there were now lakes. Where there had been roads, there were now rivers. She still couldn't make sense of it.

Scarlet sat down on the weirdly dry ground and stared. It was so close, she could almost reach out and touch it. Visions of all her belongings buried at the bottom of the ocean swam in her mind. She was pretty sure they hadn't made it that far yet.

After five minutes contemplating the new Dulshaw, she stood up, brushed down the back of her jeans and carried on along the top road. Her feet were now weighed down with dread, the glimpse of her new reality pressing claustrophobically into her brain.

The football stadium was on the other side of town, where the river meandered round, and she knew what awaited her there. There was nothing she could do for her own flat, but maybe there was something she could do for the club and the people around there. She needed something to keep her occupied today, because if she thought too much about everything that had happened, she was going to go crazy. Above her, dark clouds threatened more misery tonight — the forecast she'd seen earlier was for more rain. Exactly what they didn't need.

"Scarlet! Scarlet!"

She turned, and saw Eamonn running towards her in his regulation outfit of jeans and a bomber jacket.

"Can you believe this shit?" Eamonn's accent was pure Dublin, all lilts and swagger that had women falling over him on nights out. He was still perplexed why Scarlet had never fallen for his charms, despite Scarlet explaining it a million times before. Eamonn was one of those men who was perplexed why everyone didn't find him irresistible, which was the constant butt of their jokes.

Scarlet shook her head. "Don't," she said. "Your house is okay, though?"

Eamonn caught his breath, nodding. "Yeah, but the shop's not." Eamonn's fiancée, Steph, ran a cake shop in the town centre called Great Bakes.

"Over a foot of water, up to my knee," Eamonn said, reaching down to demonstrate the water level. "They didn't even tell us in time either, so we weren't able to save anything much, including our wedding cake which Steph had just finished icing." He ran a hand through his shiny black hair, his cheeks rosy from exertion. Eamonn hadn't shaved that morning and he had a ten o'clock shadow on his face.

"Shit," Scarlet said, before pausing. "My flat went the same way as your cake — completely gone. Underwater, never to be seen again."

Eamonn put a hand to his mouth, then he engulfed Scarlet in a hug, his arms gripping her body tightly. "I forgot you were in a basement. You could have drowned. Did they give you much notice?" He held her at arm's length now, as if checking she was still there, his breath warm on her face.

"Yeah, they knocked on my door at 4am and gave me half an hour to leave."

Eamonn shook his head in dismay. "So where are you staying? Do you need a place? Because we've got the spare room." He was still holding her, almost scared of letting her go.

Scarlet was touched, but she shook her head. "I'm good. I'm staying at the mayor's house, no less. She put a few of us up last night, said I can stay till I get sorted. She seems nice, so…" Scarlet tailed off.

Now she was saying it out loud, it sounded odd to her. Why was she turning down the offer of one of the few friends she had in town to stay in a total stranger's house? Probably because the thought of playing gooseberry with Eamonn and Steph didn't appeal. She had a lot of time for Eamonn, but she'd never considered living with him — that might be taking the friendship too far. Plus, she didn't really want to cramp their style, especially the week before their wedding.

"Mayor's house?" Eamonn stood back and regarded her. "Isn't she the snooty one who's trying to push forward the plans to build on the football stadium? You're living with *her*?" His face told Scarlet he didn't approve.

Scarlet's cheeks coloured as she answered. "It's a temporary thing, while I wait to see how the flat is. Not good, I'd say, looking down that hill." She glanced sideways towards the town, but then averted her eyes. It was best to pretend the devastation wasn't there.

Eamonn whistled to underline the devastation. "Can you *actually* believe it?" he said, shaking his head.

"Not really."

"I mean, fucking hell, it looks like a disaster movie set. Only, it's our town. My initial plan was to get drunk, but I had two obstacles to that. First, Steph wants to get plans in order — she's a Virgo, she can't help it. Second, the local pub was flooded, so that put paid to that. All the electrics and gas are out in the centre of town, too; the pipes got flooded. No lights, no cashpoints, no services. Nothing."

Scarlet's mouth dropped open at his explanation. "It's just… surreal."

"And now you're living with the mayor. Now that's surreal."

Scarlet shrugged. She didn't want Eamonn laying into Joy. She'd felt calm and content at Joy's place. She hadn't felt like she had to stand on ceremony, or be on her best behaviour. With Joy, it'd been easy, and she'd been herself. She'd *cried*, for goodness sake. And despite everything, she'd relaxed. Honest-to-goodness relaxed, *even* with everything that was going on. That said a lot. So Scarlet wasn't going to stand by and let him slate her.

"We don't know if she was involved in that development plan. It was only hearsay, and she says she's still working on it, she's on our side. She seems genuine and she was very welcoming last night." She paused, giving Eamonn a shrug. "Look at it this way: I might be able to sway her, bring her on-board."

Eamonn raised an eyebrow in Scarlet's direction. "You seem positively glowing about the mayor today — quite a turnaround," he said, nudging her with his elbow as they fell into step together, walking along the road.

Scarlet rolled her eyes. Eamonn's world was very black and white when it came to attraction, and she wasn't going to tell him he wasn't far off the mark. She hadn't fully processed the thought she might be attracted to Joy herself yet, her mind too caught up with her world falling apart to pay attention to much else.

"Somebody giving you a bed when you've got nowhere to live can do that." Scarlet thrust her hands into her jacket pockets. She wished she'd remembered her gloves, but she had a feeling they might be underwater, too.

"She left her husband, didn't she? My mate, Dean, used to work with her — rumour is she left him because she bats for your side."

Scarlet's stomach lurched when she heard that, but she kept a lid on her emotions, chewing on the inside of her cheek. Could Joy be a lesbian? It was possible, she supposed.

Eamonn shrugged. "The offer stands if you want somewhere else, anyway. I've met her once and she seemed a bit superior, a bit looking down her nose at everyone else. So if you need it, our door's open."

Scarlet's hackles rose, but she didn't respond. Defending Joy any more would just raise his suspicions even further. And when there was nothing going on, there was no need to do that. So she glossed over it.

"Anyway, I was just going to the club to see if I can help. Were you heading that way?"

Eamonn nodded. "I was. I need to see what the damage is — for next week and all." He winced as he said it.

"Shit," Scarlet said, stopping in her tracks. "I forgot about the reception. How you feeling? I was down there earlier and it doesn't look good."

"I know, they called me." Eamonn shrugged, but pain was etched on his face. "What can you do? Steph doesn't know which to be more upset about: the shop or the wedding. For now, the shop's taking up most of her time, and I need to get back to help with that. But I said I'd assess the ground first, to see if there's any hope. But Billy told me earlier he didn't think there was."

Eamonn and Steph had been planning their wedding for the best part of a year, and Eamonn had been so proud when his bride-to-be had agreed to have the reception at the football ground. Scarlet knew he'd been looking forward to having his wedding photos on the pitch, but she didn't bring it up.

Eamonn pulled his shoulders up as the wind whipped round his ears. He shivered, just as the clouds got a little bit angrier above. "It never rains but it pours. Never has a metaphor been so true," he said. The sky above them was heavy, clad in iron grey. "We've got a drowned business and a soggy wedding. At least the town hall was up high, along with the catering business. But where we're going to put all our guests to eat the food is anyone's guess."

They fell back into step, hurrying along the road, Scarlet keen to get to the ground before the heavens opened once more.

She put a hand on Eamonn's back and rubbed it up and down. "We'll figure something. Maybe Joy can help, in her role as mayor. I can ask her if you like?"

Eamonn squinted at Scarlet, considering her offer. Then he nodded. "It can't hurt, can it? Right now, we're having a street party, and I don't fancy our chances when half the streets are actually rivers."

Scarlet gave him a grim smile as they walked. "And the shop — is it bad?"

"Awful. All the equipment is buggered, all the appliances. And it's just covered in… sludge. And wet — just everything is wet. When we saw it, we both just wanted to cry. At least we're insured — there is that. Some of the businesses weren't."

Scarlet stopped walking again. She was doing that a lot these days. "I wasn't," she said quietly, the hopelessness engulfing her so that she thought her legs might cave from under her.

Now Eamonn stopped walking, too, as the rain started to fall. "Fucking hell, Scarlet," he said, pulling her to him before she fell of her own accord.

Chapter Five

It'd been a brutal day, with terrible stories of lives and businesses sunk overnight. Plus, what with having hardly any sleep, Joy had drawn on every ounce of mental toughness she had to smile her way through and reassure people the council was doing everything it could. Not even the endless stream of sandwiches and cupcakes coming through the door of the community hall could mend the damage done. The situation was very real and damaging for everyone concerned, even though they were still smiling through, showing the British spirit.

Joy had finally got away around 9pm, and was now in her kitchen, making her go-to comfort meal of beans on toast with a poached egg. Even if everything else in her world was falling apart, this meal had all the ingredients she needed to soothe her soul. She was just winding the wheel of the tin opener when there was a knock at the door. She set the tin on the counter and scooted into the hallway.

When she opened the door, Scarlet was standing on the doorstep, dripping wet. Her jacket had a hood, but the rain had managed to worm its way under it and onto her face, rivulets slaloming down her cheeks. The rains had indeed returned tonight, adding insult to injury — just as the forecasters had said it would.

"You look like a drowned rat," Joy said, standing aside as Scarlet walked in.

"I feel like one, too." Scarlet bent down and took off her boots, followed by her coat, stowing them in the correct places. She needed no telling where to put them tonight — she remembered it all from the previous day.

"How are you? You've been out for ages." Joy's arms were folded, but she immediately felt calmer, somehow better now Scarlet was home. She hadn't quite realised it, but she'd been waiting for her guest, her house not feeling complete without Scarlet in it. But she wasn't going to tell Scarlet that. She'd known her less than 24 hours, now was not the time to come across all *Single White Female*.

Scarlet breathed on her hands and rubbed them together in an effort to get warm. Then she stood by the radiator in the hallway, her hands glued to it. Her cheeks were pink from cold, her shoulder-length dark hair flat to her head. But even dishevelled, Scarlet still managed to look quietly beautiful.

That thought sent a burning sensation to Joy's cheeks.

"I've been at the football ground all day, helping to clear up the mess — it subsided from the pitch quickly but the whole place is shot. They won't be playing any football on there for a while." Scarlet shivered again. "Still, it's given me a taste of what my flat might be like — *not pretty* is the answer." Scarlet paused, shaking her head.

"Then we helped out with the houses around the ground, clearing stuff out. One guy, Dan, he has terminal cancer and is very weak, so he was particularly thankful for our help." She paused again. "It's kinda humbling seeing that; I might have lost everything, but at least I have my health, and that's far more important in the bigger picture." Scarlet shrugged. "I'm not the only one who's fucked, you know? The club are, thousands of other people are, my mate's wedding's buggered — it's a huge issue." She paused. "And you were right about the community spirit — it was so thick today, you could almost hug it. I guess this is what it was like in the war, right?"

"According to my gran, yes." Joy paused, glad her guest was feeling a little more positive than the last time she'd seen her. "I was just making beans on toast with poached egg — fancy some?" Joy didn't wait for an answer, moving into the kitchen.

"That sounds divine," Scarlet replied.

* * *

Scarlet sat at the breakfast bar while Joy busied herself with pans and toast. She should offer to help, but she'd probably just get in the way being that she didn't know the kitchen. She always preferred to do things herself when she had guests over, not that it'd happened for a while. Joy had a look of intense concentration on her face as she cracked the eggs into a pan of boiling, circling water.

Scarlet leaned forward as the eggs dropped in, not splitting. "I'm impressed," she said. "Being able to do that with poached eggs is a skill. I've never mastered it, mine always go everywhere."

Joy blushed at the compliment, which was endearing.

"My mum taught me," Joy said. "She was a chef, so poached eggs, omelettes, all of that, we learned them at a young age. Not that I get to use my skills much these days. Poached eggs is about as advanced as it gets." Joy batted her fringe out of her eye as was her habit.

"Comfort food is what this whole town needs tonight." Scarlet looked around the kitchen. "Talking of which, where's everyone else?"

The toaster popped and Joy got the bread out, flinging it onto the plates and blowing on her fingers.

"They left — they sorted out places elsewhere with friends and family." She paused, looking up at Scarlet. "I thought about offering the other room to someone else, but my guilt is assuaged having you here — I've taken in my refugee, so no fingers can be pointed."

The smell of hot, buttered toast made Scarlet realise how hungry she was; she'd hardly eaten all day. "If anyone asks, I'll say you had a family of five as well as me, okay?"

"Make it a family of seven for good measure," Joy replied, laughing. She loaded up the toast with beans and the freshly poached eggs, put them on the breakfast bar, and sat on the stool next to Scarlet.

Their knees touched as Joy jostled for position, but Scarlet said nothing, despite it causing a frisson up her body. She wasn't sure what had happened since yesterday, but there was something underlying tonight.

But she wasn't going to dwell on it — dwelling wasn't Scarlet's style. She was going to eat her dinner and chat politely to the mayor. Only, she didn't look at Joy as the mayor anymore. Now, Joy was her friend, as well as being her temporary saviour. And a friend was exactly what Scarlet needed after everything that had happened.

"So the stadium was terrible?" Joy asked, in between mouthfuls. Joy did not speak with her mouth full, which Scarlet appreciated. It wasn't an appealing habit, and it was something Liv had done *all the time.*

"Awful," Scarlet said, resting her cutlery as she swallowed. "They only just put the new gym in, and all the equipment is ruined. Plus, the stands are going to need replacing, the turf, the flags, the goals — everything. And when the water subsided it was just... grim. Mucky. Same goes for all the houses around it, too. And the smell..." Scarlet winced, then picked up her knife and fork. "Anyway, let's not talk about it while we're eating." She paused. "Let's talk about something more cheery. How was your day?"

Joy sighed. "I'm not sure you've come to the right place for cheery," she said. "You want the real version or the fake one?"

"Which one's lighter?"

"The fake one, of course."

"I'll go with the fake one, then," Scarlet replied with a definite nod.

A mischievous grin worked its way onto Joy's face, then she raised both eyebrows at Scarlet before answering. "How was my day?" she asked, using a tone way higher than normal. "Well, dear," Joy continued. "I dropped the kids off at nursery, the dog got his shots, and I've chosen our new wardrobes — I've gone for shiny burgundy, I hope that's okay." The smile that creased Joy's face lit up the room.

"Burgundy is my absolute favourite," Scarlet said, her mouth dropping open in wonder. "And did you remember to pick the kids *up* again?"

Joy's eyes shot open in mock alarm. "OMG! I *knew* there was something I was meant to do…"

And then Scarlet was laughing too, just like Joy. So hard that a baked bean spilled out of her mouth and landed on her top.

Which only made the pair laugh harder, as Scarlet popped the bean back in her mouth, licking her finger of bean juice as she did. Their laughter was infectious and just got louder — it'd been a long day, and they both needed this.

Tears were now rolling down Joy's face, and she wiped them up with the back of her hand, almost hysterical. And then she began to hiccup, softly at first, then more often, and louder.

"Shit," Joy said, then hiccupped again. She hopped off her stool, hiccupped, then ran to the sink. She filled a glass with water, hiccupping the whole time, and began to gulp at a rapid pace.

Scarlet blew her nose and carried on eating, glancing at Joy who was now gulping water from an upside down angle. It didn't surprise Scarlet. She'd seen many tricks to get rid of hiccups in her lifetime, and this was tried and tested. Eventually, it worked and Joy retook her seat, eating her now-cold plate of food, with Scarlet mopping up the last of hers.

Joy swallowed a mouthful down, then held her fork in the air and waited. When no hiccup came, she raised her fork in triumph. "I win!" she said. "I hate hiccups."

Scarlet grinned. "You looked very cute while you had them, if that's any consolation." And then she wished she could just shut up: that comment had just flown out of her mouth with no recourse.

Joy eyed her, clearly trying to work her out. But thankfully, she decided to let it slide.

Scarlet crashed on, ignoring the noise of her heart in her ears. *Thump, thump, thump.* "I heard about one kid in America who had hiccups for, like, four years. I mean, that's brutal. Imagine — I get agitated after four minutes."

"I don't think I'd last four hours," Joy said, smiling. Then she carried on eating, and a comfortable silence settled on the kitchen like a warm blanket.

"So, you said you were married. When did you get divorced?"

Scarlet eyed Joy. This was her moment to come out, she supposed. It wasn't a big deal, Scarlet was out to everyone in her life. It wasn't an issue; it was just a part of who she was. Yet saying it to Joy felt like it was a big issue. Like something would shift, and perhaps not for the worse. And that was something that made Scarlet's heart race just that little bit faster still.

"Three years ago. It was messy — my wife," Scarlet said, checking Joy's face for any trace of surprise.

There was none.

She carried on. "My wife turned out to be a secret gambler. Might have almost been easier if she was unfaithful with a person, rather than money." Scarlet shrugged. "That's my sorry tale."

Joy nodded, licking her lips. "So you were married to a woman?"

Was this going to be an issue after all? Scarlet's cheeks flushed red as she nodded her head. "I was. I'm a lesbian, in case you hadn't worked that out yet."

Joy looked her in the eye, then looked away. Joy was flustered.

Scarlet put one foot on the ground. Had she read this wrong? Was Joy not a bleeding-heart liberal like the rest of her friends? If she was a right-wing Tory, this living arrangement might be problematic. Perhaps she *might* have to take Eamonn up on his offer. "That's not a problem, is it?"

Joy shook her head. "No!" she said, her voice high-pitched. "Of course not, not at all." She paused. "It's just... I thought you might be, but I wasn't sure." Another longer pause. "It's the reason I left Steve — because I think I'm gay." She still wasn't looking at Scarlet. "Actually, I don't think it, I know it. I just haven't had much practice. I was a bit of a late bloomer. Didn't clock it till I was in my thirties, and by that time, I was married." She finally looked at Scarlet. "And that's the first time I've said that to someone who wasn't my ex or my gran." Joy paused. "Does it surprise you?"

Scarlet smiled at Joy, relief washing through her body. So Eamonn had been right in what he'd told her. "It takes a lot to surprise me these days," she replied. "But well done on your first coming out to a stranger. It wasn't so hard, was it?"

Joy shook her head. "It wasn't," she said. "Although, I wouldn't call you a stranger."

Warmth swept through Scarlet: neither would she. "I know, but we have only known each other for 24 hours, even if those 24 hours have been counted in dog years." Scarlet laughed. "How did your ex take it?"

"Surprisingly well, we're still friends. On some level, he said he'd always known." Joy laughed a hollow laugh. "I just wish he'd have told me, save me wasting a good chunk of my life." Alarm spread across her features as she glanced at Scarlet. "Not that he was a waste, far from it..."

Scarlet held up a hand. "I get it," she said. "You don't have to explain. I'm not going to put a report in the local paper saying we've got a lesbian man-hating mayor." Scarlet shot Joy a grin.

Joy returned it with a wry smile of her own. "That, at least, is good to know."

"So you were married to a man, but now you're a lesbian. I don't know much about you, do I?"

And Scarlet didn't. She'd been in Joy's house for a day, but the spotlight had been on her — with good reason. But now it was time to discover some more about her host. What she'd already found out had been enlightening. *Truly enlightening.*

"Do your parents live nearby? You said your mum's a chef — does she work anywhere I'd know?"

Joy shook her head. "No — they used to run one of the pubs in town, but they sold up and moved out to Spain a couple of years ago. Mum said she put in enough hours in the kitchen, and it was time to enjoy what years she had left. I agreed whole-heartedly. My brother, however, had a different opinion. But then again, that's the story of my brother. Michael generally has different views from me."

"Does he still live around here?"

Joy nodded. "Lives in a village about half an hour away, but I probably see my parents more often than I see him. He sent me a text to ask if I'd drowned today, but that's as far as his brotherly love stretches." Joy shrugged.

"We get on okay when we don't see each other too often, and that suits us both fine."

"Whatever works," Scarlet replied. Images of her twin brothers flashed through her mind, but she pushed them to one side. She hadn't spoken to either of them for months either, but that was her doing, not theirs. Her brothers were constantly in touch; it was Scarlet who'd decided to step out of the loop, to press pause on family life. What did she have to offer them, after all, apart from self-pity and misery?

Joy nodded again. "I go to see my parents at least once a year, usually twice, and they come over at least once to see Gran. They tried to convince her to go out, but she's not keen on flying." Joy paused, looking wistful. "In fact, when the town is back on its feet, I may just fly off there to get a sunshine injection. I might need it after the next few weeks."

"I think you might be right."

Scarlet bit her top lip, still thinking about her brothers. She really should let them know about her flat and where she was, but she was putting it off. Ever since her mum had died and Liv had left, she'd been putting *life* off. But after the flood, she might have to start tackling life, get her hands dirty again. She'd lived in a sterile world for long enough. And sitting here in Joy's kitchen, she could almost feel the fanfare of living being pressed back into her being.

"Seeing all the devastation today, I just want to say it's brilliant to come back here and feel at home." Scarlet paused. "Because I really do feel at home here, and that's an amazing thing for me to say. I don't usually feel at home anywhere. Sometimes not even my own home."

Scarlet held Joy's gaze, and there was something in the way Joy was looking at her. Joy's gaze held weight, like there was something else she wanted to say, but was holding back.

Embarrassment crept onto Scarlet's cheeks because of that *and* because of what she'd just admitted. It was shameful that she didn't feel at home in her own house sometimes, but it was the truth. Scarlet had felt uninvited, uncomfortable in her own skin for most of the past few years.

But now, there was none of that. She was just being truthful, being Scarlet. And that was amazing.

"You've been so welcoming, far more than I might have been had someone turned up on my doorstep at five in the morning." Scarlet bounced her gaze around the kitchen, anywhere to get it away from Joy's kind eyes. She took in Joy's old-school kitchen clock, her bright green splashback, her neatly hung utensils.

But when she did look back, Joy was smiling at her.

"You're welcome. To tell you the truth, it can be a bit lonely being mayor and having so much to deal with, so it's nice to have the company." Now it was Joy's turn to look away. "And it's weird to think we only met properly last night, isn't it? And here we are eating beans in my kitchen."

Scarlet nodded. It really was. She couldn't believe it'd been less than 24 hours since she'd turned up on Joy's doorstep. So much had happened. So many emotions. In reality, more emotions than Scarlet had let herself feel in years. Keeping a lid on feelings was far easier than allowing them to roam free. Open yourself up, and people punish you, leave you. Scarlet had learned the lesson and toughened up.

Until last night.

"It is weird, but it's lovely," Scarlet replied. "And you were right — the kindness of strangers today was overwhelming. At the stadium, the guys who run the local Indian restaurant round the corner brought over a whole pot of curry. They set up a makeshift table and served it with rice and naan bread. Nobody asked them, they just did it." Scarlet shook her head. "And the amount of people at the club — supporters, footballers, coaches, and just locals, all helping to do the clean-up of the stadium and the surrounding area. People power in action."

Joy smiled at that. "You see, what did I tell you? Never underestimate the power of people and the kindness in the world."

Tears pricked the back of Scarlet's eyes, but she swallowed them down. Kindness wasn't something that had been in her life much lately, but recent events had restored her faith in humanity. It was going to take more than one day, but Joy was living proof it was out there, as was everyone she'd met today. Her parents would have been part of it, too, if they were alive.

Oh no, why did she start thinking about them? She

didn't want to cry again in front of Joy, not two nights running. But her body had other ideas. A tear trickled down her cheek and she wiped it away quickly, turning her head away. She took a huge sniff and wiped her sleeve across her nose, a trail of snot glistening there. Attractive.

Scarlet held it together in life; it was what she did. But where Joy was concerned, that seemed like it was impossible. Joy tugged down her defences, laid Scarlet bare.

And Joy was a lesbian. A newly out lesbian. Scarlet wasn't truly sure what implications that held. Whatever they were, she wasn't sure she was ready for them. From moving at a snail's pace, life was suddenly hurtling around her senses and through her veins at 100 miles an hour.

* * *

Joy could see Scarlet was floundering. She raced back over the conversation, not sure what she'd said to provoke tears, but they were there in Scarlet's eyes. What could she do to make it better? Perhaps a change of subject, or a cup of tea. Was it talking about Scarlet's marriage that had set her off? Or talking about Joy's family?

Joy jumped up and put the kettle on, turning to Scarlet, who was still sniffing. Maybe she could even up the family score by asking about Scarlet's nearest and dearest. Yes, that was a good plan.

"Are your family from round here? I take it not, with your accent."

At the question, Scarlet's face went from sad to alarm,

and Joy could have kicked herself. Clearly, this change of subject wasn't welcome.

Scarlet began to bite her nails, then shook her head slowly. "I'm from down south originally, Dorset. My parents are both dead, and I've got twin brothers — one in Australia, one near Preston, but I don't see him that often." Scarlet hugged herself with both arms, exhaling deeply before she spoke again. "I've got some aunts, a few cousins, but we don't really keep in touch." She shrugged. "You know how it is." A pause.

"Then my relationship went kaput, so I moved here a few years ago because everyone told me people up north were friendly. But when I got here, I found the people were the same as they are everywhere else." She shrugged again. "I live in a basement flat and I barely even know my neighbours." She paused. "*Lived in a basement flat.*"

"But you were out with friends today?" Joy was trying to halt the evening's slide into melancholy. She'd been enjoying this new side of Scarlet, the more care-free, open side. The one who giggled and smiled broadly. Her whole face lit up when she laughed. Joy didn't want to lose it, but she could already feel the mood slipping through her fingers like sand.

"They're my football friends — I only ever see them on matchdays, never at any other time. One of them offered me his spare room, but I don't want to be a spare part in his house with him and his fiancée. And that's how I feel most days, really — a spare part." Scarlet shook her head, her every action appearing heavy, grating. "I've never really fitted in anywhere, so I guess that's just me." She picked up her knife, then quickly put it down again. "I'm a misfit, but I live with it."

Joy didn't think Scarlet was a misfit, not by a long shot. Scarlet was strong and bold, living her life just the way she wanted it. She'd got married to a woman she loved, she'd endured loss, but she was still standing, coming out the other side. If anything, Joy was the misfit in this situation, not Scarlet.

Definitely not Scarlet.

Scarlet got up abruptly and took her plate to the kitchen, stacking the dishwasher. Then she stood next to Joy, clearly not sure of her next move. The tension of the moment hovered in the air around them. Joy could feel Scarlet packing up the conversation, sweeping it under the carpet and wiping her hands on the way out already. But she didn't want Scarlet to disappear — literally or metaphorically.

Joy had been enjoying her company and wanted her to stay, so she jumped in, determined to lift the mood back up. "We're all misfits of some sort. I hardly fit the mayor role, do I?"

She touched Scarlet's arm, and her guest almost jumped out of her skin. Whatever was going on inside Scarlet's head, Joy would love to know. She wanted to sit Scarlet down, get her to tell her everything, make her see that her life wasn't worthless, meaningless, and that she could easily have exactly what she wanted. Because what Scarlet was searching for was probably the same thing everybody was searching for: love, happiness, friendship, and connection. All anybody needed, when it came down to it, was connection. That, and a reduced email inbox.

"You fancy a nightcap in the lounge?" Joy asked, keeping her voice light, trying to take the edge off the situation. "I promise, no depressing talk, only light, upbeat chat." Joy turned on her special smile saved for special occasions.

It didn't work. Scarlet had already shut down.

There was a short delay, as if they were speaking on a really bad international phone line.

"I should try to get some sleep tonight," Scarlet replied, shaking her head. "I might be able to get to my flat tomorrow, so I'll need to be rested for what's to come." Scarlet paused. "Thanks anyway."

Joy nodded, resigned, her shoulders slumping. She knew when she was beaten, that she should let Scarlet go and be alone, even if Joy desperately wanted to carry on talking. She hadn't talked truthfully in years, and now she saw her chance, she craved it like an addict.

But it would have to wait.

"I've moved your stuff into the room at the top of the stairs. I've changed the sheets, too, so it's all ready. Let me know if you need anything else."

Scarlet nodded, unable to hold Joy's gaze. "Will do," she said, brushing past her.

"And Scarlet?"

She turned and gave Joy a heart-breaking look. Whatever or whoever had happened to Scarlet, it'd left its mark, one that would be difficult to erase. The mark on Scarlet's heart was clearly done in permanent marker.

"You're very welcome here till your flat gets fixed up, so don't worry about that, okay? I mean it."

Scarlet gulped, then bit her lip. "Thanks," she said, her voice a whisper, before leaving the room.

* * *

The conversation with Joy had knocked Scarlet out. If you could call it a conversation. Words in a room, maybe. Scarlet had been rude, and Joy didn't deserve that: she was thoughtful, understanding, compassionate. Plus, it was becoming clear to Scarlet, *attractive*.

Scarlet slammed her head into her pillow as her libido pepped up, agreeing with her thoughts. Yes, Joy was attractive. And gay. And available. But the thing was, Scarlet really wasn't sure whether or not *she* was available. On the surface, sure. But underneath? She was too damaged, and she didn't want to inflict that on someone else. And that was even supposing Joy was amenable to it.

To her.

And Scarlet wouldn't blame her if she wasn't.

Scarlet had noticed Joy was good looking previously, of course she had. But back then, she'd just been 'the mayor', and everyone knew you didn't fancy the mayor.

Who the hell fancied their mayor? The mayor was normally a sweaty, older man with a patronising manner. A million miles from Joy.

And what if Scarlet told Joy? What then? If she let her guard down and acted on any feelings that might be stirring towards Joy, she knew the way it would go. The way it had gone with all of her previous encounters with women since Liv. It would start off fine, with Scarlet on her best behaviour. She would be courteous, and they'd be keen. And they'd have dinner, have sex, have drinks. Perhaps not in that order. It would be nice. *Nice*. What sort of a word was that?

But Scarlet would never really commit, unbeknown to them. And then gradually, slowly but surely, she'd begin inching out the door, unhooking herself from the unsuspecting woman, until before the other person knew it, Scarlet wasn't returning their calls, she wasn't answering their texts. Scarlet had left the building, leaving the other woman totally confused.

Because as soon as the other person wanted to know more about her, Scarlet was gone. Scarlet had been down that road before, and she knew where it led. Love, dependency, hopes, dreams. When you opened yourself up, people took advantage. When really, all it took was some gumption up front, some strength, and you need never let yourself get into such a vulnerable position. Simple.

Only, this time, Scarlet had begun differently. This time, there was no beginning, no dating, no pretence. This time, life had thrown Joy and her together, and Scarlet's defences had been breached, much like the town's flood defences. Scarlet didn't stand a chance, and the only plan she'd come up with was to run out of the kitchen, because if she didn't run, who knew where it might lead? Yes, she was upset about her parents, but also about what was happening. Was 'upset' the right word? Perhaps 'confused' covered it better. Or even 'scared'.

Scarlet wasn't ready to take a chance again.

At least, that's what she *had* thought. The only thing was, Joy made her feel like she *could* be ready, at some point. Around Joy, Scarlet was smiling again. There was a kernel of friendship budding, and Scarlet hadn't had one of those in years. Not with another woman. Not with another *gay* woman. She didn't want to scupper the chance of that with her libido, which needed tending. She could handle that herself.

She needed a friend way more than she needed a lover, and she didn't dare to dream the two could be interlinked. Opening herself up to any possibility was just too scary to consider, so she held back; it was the best way. Yes, she was living life on cruise control, between the lines. She had no relationship ups, no relationship downs. She simply had time, hours and hours of time, with nobody to spend them with and nowhere to go. The chat about her family had truly brought that home to her — she'd tried to come off as nonchalant, but every word had shredded her heart.

Scarlet exhaled. Joy had even made up a new bed for her: where had she come from? She was so normal, so grounded. Everything Scarlet wasn't.

Scarlet couldn't go there — she simply *couldn't.*

Yet, all the while, despite the ticker-tape of doubt playing in her brain, there were also rays of hope sliding through. Hope, laced with fear and excitement. The usual feelings when it came to meeting new women. Would Joy even entertain the idea of her and Scarlet? The town mayor with the town misfit?

Scarlet shook her head, then covered it with her pillow.

Chapter Six

Joy woke up the next day raring to go; it was amazing what a full night's sleep could do for you. She lay under her heavy winter duvet, phone in hand, checking Twitter to see what damage the overnight rain had done. It didn't seem as bad as they'd expected, which was something. However, there was more rain forecast for today, and the extra water meant the floods hadn't receded as swiftly as anticipated. It was going to be touch and go whether Scarlet would be able to get back into her flat today, and Joy could only imagine how she'd take that news. She hoped she'd had a good night's sleep, too, and woken up refreshed after last night's meltdown.

And what would Scarlet make of Joy, now she knew the truth? Of course, she wasn't going to judge Joy for being a lesbian: Joy wasn't worried about that. But Joy had been married to a man — how did that sit with Scarlet? She hadn't reacted adversely, so Joy hoped she was fine with it; she had to believe she was.

Scarlet was the first person outside her close circle Joy had come out to. Her gran knew, Steve knew, her friend

Wendy knew, but it wasn't out in the wider world. Joy had meant to do it gradually, but it'd been harder than she thought, with 38 years of denial to unpick. Then, when she'd been selected as town mayor, Joy had been scared to go public fully.

Scarlet was the first new person she'd felt comfortable enough to share with.

Scarlet was significant.

Joy threw back her covers and hopped into her ultra-fluffy dressing gown, a Christmas present to herself. Without a husband or girlfriend to buy for her now, Joy put extra effort into buying for herself on big occasions these days, especially now she had a public image to maintain. She worked hard so she deserved it, and this dressing gown was perfect. Because the other plus point about buying gifts for yourself was that you got exactly what you wanted *every single time*.

Joy was just about to turn the handle on her door when she heard movement on the landing. Scarlet was up. She hesitated. Was this the best presentation of herself, pyjamas and a dressing gown?

She stepped back and checked herself in the mirror. Her hair was flat, not sticking up, and she'd already cleaned the sleep from her eyes. Natural, that was the look she was going for. If she suddenly began getting dressed and putting on make-up to go to breakfast, that would be even weirder. It was *Scarlet*, not the queen.

Joy gave herself a pep-up wink in her bedroom mirror,

before heading down the stairs and into the kitchen. Grey clouds were still looming, visible via the skylight overhead. But crucially, they didn't look quite as foreboding as they had the day before. Perhaps today would be a better day in the town. She was crossing her fingers, her toes, her eyes — whatever could be crossed, Joy was crossing it.

"Morning," Scarlet said from behind her, making Joy jump. She replaced the kettle in its holder and twisted around. Scarlet was fully dressed; Joy guessed she hadn't had time to pack a dressing gown.

"Morning," Joy replied. "How you feeling?" Scarlet appeared refreshed, her skin less taut than it had been when she ran out of the kitchen the previous evening.

Scarlet plonked herself down on one of the breakfast bar stools, reprising her position from last night. "Loads better after a proper night's sleep," she said, yawning. "You shouldn't have such comfortable guest beds: rule number one, my mum used to say." Scarlet shifted her position on the stool.

"I shouldn't?"

Scarlet shook her head. "Nope. Makes guests stay longer and come back more often. My mum would have had them sleeping on barbed wire camp beds if she'd had her way. Luckily, my dad was a bit kinder."

Joy smiled. "Your mum sounds like a right character."

Scarlet smiled right back, beaming at the thought of her mum. "She really was." Then she paused. "But I also feel like I made a right tit of myself last night." Scarlet winced, before meeting Joy's eyeline. "Sorry I was rude, it'd just been a long day."

Joy waved a hand through the air to demonstrate how little it mattered. "You weren't rude at all. If anything, you're holding up remarkably well." Then she busied herself making tea, before setting it down in front of Scarlet. "So what are your plans today? Apart from letting me make you a slap-up breakfast, in celebration of your first Sunday here."

Joy leaned against the counter, folding her arms across her chest. She wanted to spoil Scarlet, to support her, to show her that the whole world wasn't out to get her. She had her fingers crossed Scarlet would let her, but she was aware it'd be a hard sell.

Scarlet stared up at the skylight, furrowing her forehead as she did.

"Depends on that," she said, pointing upwards. "If it decides to chuck another load of water on us today, I still might not be able to get into my flat. But if the weather gods are smiling on us, who knows?" She sighed. "Failing that, I thought I'd go back to see Dan, the one I mentioned who has cancer, see if he needs any more help." Scarlet paused. "How about you?"

Joy pursed her lips. "More emergency meetings after lunch, and when I'm not at those, I'll be helping out where I can."

"If you make it back in time, do you fancy watching a film later? I feel like I need a shot of normality in my day."

"I like the sound of that *a lot*," Joy said, burying her head in the fridge, before emerging with bacon, sausage, eggs, and tomatoes. "Feels like we've been running around chasing our tails forever, and today I've been summoned to the town hall again. I'm sure we can find something suitably trashy on Netflix. Maybe even a dredge up an old lesbian film from my limited collection. I went on a spree and bought a ton when I left Steve." Joy flashed Scarlet a grin.

Scarlet raised an eyebrow at her. "Oh really?" she said. "I hope you've watched all the classics."

"Let's see," Joy said, beginning to count on her fingers. "I bought *High Art,* and that was a barrel of laughs," she began.

Scarlet snorted. "You should have checked the reviews before you bought that one. That was from an era when all lesbian movies had to end with someone dying. Luckily, we've gone beyond that now. Well, sort of."

"Thank goodness!" Joy said. "It was beautifully shot, but I was utterly depressed by the end. Heroin chic to the hilt, mind."

"Absolutely."

Joy continued counting on her fingers. "Then there was *Imagine Me & You*, which I loved, and *Better Than Chocolate*, which I believe falls into the so-bad-it's-good category. *But I'm A Cheerleader* was fab, but then I watched *The Kids Are Alright* and wanted to slap Julianne Moore, even though I love her. What was she doing sleeping with that bloke?"

Scarlet laughed. "That's something else that had to happen in lesbian films of yore, the woman runs off with a guy. I know it *does* happen, but not as often as Hollywood would have you believe." Scarlet paused. "Have you watched the *L Word* yet?"

Joy shook her head; she knew she should have, but she just hadn't had the time. Her friend Wendy had even bought her the first series, but it was still sitting on her shelf, waiting to be watched. "I haven't yet, but it's on my list."

Scarlet let her mouth hang open in mock-shock. "Well there's our evening sorted — we can watch the entire first series, the best by a country mile. And you get to have an education on how impossibly glamorous and rich lesbians live in LA. It's very close to how we all live here, obviously."

Joy let out a bark of laughter. "I'm sure it's exactly like living in Yorkshire," she laughed. "I take it you want a full English, by the way?"

Scarlet nodded, a smile slowly spreading across her face. "I really like this hotel, have I mentioned that?" She blew on her tea before taking a sip.

"Make the most of it," Joy said. "I've cooked for two days in a row now — unheard of." She sliced open the packet of bacon with a knife. "I'm also planning on going up and visiting my gran today, if you fancy a change of scene," Joy added, glancing up at Scarlet. She hadn't planned on inviting her, but now she'd said it, it seemed to make sense. Scarlet didn't know many people in the town, and the Grasspoint residents were a friendly bunch who always made her smile, so she assumed they'd do the same for her guest.

She couldn't gauge Scarlet's reaction as her face stayed blank.

"Just to check and see how everyone is," Joy continued. "I worry about them more when something like this happens. But if you don't fancy it, no problem at all."

Scarlet shook her head. "I'd love to come," she said. "I'd give anything to still have my grandma here, so I'd love to meet yours. She sounds important to you."

"She is." Joy smiled, a warmth flowing through her. Somehow, it was important to her that Scarlet meet her gran, even though Joy was well aware that introducing Scarlet to Clementine was going to send her grandma's eyebrow-raising into orbit.

* * *

After breakfast, Joy and Scarlet sat at the breakfast bar with two fresh mugs of tea, getting in an extra shot of caffeine before facing the day. Joy was semi-smart today in black trousers and a green shirt paired with a silk scarf: she was being mayor later, after all.

"You know, I really do feel like I owe you an apology about last night," Scarlet said, after taking her first sip of her new tea. She clasped her hands before continuing, as if wrestling the words, moulding them between her fingers. "We were having a laugh and you'd cooked me a lovely dinner, but then I went a bit weird and wandered off, so I'm sorry. I'm still a bit touchy when it comes to talking about my family. Plus, you were just being really lovely to me, and I didn't want to break down. Not again." She risked a glance at Joy, who was listening intently, her face a portrait of compassion.

Scarlet ploughed on. "It's just hard when something like this happens and you don't have the normal support systems in place. It's been a bit overwhelming and made my barriers come down, which is unnerving." She took a large gulp of air before continuing. "Barriers haven't been kind to me in the past few days, have they?"

Joy smiled. "You might say that."

"But this is too big to face alone, so I know I shouldn't try to…" Scarlet looked away, composing herself, trying to fight back the tears, but it was impossible. Since the flood, tears seemed to have moved into the spot in her make-up where cynicism and pessimism used to live.

Joy reached over and gave her a tissue, before squeezing Scarlet's knee to comfort her.

Scarlet wobbled on her stool, the contact taking her by surprise. Now she knew Joy was a lesbian, every bit of contact had taken on new meaning. She took another deep breath before carrying on. Her brain was even more scrambled now than it had been before. Adrenaline fizzed round her body and all she could focus on was Joy's hand. On her knee.

Contact.

With another woman.

Who she was attracted to — she had no doubt about that now.

"I really do appreciate everything you've done for me. I don't know what I would have done otherwise." Scarlet blew her nose as she finished, taking in Joy's open, honest face. And now, for the first time, her soft, pink lips. It would be so easy to lean forward and kiss them now, but also slightly inappropriate when she still had snot and tears dripping from her eyes and nose. She had a feeling she wasn't at her prettiest.

"You have to stop thanking me, you know," Joy said. "It's been great having you, and I plan to help you get through this in any way I can, I mean it." Joy leaned forward and took Scarlet's hand.

Scarlet forgot to breathe.

"You're not alone in this. I'm here for you 100 per cent, okay?" Joy ran her thumb lightly over Scarlet's knuckles, but the gesture was so intimate, she might as well have just slipped her fingers inside her. Scarlet's body went into high alert mode, all systems blaring. She concentrated on not hyperventilating or collapsing on the floor, which could be construed as a slight over-reaction.

All that stuff she'd said about not wanting to get involved with Joy, not acting on what she was feeling? She was ready to chuck it aside at any moment, she knew that now. One move made by Joy and her resolve would crumble like a shortbread biscuit.

Scarlet was pulled out of her reverie by a sudden

knocking at the front door. She blinked and shuddered, and Joy did the same. They both locked eyes on their intertwined hands at the same moment, staring at them as if they were a bomb. Then Joy let go of Scarlet's hand, before jumping up and running to get the door.

Scarlet stared at her red hot hand. She clung to the breakfast bar to steady herself, then took a hefty slug of tea. She had to concentrate and remember to breathe.

In, out; in, out.

Scarlet heard the door open, then muffled voices, then the door shut. She turned on her stool, not quite sure what to say to Joy after their brief moment had been interrupted, but any words that had been forming fell away when Joy returned.

She wasn't alone. Standing beside her was a man in running gear, breathing heavily. He'd clearly just been out for a run, even in this dismal weather. That was commitment for you. Or madness.

"Oh, I didn't realise you had company," he said, glancing at Joy.

Then he looked at Scarlet and his face became a question mark.

"This is Scarlet, her flat was flooded so she's staying for a while till it dries out," Joy said, walking over to the kettle and refilling it. It didn't escape Scarlet's notice that Joy wasn't looking at either of them as she spoke. Plus, Joy's voice, which had been light and airy, now had a sharp edge to it.

"Scarlet, this is my ex-husband, Steve."

Scarlet accepted Steve's outstretched hand, before grabbing another tissue from the box and blowing her nose. She must look a state; she hadn't intended to have an audience for her tears. Especially not Joy's ex-husband.

"Sorry to hear about your flat," Steve said, leaning against the kitchen counter like he belonged there. Which, Scarlet realised, he used to. But he didn't anymore. In fact, he looked starkly out of place, all hot air and breathlessness in a kitchen where a moment had just been shared.

"Terrible what's happened." He paused, glancing at Joy. "We're the lucky ones, aren't we? There but for the grace of god and all that."

Joy didn't respond, just made Steve a cup of tea. Steve had waltzed in at exactly the wrong moment. It had been their moment, and then Steve had gatecrashed. Was this a regular occurrence? Scarlet had no idea.

"So how much water got into your flat?" Steve was helping himself to biscuits from the tin on the side, like he lived here. "I was just on my way home from my jog and thought I'd check on Joy, see if she was okay. We might not be husband and wife anymore, but I still care," he said with a smile. "Better to be safe than sorry." He took a bite into his biscuit and grinned at Joy. "Glad to see you're still stocking my favourite," he told Joy through a mouthful of chocolate chip.

"They're my favourite, too." Joy's voice sliced through the air like a machete.

Scarlet gave Joy a weak smile, which she hoped portrayed that she understood. Scarlet was picking up the vibes that Steve wasn't welcome far quicker than Steve himself. Again, Scarlet pondered if this had been a regular occurrence in their marriage. She had a feeling it might have been.

"In answer to your question," she told Steve, "all of the water got into my flat. I live in a basement flat on Colville Road. My flat drowned."

Telling a stranger was totally different to telling Joy. Telling Steve felt like it was somebody else telling him, like it hadn't really happened to her. She was distancing herself from the reality and his reaction. She was going to have to get used to this reaction, she knew. Scarlet wasn't one to take other people's sympathy well. She remembered it from when her parents had died. What the hell did anybody else know about the situation she was in? It was her living it, after all.

"That really sucks," Steve said, his face contorting into a mask of sympathy. "Good job Joy was around to save the day. She's like that, though. A model citizen, which is why she was the perfect choice for mayor." He shot Joy an affectionate smile, before speaking with his mouth full again. Did it bother Joy as much as it bothered Scarlet? Some crumbs fell from his mouth and hit the floor. "So you just met the other night?"

Scarlet shot Joy a glance, and she spied a fleeting panicked look gloss over Joy's face. She didn't blame her

— Scarlet was confused by what was going on, too. The answer to Steve's question was a simple yes, but somehow after the last 48 hours, it wasn't so simple anymore. The playing field wasn't level, and their relationship was so much more already than strangers who were being kind to each other.

Steve looked from one to the other, then stopped chewing, his mouth now hanging open.

"Oh," he said. "Are you two… together?" He flicked his index finger towards Joy, then Scarlet, as reality dawned.

"No!" Scarlet said, at exactly the same time as Joy, and both of them a little too sharply.

Scarlet might as well have slapped the kitchen counter with her hand to accompany the words, such was their force. All three of them winced at the tone.

"I mean, we've met before," Scarlet said, blushing like they'd just been caught with their pants down. "I work at the council, so…" She tailed off, leaving Steve to fill in the rest of the blanks.

Steve finally swallowed the biscuit he'd been chewing extra-slow, his chat now dried up. He shot a questioning glance towards Joy, but when she ignored him, he busied himself by tweaking the waistband of his track pants, then brushing down the front of his fluorescent top.

"Look, don't worry about that tea — second thoughts, I should really get home and change out of this gear. Plus, I'm meeting Sharon for lunch, so I should get moving." He offered a hand to Scarlet. "It was lovely to meet you, and I hope you can get back into your flat soon," he told her.

Steve's eyes searched her face for a clue to his earlier question, but Scarlet concentrated on giving nothing away. She had nothing to give away, but she was sure her face was lit up right now, with the words *I like Joy!* tattooed on her forehead.

"Thanks," Scarlet replied, shaking Steve's hand.

"And I'll call you in the week," he told Joy. Then Steve almost sprinted for the door. "I can see myself out," he shouted over his shoulder.

They both waited for the front door to slam, before they relaxed, shoulders slumping downwards. They were silent for a moment or two, weighing up what had just happened. Scarlet wasn't exactly sure herself.

It was Joy who spoke first. "You know sometimes, when you see your ex, and you wonder what you ever saw in them?" she said, barely containing a smile now she was able to unclench her muscles.

Scarlet let out a bark of laughter. "Oh, I know that feeling." She locked eyes with Joy, and desire swept through her body. Yep, no doubt about it, the gears had shifted in Scarlet this morning.

"And the way he just stood there chewing his food so loudly in my kitchen," Joy added with a shake of her head.

When she heard that, Scarlet could do nothing but grin.

* * *

After Steve gatecrashed their breakfast moment, something changed. Something slight and nothing Joy could pinpoint, but it was there, this unnameable thing. And Joy was glad of its presence, its bulk. It couldn't be ignored, which simultaneously scared Joy and made her want to vomit with anticipation.

Joy led the way into Grasspoint, waving at Celia, who was on her phone as they walked in. The air was thick with the smell of Sunday roast being readied for the residents, and Joy's stomach rumbled, even though she was still full of her fry up. The residents were being entertained with bingo, which Joy should have remembered. Sunday lunchtime was always bingo time, and her grandma was a big fan.

However, when she looked up and saw Joy and Scarlet walking towards her, Clementine's curiosity was piqued enough to abandon her game and join them. And where bingo was concerned, that was a first.

"So *you're* the flood refugee," Clementine said, giving Scarlet the once over. Her grandma's barely concealed scrutiny of Scarlet made Joy cringe, but there wasn't much she could do. As she'd learned many times, old people simply didn't care what anybody else thought; they did what they liked.

"Joy didn't say you were attractive, although I should have guessed, I suppose, what with her being evasive when I asked if you were single. Now I can see why."

Joy closed her eyes as her cheeks flamed red. She wasn't even going to bother looking over at Scarlet. Had her gran really just said those words, out loud? Coming so soon after Joy and Scarlet's earlier moment in the kitchen, it was as if her gran was jumping up and down on the eggshells Joy had artfully laid out.

"Grandma! I thought we agreed that you embarrassing me should have stopped by now. Is this going to continue until I'm 50?"

Clementine flashed Joy a wide grin. "And beyond, if I'm still alive, dear. It's Grandma's right to do so, isn't it, Scarlet?"

Scarlet grinned. "Apparently it is," she said. "Lovely to meet you, I've heard a lot about you."

"Have you now?" Clementine said. "I'd like to say the same, but I'd be lying. My granddaughter only mentioned you yesterday, but then you are a recent development." She turned to Joy. "What are you doing here again, anyhow? You only came yesterday."

"Just thought I'd check if everything was okay up here."

"We're fine — it's the people at the bottom of the valley you need to worry about. Them, and Iris Heaton's granddaughter, who was meant to be getting married this Saturday at the football club. Crying shame, as apparently it's all underwater."

"It is," Scarlet said, her ears perking up. "Are you talking about Steph and Eamonn?"

Clementine's eyes widened. "I am, dear. You know them?"

Scarlet nodded. "Eamonn more than Steph, but yes."

"Well, you tell him he should think about having the reception here, at the new function room. Ask Celia, I'm sure she'd say yes. Iris said she'd tell them, but her memory isn't what it was, if you get what I'm saying." Clementine inclined her head towards them to emphasise her point.

"That's not a bad idea," Joy said, glancing at Scarlet. "You think your friend would be interested? We could have a look now and take some pictures."

"I'm sure he would be — he's desperate to find somewhere, and somewhere high and dry would be the ideal place."

"High and dry we can do — that describes us to a tee," Clementine told Scarlet, laughing. "Now Scarlet — what a name. Is it after Scarlet O'Hara, *Gone With The Wind* and all of that?"

Scarlet nodded. "It is — my mum was a big fan of her movies, so I got the film star name. It was either Scarlet, Grace, or Barbara. She didn't like Vivien, so she decided against that. When I was in school, how I yearned to be called something different. But now that I'm older, I kinda like Scarlet."

Clementine patted Scarlet's knee. "She was a beauty, too, so your mum clearly knew what she was doing."

Joy shot her grandma a look, but she ignored her. Gran was on a roll, and Joy knew there was nothing she could do apart from sit back and watch her play out, like an old movie she'd watched numerous times.

"My brothers are called Fred and Clark, after Clark Gable and Fred Astaire. I don't think my dad had any say in our names — I don't think he'd even seen any of their films before he met my mum. She always used to say she was born into the wrong era, born too late."

Clementine nodded her head. "It was a great era for many things, especially films." She paused. "So how's my granddaughter treating you? I hope she's given you the room with the view — gorgeous sunshine in that one." She didn't wait for an answer, turning to Joy while she took a breath. "And have you got coasters yet so your guests don't feel like they're crashing their glasses on your precious coffee table every time they move?" Clementine narrowed her gaze towards Joy.

Scarlet smiled as Joy floundered like a fish out of water.

"I haven't yet, what with coping with the flood and being the mayor and everything, but it's on my to-do list. Anything else you want to bring up now I've brought a friend along?" Joy asked, pursing her lips.

But Clementine knew this was a battle she'd already won, so she simply gave Joy a sweet smile. "Nothing else," she said, patting Joy's knee. "But give me a moment and I'll try to dredge up something else." She put a finger to her lips. "Of course, if I'd known you were coming, I'd have got your old baby photos out, and the ones from school. Especially the one of you with that terrible fringe your mother insisted on. But maybe we can save that for next time."

"I'd like that very much," Scarlet replied with a grin.

Joy sighed, shaking her head with a smile. "Oh please, don't encourage her."

Clementine laughed gently, clearly enjoying this a little too much. "Anyway," Clementine said, grabbing onto her armchair and levering herself up in one almost-swift move, "you want to come and have a look at the function room for your friend? I can get the key from Celia, and then we can have a cup of tea and you can tell me all about yourself, Scarlet."

Joy watched a brief flash of alarm cross Scarlet's face before she replaced it with a more general mask of normality. "Love to," Scarlet said.

But knowing Scarlet as she did, Joy was pretty certain that was a lie.

Chapter Seven

"You about ready to go?"

Joy nodded, looking around the community hall. "Yep — it's been a long day, but at least we've got a home to go to. Shall we pick up a takeaway on the way home?"

Scarlet wrinkled her face. "I was thinking we could swing by my road on the way home, see how they're doing, and if I might be able to get in tomorrow," she said. "And then maybe we could go to the pub for dinner — my treat as a thank you for having me." She paused, her eyes flicking up and down Joy's face. "What do you say?"

Joy nodded, a smile warming her face. "Let me get my coat."

Joy fell into an easy stride beside Scarlet, flipping the collars of her thick blue coat up to shield her neck from the biting January wind. Joy had spent the day in meetings as well as just listening to people's issues, while the town leaders and emergency services had been flat out all weekend in an effort to get the town cleaned up and people back in their homes as quickly as possible. Scarlet, meanwhile, had spent the day at the houses near the football club again, helping the clean-up effort as best she could.

"You think we're going to be able to see much in this light?" Joy asked, their footsteps echoing in the empty street. It was just gone 6pm, but the sky was already charcoal grey, the streetlights casting an insipid golden glow onto the evening.

"Dan told me the signs have gone from Slater Street, so I just wanted to see for myself."

"Dan?" Joy tugged her coat collar up some more.

"The one I was just talking to at the hall — I told you about him earlier, he's the one with terminal cancer?"

"Now I know why he looked so thin."

Scarlet nodded, looking straight ahead. "He's only 45, it's tragic." She stamped her hands firmly into her coat pockets. It was bitterly cold tonight and she could see her breath in front of her.

They turned the corner into Acron Street and Scarlet stopped walking. There was water shimmering in the road that crossed the bottom of the hill. Her road, that was now a mini-river. The road she'd called home for the past two years, that was no longer there. Underwater. Submerged.

She went to speak, but nothing came out. It was still a short, sharp shock, seeing it with her eyes. Sure, she'd seen the other streets, the main road, the football stadium. But seeing the street *she* lived on completely took the wind out of her sails. There was nothing inside her but lurching wind, threatening to topple her at any moment.

It wasn't often she missed the loving arms of her parents, but today was one of those moments. What Scarlet would have given to run home and fall into her mum's arms, but she knew she couldn't; Joy was as good as it was going to get.

Joy put an arm around Scarlet's shoulders and squeezed hard. "You okay?"

Scarlet wasn't, but she nodded her head anyway, knowing it would make Joy feel better.

Then she took a step away, shaking herself down, as if trying to shake off what she was seeing. "It's just that the water's still there. Over *two days* later, it's still there. And I know my flat's buggered," she said, tapping her index finger to the side of her head. "They told me that from the beginning, so I know it in my brain. But knowing it and seeing it are two completely different things."

Scarlet took a few steps forward, pausing at the top of the incline.

Joy tugged on her arm again. "Are you sure you want to go down there? You won't be able to get anywhere near your place still," Joy said. "Plus, it's freezing."

Scarlet turned and smiled at her. "You're right on the last bit," she said, shivering. She sucked on the inside of her cheek. She was touched at Joy's concern, but this was something she had to do, even if she couldn't really do much at all. She had to get as close as she could, and take it in. She was sure it would help when the time came for her to face the carnage up close. "You stay there. I'm just going to run to the bottom of the hill. I'll be back in a minute."

Scarlet took off, jogging slowly down the street lined with terraced houses, their front doors opening directly onto the pavement. Lights flickered inside the houses at the top of the street, with TVs visible, sofas occupied, mugs of tea steaming. This road had been affected, too, but only those at the flatter, bottom end. The houses at the top were still breathing sighs of relief they'd escaped.

But soon enough, Scarlet reached the less fortunate, and then she slowed right down. There was no way she could run on these pavements; they were too cluttered with the debris from people's lives. Sofas ruined, fridge-freezers discarded, tables smashed to bits. Piles of shoes and clothing lay sodden. Kitchen cabinets and a cooker stood outside one house, along with paintings and curtains. There was so much else Scarlet couldn't make out in the twilight, but the pavements weren't passable. There was just too much of people's former lives on show.

And the smell was making Scarlet gag. Mud, dirt, and sewage were compressed into every object the flood had come into contact with. It'd been drifting around the place ever since Friday night, but being up so close almost made Scarlet hurl.

She hadn't smelt it everywhere she'd gone; the overriding smell in some areas was bleach, council supplied and being liberally used. However, in some places, the sewage smell was nauseating, and this was one of them — right near to her flat. What's more, these houses could open windows and let loads of light and air in. In her basement flat, it wasn't going to be quite so easy. But she wasn't going to think about that now, because then she might make her own waterworks turn on again.

Positive thoughts, positive thoughts, positive thoughts.

Scarlet stopped at the barriers, around six feet away from the still waters. They'd been rushing in the previous few days, but now they were still, waiting to be told where to go, what to do next. If only the waters had been as obedient two days earlier.

Scarlet took a deep breath, then wished she hadn't. The smell was overwhelming. Coughing, she turned and stumbled up the hill and walked straight into Joy, who'd come halfway down.

Joy put her arms around Scarlet and held her tight.

Scarlet bit the inside of her cheek again, took another deep breath and cleared her throat. "Let's get to the pub, shall we, before I start to bawl on you again."

Joy hugged her a little bit tighter.

* * *

They were in what Scarlet's brother Clark would describe as her local, even though it wasn't, seeing as Scarlet hardly ever left her flat. When Clark had visited after she'd moved in, they'd come here for dinner, but that was the first and last time. It took seismic life changes for Scarlet to come here, it seemed.

But looking around now, Scarlet was thinking she should come in more. It was a homely pub with a modern touch, and the tables and chairs were reassuringly heavy. This pub reminded her of the many establishments she and Liv used to frequent in their life together: it was lived in and loved.

"You want to talk about it?" Joy was leaning back in her chair, giving Scarlet her comforting, warm stare. It wasn't helping.

"If you keep looking at me like that, I will cry again. Is that what you want?"

Joy held up both hands. "How should I look at you, exactly? Would you prefer it if I scowled?" A smile tugged at the corner of her mouth.

Scarlet laughed. "Maybe. Just stop looking so bloody... *concerned*. You're killing me with kindness."

"I will make an effort to be meaner." She paused. "But only if you tell me what's going on in your head."

Scarlet regained her composure and sat up straight in her chair. "We could be here for days."

Joy shrugged. "I've got time. And remember, I'm a life coach, so I don't get weird with silences. In fact, I embrace the silence. I love silence. So I won't change the subject, however much you hum and ha."

Scarlet narrowed her gaze. Joy wasn't giving up, even though Scarlet had been more than open with her since they met. "You want me to talk about it, here in this pub? I thought this was a friendly drink."

Joy nodded. "I do and it is. That's what friends do; they come out to the pub and talk about how they're feeling." Joy paused, fixing Scarlet with her stare. "Plus, I think you'll tell me more. We're in public, there are less places to run and hide."

"Run and hide? You already know way more about me than most." Scarlet paused. "I don't know what else to say. It's like I told you — I'm 39 years old, 40 this year, and everything I own can be fitted into a suitcase. I'm homeless and an adult orphan." Scarlet sighed. "I'm like a tragic case from the Victorian era. They might make a documentary about me or put me in a zoo."

Joy stroked her chin, one elbow on the table. "You know what I think?"

Scarlet shook her head.

"I think you're a glass half empty person and you need to switch your mindset around." She held up one hand, telling Scarlet she hadn't quite finished yet. "Hear me out on this one," Joy said. "I'm not going to contest all those things you just said. Yes, you are nearly 40 and yes, you are homeless. But you have a roof over your head, and your homelessness is temporary. You have friends. You have family, you just choose not to include them in your life, from what I can tell." She paused, holding Scarlet in place with her sharp examination of character. "You have a job and you have a new friend in me. So I would say, even though things aren't perfect, they're not a disaster just yet."

Scarlet didn't reply, but she didn't look away from Joy either. She didn't particularly want to hear what Joy had to say, as Joy seemed to favour logic, while Scarlet's natural outlook was pessimism. But Joy was giving her no choice, and it would be churlish of Scarlet to just cover her ears, which is what she wanted to do. Which meant she had to listen.

"Since when did you become my therapist, too?" Scarlet asked eventually.

Joy shrugged. "It's my job. From everything you've told me, maybe this flood is just the tonic you needed to kickstart your life. You've been in hiding far too long." She sat forward in her chair and pointed a finger at Scarlet. "I think the world deserves to see a bit more of Scarlet Williams, don't you?"

"I'm not sure Scarlet Williams agrees," Scarlet mumbled. She didn't like this side of Joy. The one that was poking her into action. She preferred the side that poured her whisky and let her wallow.

"And since when are you a life coach?" Scarlet furrowed her brow, trying to wrap her brain around this information. "What is a life coach, anyway? I thought it was one of those made-up terms that was strictly kept down south. You're a life coach and you live within half an hour of Manchester. Do they even allow life coaches this far north?"

Joy laughed, a loud, throaty laugh. "People need life coaches wherever they live. And I deliver it to business leaders and CEOs, as well as individuals. So you could say landing up with me is a double win. I'm determined to chip away at you and make the real Scarlet Williams stand up."

Scarlet folded her arms across her chest. Discontent bubbled up inside her. She wasn't sure she was wholly down with what Joy was saying. "And what if this is the real Scarlet Williams? What then?"

She'd managed the last few years burrowing herself into a liveable rut; she wasn't sure she wanted to come out. It was often too bright outside, and everyone was far too cheery for Scarlet's liking, even in the face of adversity. She thought about all the people at the community hall with their 'Keep Calm And Carry On' attitude. That community hall should have been a tin of condensed misery, but instead, it was a breeding ground for optimism.

Joy shook her head. "It's not, trust me. And deep down, you know that. You need to start living." She paused, before clicking her fingers together. "Take this weekend. It hasn't been a normal weekend for anyone. What would your normal weekend have looked like?"

Scarlet pointed a finger at her chest. "My weekend?"

Joy nodded.

"I'd have got up, had breakfast, gone to football, had a couple of pints with Matt and Eamonn, then come home and watched TV with a takeaway." Scarlet mumbled the last bit, embarrassed by how mundane her life sounded.

"And Sunday?" Joy's tone held compassion — she wasn't attacking Scarlet.

Scarlet drew on her pint, feeling the alcohol coat her system and pump up her confidence. "Do you put your clients on a couch?" Scarlet never liked being the centre of attention, and Joy was hitting far too many bull's eyes. Scarlet would try to steer her down another path, get her to talk about herself.

Come to think of it, Joy hadn't done much of the talking since Scarlet had been a guest at her house, but Scarlet had assumed that was because she was being kind and listening to her. She hadn't realised she was being assessed the whole time. It made her feel a little exposed.

"No, I don't," Joy replied. "But that's off the topic. What do you do on Sunday?"

Scarlet squirmed in her chair. "Why is it so important?"

Joy smiled at her. "You don't have to answer if you don't want to." She paused. "But I think you might feel better if you did."

Scarlet chewed the inside of her cheek. "Nothing, really," she said, eventually, the words sliding out of her mouth in slow motion. "I might go for a walk. I might watch football. I might read the paper. Normal Sunday things."

Joy nodded. "But you don't see anyone."

Scarlet trailed her finger up and down her pint glass. "I say hello to the man in the newsagents."

Joy raised an eyebrow. "Do you?"

Scarlet was rumbled and she shook her head. Joy was much better than the shrink she'd seen once after her mum's death.

"What I'm getting at is there's no human interaction."

"Human interaction is over-rated."

Joy's face lit up with laughter. It was a good look, Scarlet had to admit. The alcohol had infused Joy's cheeks with rouge and she looked happy and alive.

"I totally agree, but we all need it from time to time." Joy paused. "And how about this weekend? You've been out and about, chatting to people, staying with me. I know the circumstances aren't ideal, but if you take the flood out of the equation, how's this weekend been? How has it made you *feel*?"

Scarlet scanned through the days in her mind, from the time she left her flat in the early hours of Saturday morning. Sitting drinking whisky with Joy, joining in the clean-up at the stadium, chatting with people at the community hall, sharing breakfast with somebody else. And now here she was, out at the pub with another woman.

Scarlet was *living*, and that hadn't happened on a weekend in years, no matter what weekend it was.

"It's been... nice." Scarlet's voice was at a whisper. Joy wasn't going to let up, was she? Joy waited for her to continue, as Scarlet knew she would. "It's been social," she said, this time staring at Joy defiantly. Joy had her number, so what was the point in lying? "So, yes, apart from the

'I'm homeless and nearly 40 bit', I've even enjoyed it a little." Which sounded like a terrible thing to say.

"It's been your best weekend in ages?" Joy asked.

Scarlet gave a wry laugh. "You make me sound like a right sad case. My best weekend in years was the one where I got flooded?"

Joy smiled. "It's not that uncommon — adversity brings people together, makes you re-evaluate. Things you thought you couldn't live without, suddenly you can because you have to. They're simply not there anymore. That's why the 40s in Britain were seen as one of our happiest decades." She paused. "If you take out all the war, along with the death and bombs."

They both laughed at that.

Scarlet was silent for a moment, contemplating what Joy had said. She was right, Scarlet had enjoyed this weekend. Most of the time, she savoured Saturdays, but hated Sundays. But this weekend had been her most exciting in years, filled with drama, pep, and excitement. If it was turned into a film, it'd be a box office smash.

Scarlet flicked her gaze up at Joy and studied her face. "What about you?"

Joy was startled. "Me?" She furrowed her brow. It didn't wrinkle much, which Scarlet had noticed in their time together. How old was Joy again? Scarlet was fairly sure she was younger than her, but she had flawless skin. Scarlet used to work with a woman just like that and she'd been impressed daily.

"What do you normally do at the weekend, and how has this weekend been for *you*?"

Joy smoothed down her trousers, avoiding the question, then took a sip of her pint.

Did Joy normally drink beer? Somehow, it didn't sit right with her. But Scarlet decided not to ask that question right now. She was more interested in the answer that Joy was studiously trying to avoid. She could give it out, but could she take it?

"Well, I usually have mayoral engagements on a weekend. Other than that, I might read the paper, go to the gym, see Steve…" Joy tailed off, not looking at Scarlet.

"So essentially, take the 'being the mayor' bit out of the equation, and we have quite similar weekends." Scarlet sat back, her arms folded.

Joy sat up straighter, shaking her head. "No, I *see* people. Steve pops round most Sundays, and I go to friends' houses for dinner parties and drinks."

"When was the last time you did that?" Scarlet wasn't giving her time to wriggle out of this one. If Joy was going to ambush her about her life, then she could give as good as she got, life coach or not. The fact Joy looked adorably cute when she was flummoxed was an added bonus.

Joy cast her gaze up to the ceiling, then shrugged, looking down and studying her fingernails. "I don't know, not for a while. Three months ago?" She blushed as she said it.

Scarlet drummed her fingers on the table. "So once

every quarter, you go out with friends on the weekend. The rest of the time, you hide behind being the mayor, and occasionally see your ex-husband who's still in love with you."

"He is not still in love with me!" Joy said, slamming her fist down on the table. She had the good grace to look embarrassed by that. "Ouch," she said, shaking her hand. "Sorry, that was accidental." She lowered her voice, leaning into Scarlet. "Steve is *not* still in love with me. He's had a new girlfriend, Sharon, for months now." But even Scarlet could see she didn't believe her words 100 per cent.

"Uh-huh," Scarlet replied. "I don't want to argue about it, because it's a fact. Steve is still in love with you. And he was hurt when he turned up on the doorstep and you had another woman in your kitchen — the look on his face was a picture. I take it that's never happened before?"

Joy shook her head slowly. "No."

Scarlet raised an eyebrow. "Never once? Since you two split up — how long ago?"

"Two years," Joy replied.

"And he's never seen you with another woman?"

Joy shook her head. "I don't really parade them around the town when I get together with someone." She paused. "Besides, I figured I'd give this year over to being mayor, and that comes with responsibilities. I don't want to drag someone else into that, so I haven't really been on the market."

Scarlet coughed. "You've not been dating because

you're mayor?" Her tone was incredulous. "And you've been having a go at *my* life." She raised her second eyebrow in as many minutes. "You realise how stupid that sounds? I think Dulshaw could cope with you having a girlfriend. The town would not grind to a halt or go into shock. It's the 21st century, not medieval times."

Joy put her head down and didn't move.

Scarlet was blindsided. Was it Joy's turn to cry now? She hadn't expected tears, she just wanted Joy to see that nobody's life was perfect, and that she should be living the life she wanted, too.

"You okay?" Scarlet said, leaning over and putting a hand on Joy's arm.

Joy jumped like she'd just been shot. She rubbed her palms up and down her face, before nodding. "Yes, I'm okay. At least, I will be when I get over the shock of having my life dissected for me." She laughed, but it was hollow. "You don't pull any punches, do you?" Joy flicked her gaze up at Scarlet, then back down again. "Maybe you should consider being a life coach."

Scarlet shook her head. "Nah, too much talking and touchy-feely involved for me." She paused. "But I'm sorry if I hurt your feelings; I didn't mean to. But maybe it's time to start being the real you, too. Get a girlfriend, get on with your life, and don't worry about what anybody thinks, including Steve."

Was Scarlet really lecturing Joy on relationships? Apparently, she was.

Joy nodded her head slowly. "I know all of that, and believe me, it's not something I haven't told myself. But it's easier said than done, seeing as I don't exactly have a string of women banging down my front door."

"You and me both," Scarlet said, her gaze lingering on Joy's face. "Not that I've got a door for them to knock down anymore."

"There is that," Joy said, wincing in sympathy. "For me, it just felt easier this year to be the mayor, get my life back on track, and *then* think about getting back in touch with friends and perhaps a relationship after that."

"And what does your grandma think of that plan?"

"Oh, I think you could tell when you met her, she's on your side. She says I should get myself out there and get back in the game. This was a woman who was married three times in her life as she always tells me, so she's got experience of starting over. She liked Steve, there wasn't much to dislike, but as she told me, she probably liked him more than I did. Sadly, she might have been right." Joy sighed.

"Grandmas are normally right, even if they have a very direct way of saying so," Scarlet replied with a smile. "Have we really both just agreed that getting flooded has been the most exciting thing that's happened in our lives in the past two years?" She began laughing gently. It was the craziest thing to say, but she was pretty sure it was a correct assumption for the pair of them.

Joy gave her a grin. "Sadly, I think we have," she said, letting out a sneeze in the process. She wrinkled her nose to recover, before continuing. "Can this be our little secret?"

Scarlet nodded. "Absolutely — need-to-know basis. By which I mean, nobody ever needs to know."

"Perfect."

* * *

Scarlet placed two more pints of Peroni on the table in front of them, along with two packets of crisps. "Pre-dinner snack," she told Joy, handing her a menu. "You know what you want?"

Joy shook her head. "Not really." She put the menu down without looking at it.

Scarlet opened one of the bags of crisps, tutting as she did so. "Why can't you just get salt and vinegar anymore? Why does it always have to be sea salt and cider vinegar? Poncey crisp companies."

Joy smiled at her weakly. "I need to stop Steve coming round all the time and being my saviour, don't I?"

Scarlet held up a hand. "Whoa, where did that come from?"

Joy laughed. "I've just had five minutes of thinking while you were at the bar buying beer and poncey crisps."

Scarlet grinned at her, taking a handful of crisps. "You just need to set up new boundaries with him, that's all. Does he have a key to your house?"

Joy nodded. He'd been the obvious candidate for her

spare key when they'd split up. Their break-up hadn't been acrimonious, just sad.

"Is that the house you both used to live in?"

Joy shook her head. "No — he's still in that one, he bought me out. Moving out seemed like the right thing to do, seeing as it was me who was breaking up with him." Plus, Joy hadn't wanted to hold on to the memories they'd made in that house. She'd wanted a clean break, a fresh start, and starting over again in a new house was all part of that.

"I'll add 'noble' to your list of attributes." Scarlet said. "And do you have a key to his house?"

"I do," Joy replied. "He's never used my key, it's just in case I get locked out. You saw yesterday — he knocks when he comes round, doesn't just march in. We're each other's emergency key place." She paused. "He doesn't overstep boundaries, he's respectful." She might not be married to him anymore, but she didn't want to badmouth Steve when it wasn't necessary.

Scarlet crossed her legs and snagged more crisps. "Okay. Then maybe you need to get a girlfriend and have her there when he next turns up. He'd soon get the message that his Sunday morning call is one routine he needs to change. If you look at it in another way, it's a little bit controlling — he likes your life the way it is because it fits with his." Scarlet paused. "Or else, you could say he's trying to hold on to you and the past, and this is the last crumb of you he has. But you both have to move on."

Joy recoiled. She was sure she was meant to be the

wise one here, but Scarlet had turned the tables. "Tell me again when you turned into a sage advice-giver?"

Scarlet rolled her eyes. "Clearly living with you for two days has rubbed off," she said. "But honestly, you can change your relationship with Steve step by step, that's not hard. The putting yourself out there is the more difficult part. I should know, I've been avoiding it for the past few years, too. What's the point when all relationships end in heartbreak or death?"

"Now you've gone from being wise to the bringer of doom."

"It's a talent I have."

Joy smiled at Scarlet, admiring again her eyes, the colour of rich cocoa. She could interrupt her routine for those eyes, of that she had no doubt. "Putting myself out there — properly putting myself out there, not just dipping my toe in the water? That's a scary thought. Don't forget, I'm new to this."

There was nothing Joy would like more than to find a girlfriend, someone to call at night, wake up with in the morning, share things with. But she was so new to this, it scared her. Sure, she'd slept with a couple of women, and that had been a real eye-opener, but neither of them had been girlfriend material. Joy wanted to meet someone she connected with. Someone local. Someone like... Scarlet? When that thought clattered into the front of her brain, Joy jolted with the weight of its meaning. She blinked a few times to try to erase it, then focused again on... Scarlet.

Nope, there was the thought again, throwing stones at her window like a lovesick teenager.

"It's a doddle," Scarlet replied. "Look at me, I'm a walking example of how easy girlfriends are to get. I can't stop the women turning up. Especially at weekends, as we've surmised." Scarlet let out a long, low laugh, before leaning forward, hooking her gaze around Joy.

Joy was transfixed.

"To clarify: when you say new, you've slept with a woman, right?"

Joy nodded, embarrassment burning through her body. "Of course!" she replied, like that question was preposterous.

"Okay, good, I was just checking you weren't an absolute beginner." Scarlet cocked her head. "And I take it that went alright, otherwise you wouldn't be coming back for more."

Joy took a slug of her beer. She wasn't normally a beer drinker, but she'd said yes to a pint when Scarlet ordered her own, not wanting her to think her any less of a woman. Which, now she thought about it, was frankly ridiculous. Joy should have just ordered a rum and coke like she normally would. But right now, when she needed something to deflect attention from herself, having a pint of beer to hide behind was perfect.

"This is getting a little more personal than I imagined," Joy said, her cheeks reddening that bit further.

She recalled the woman who'd taken her second

virginity — her name had been Heather, and she'd had a cute dimple and split ends. They'd met online, had a couple of drinks, and shared some tacos in a tex-mex place in Manchester. Heather had chewed the tacos with her mouth wide open, and right from the start, Joy had known it was going nowhere long-term, but she had been determined to get what she needed from the encounter. And she had.

"Let's just say, it was a promising start, but I want to meet someone I connect with. I mean, I kinda had that with Steve, but not really." She paused, rolling images of her life with Steve around her mind. It had so nearly been there and she'd kidded herself for years it was what she wanted.

She sighed. "I don't know. Getting out of my marriage seems like the easy bit now. Meeting someone I want to be with is *way* harder than I thought."

Scarlet frowned, studying Joy. "But have you even tried? I mean, really tried? Have you been on dates?"

"I went on two dates."

"With two different people?"

"Yes." Joy exhaled, annoyed.

"So you've never had a second date with a woman?"

"No. I've had two dates and slept with two women."

"Ouch."

"What?" She narrowed her eyes. What exactly was Scarlet getting at?

"You need to sleep with someone who gives you better

sex. You slept with two women, which should have been a eureka moment."

"It was!"

"I'd say it wasn't that much of one, otherwise you would have gone back for more, am I right?"

Joy shook her head. "Not really — I wanted to try it out, see if I was right in my assumption that I'm gay. And believe me, I was right. It just felt… right. Better. Different." She paused. "But neither of the women I slept with were women I'd want a relationship with. I was attracted to them on some level, and I thought they'd be good for me to break my duck. And they were, but nothing more."

"Wow, you make sex sound like a science experiment. You're way more matter-of-fact about these things than I've ever been. Maybe that's where I've been going wrong."

"I don't know about that," Joy said, with a frown. "I don't want you to think I'm cold-hearted and clinical about this — I'm not. I want what everyone wants, the full package, but I wanted to get the 'first time' bit out of the way before that. Because nobody likes a 38-year-old virgin, do they?"

"Wasn't there a film about that?"

"They rounded up the age, it sounds better," Joy replied.

Scarlet let out a bark of laughter. "I'd have liked it more if you'd been the lead, though — you're way prettier than Steve Carell. And I think you'd have lasted longer than 30 seconds on your first time, too."

Desire flooded Joy's system as she formed an image of her and Scarlet in bed together, Scarlet under Joy, Joy taking full control. Her clit twitched as she did, and she couldn't look Scarlet in the eye. Joy wasn't sure when this conversation had taken the turn it had, but now she was all riled up and confused, too.

Was Scarlet a possibility for her? Was she thinking the same thing? Joy had absolutely no idea, and if she was, that scared the hell out of her. Because if Joy had the possibility of having a relationship with someone who she liked *and* connected with, she might have to surrender herself: she might have to let herself go, live for the moment, fall in love. A compatible partner might just explode her world. Just like the image of a naked Scarlet was doing to her mind right now.

"Anyway, let's get off the subject of my sex life, or lack thereof, shall we? Enough embarrassment for one night." Joy paused. "But despite everything, this weekend has been kinda fun, and meeting you has been the highlight. Even if you do give me the third degree. I can't believe we've lived so close to each other and yet never really met, not properly."

"We did meet at the football, but you ignored me."

"I didn't ignore you!" Joy said, frowning. "The stadium deal has just been difficult. *Really difficult.*"

She'd known what the football club and the stadium meant to Scarlet and the others when she'd met them, but it hadn't been her decision to approve the development, due to begin in three year's time. If it was up to Joy, the plans would have been thrown out on the first hearing, but the building firm had some council connections, and she could always see the way it was going. Modern politics was a bit like life — it wasn't about what you knew, it was who you knew. Whatever, Joy was glad she'd had the chance to meet Scarlet again.

"Meeting you has been far from difficult. It's certainly made a change from reading the papers and going to the gym." Joy circled her hand above the table. "I mean, look at this — I'm out on a Sunday night, drinking in a pub. Unheard of!"

Scarlet's face crinkled as she laughed.

"You should do that more often, you know."

"What?"

"Laugh, smile, let go. You light up when you do." Joy felt a rush at her core as she said it, and she crossed her legs to take her mind off that fact. It was true, though: Scarlet had spent the weekend wallowing in misery, but when she changed her focus, her whole being changed.

"If you're trying to embarrass me now, you're doing a good job."

Joy shrugged. "Just being truthful."

Scarlet studied her before replying. "And did I tell you about Dan, the guy at the hall today? He was offering me money to get back on my feet again. He's the one with cancer and he was going to leave it all to a charity, but he's decided to come to the community hall and give it away. I told him I couldn't take it, but he was insistent." She shook her head again. "All this kindness, it flies in the face of everything I've known over the past few years. And now I have it, I'm not sure what to do with it."

Joy understood. When the world was against you, it was easy to fall into a pattern where you believed that's how it always was and always would be. You tended to bunker down, just as Scarlet had. But it didn't have to be so, and sometimes, you needed to look up and take a risk. She'd done it when she left Steve, and the world hadn't ended. Sure, there was still a way to go until she was fully out, but Joy had a feeling Scarlet could help her find the courage to complete that journey.

"Bottom line is, people are generally nice," Joy said. "That's human nature."

Scarlet smiled at Joy. "You know what, I think you were aptly named."

Joy laughed. Yes, she could be sweetness and light, but she could be other things, too. "You do? Tell that to Steve."

"Steve will get over it," Scarlet said, laughing gently. "But you — you're definitely a glass half full kinda woman. I might give it a try, but don't expect miracles overnight."

"I won't," Joy replied, just glad Scarlet wasn't crying anymore. "And what about you?"

Scarlet wrinkled her face. "What about me?"

"Your name," Joy said. "Is it an apt name for you?"

Scarlet let a slow smile spread across her face, then

gave Joy a flirty wink. "Am I a scarlet woman? Now that would be telling."

* * *

They got back to the house warm and full after another drink and a late roast dinner.

"I assume you want a whisky, even though I really shouldn't as I have a very busy day being the mayor tomorrow." Joy turned her body to Scarlet.

Scarlet let out a satisfied groan as her tired body hit the sofa. She checked her watch before nodding. "I don't know why I was checking the time, the answer was always going to be yes," she said.

"I knew that anyway, I was just being polite."

A warm glow oozed through Scarlet's veins. She loved that they were already quipping with each other, laughing at each other's jokes. In fact, she loved a lot of things about Joy. Her deep blue eyes. Her soft features. Her honey-blonde hair. Joy was a genuine person, but more than that, *she got Scarlet.* And that hadn't happened in a very long time.

The sound of crystal on glass interrupted her thoughts, and Scarlet looked up into Joy's arresting, blue eyes.

"Remind me tomorrow, in between doing what we have to do, to get some bloody coasters for this table, will you?" Joy was pointing at the coffee table. "You promise?"

Scarlet smiled. "I promise."

"Good." Joy sat down on the sofa next to her.

The previous times they'd sat in the lounge together, they'd always taken a sofa each. Scarlet wasn't complaining as they sat, almost thigh to thigh.

"You know, the last person I was this relaxed with was my wife." Scarlet paused. "And that didn't turn out so well."

"Join the club," said Joy. "Aren't we a pair? Both divorced and hiding from the world." She paused. "So you just upped and left?"

Scarlet nodded, an image of Liv in her mind. Liv crying, saying how desperately sorry she was for all of her gambling. For gambling away the money Scarlet had diligently saved up. Scarlet was just glad she hadn't transferred the inheritance money into their joint account, otherwise that would have gone as well and then she'd have been left with nothing.

"Yep, packed up my stuff and got out. Once I'd secured my job of course — I needed an income. Especially after Liv gambled away all our savings, leaving me broke." She shook her head, throwing a wry smile. "So that's my sad story of how I ended up here." Scarlet tucked a leg under her body, then pushed her hair behind her ears. "I wanted to get as far away as I possibly could, and escape the endless circle of sympathy. I couldn't take it. So I made a fresh start by moving 200 miles up the country."

"How did that turn out?"

Scarlet grinned. "Swimmingly."

"Ha," Joy replied.

Joy's focus was all on her — Scarlet wasn't used to it, but she liked it. "What about you? How did you end up in Dulshaw?" she asked. "You don't sound like you're from here."

Joy ran a hand up and down her thigh. "Actually, I grew up here."

"In Dulshaw?" Scarlet was surprised — Joy's accent or attitude didn't seem strong enough. The locals were all fiercely proud northerners, with accents as thick as their coats.

Joy nodded. "Born and bred. But then I went to uni in Manchester and stayed, so my accent mellowed. Plus, I deal with international clients, so it helps if they know what you're saying." She shrugged. "My brother says I'm the posh one of the family, as does my dad. But I still shop at Aldi, so I don't think I'm too out of touch."

"That means you're on-trend. Aldi is the supermarket of choice. I read it in the paper, so it must be true. My colleague at work calls it her European delicatessen."

Joy let out a bark of laughter. Scarlet had heard it before, but tonight it seemed… cute. Joy was different to anyone she'd met yet in Dulshaw. And even though she was from here, she had a wider perspective on life, which Scarlet appreciated. Speaking to Joy was like throwing open the windows on Scarlet's world, letting some air and light in. She sipped her whisky and smiled at Joy, who smiled right back.

A longing sensation fizzed down Scarlet's body, causing her to shudder slightly. Scarlet steadied her breathing, but didn't look away from Joy. Scarlet hadn't been sure before, but she was definite now: she was attracted to Joy. The problem was, she had no way of knowing how Joy felt about her without asking her, and that was out of the question.

Nevertheless, an image of leaning over and kissing Joy on the couch whizzed through Scarlet's mind, like a drive-by. It took her by surprise, but she suppressed the gasp that formed in her throat.

"And are you still in touch? With your ex, I mean?" Joy's voice cut through Scarlet's daydreams and she blushed. Caught in the act. She blinked, then refocused.

"With Liv? God, no. After the initial shock and devastation, I cut nearly all ties with her, bar a few financial things that took longer to sort out. She fucked me over so badly, it seemed like the easiest thing to do — even after eight years together. Plus, I was embarrassed. I mean, how did I not realise, not see what was happening right in front of my nose? It still wakes me up at night on occasion." Scarlet shuddered.

"Sounds awful," Joy said. "And did she ever say sorry, apologise for what she did?"

Scarlet let out a strangled laugh. "Fat chance," she said. "No, I was just the latest in a line of suckers that fell for Liv's charms — and she had some charms." An image of Liv lavishing Scarlet with jewellery sprang to her mind, of wining and dining her in Michelin-starred restaurants, of bringing her home to complete the evening in their bed.

"I always thought she had piles of money, the cash

always seemed to be there. Turns out, she'd run up credit cards and our overdraft, and I was liable for it." Scarlet shook her head, then sat up straighter. "But it's done now, the money's paid back, and I can get on with my life. Life is duller on your own, but it's also a heck of a lot more predictable, which is exactly what I've needed over the last couple of years."

Joy smiled, her eyes radiating kindness. "For what it's worth, I think you've done a sterling job. Makes mine and Steve's break-up look like child's play."

Scarlet smiled right back. "All break-ups have their tough points, but the toughest one is learning to be on your own again, making every little decision on your own." She took another sip of her drink and let it go down before continuing. "But you get used to it. Now I worry I'm too set in my ways to have a relationship."

Joy laughed, nodding her head. "I have that chat with myself most weeks."

Scarlet rolled the last of her whisky around her glass, loving the way it clung to the sides. She tilted her head at Joy, raking her body with her eyes. She swallowed down hard as emotion washed over her. She wasn't sure what she was feeling, but whatever it was, it was powerful, almost too powerful to ignore. Scarlet put the lid on it for now, but she wasn't sure how secure it was.

"I know you see him all the time, but do you miss him? Steve, I mean. I know you don't want to be with him anymore, but you were together for how long?"

"Ten years," Joy replied, a far off look in her eye. "But the honest answer, now, is no. I mean, I miss the companionship of being in a couple, but we were never right; I could just never work out why. He never made my toes tingle, I never craved him." She paused, making sure she had Scarlet's full attention.

Joy absolutely did. Scarlet was all ears, eyes, nose, mouth, whatever Joy wanted.

"My next partner is going to be all of the things — friend, lover, my one and only. Which is why I've hesitated and put it off, because it's a lot to put on one person, isn't it?"

Scarlet shook her head, allowing herself to wonder if she could be that person for Joy. Was it too far-fetched that she might end up with the town mayor, a pillar of society? Was it even more far-fetched she might be entertaining the idea of loving someone again?

"Not at all," Scarlet said. "It means you've reached a stage in life where you know what you want, and you're not going to settle for anything less. And that's admirable if you ask me."

Joy looked her in the eye. "That's it," she said softly. "I know what I want. And when I'm 100 per cent sure, I won't hesitate, believe me."

Her words rolled through Scarlet's body like a thunderbolt.

Bang.

Chapter Eight

Scarlet met Eamonn at one of the few cafés that hadn't been affected by the flood the next day. He gave her a hug as he sat down opposite her. "How are you?" he asked, scraping a hand across his grey-flecked stubble.

Scarlet gave him a brief smile. "Surprisingly okay," she said. "Joy's been brilliant and it's been lovely getting to know her. I know the flood's taken my home and your business, but that's the one positive to come out of this — I've met some new people who I think I'll stay friends with. Look on the bright side and all of that."

The waitress appeared and they placed their orders of coffee and toasted teacakes, then Eamonn leaned back, assessing Scarlet. "Look on the bright side? That's not the Scarlet I know and love. You never have a bright side."

"I do," Scarlet replied, affronted.

Eamonn laughed, a dimple showing on his left cheek as he did. "Nope," he said. "You don't. *Ever*. Ask Matt, he'll back me up. Even when we were five-nil up against Bridgetown in the cup that time, you were still convinced we'd bugger it up somehow."

"That's got nothing to do with looking on the bright side. That's just football." Scarlet sat back and crossed her arms, trying not to bristle. It wasn't working.

"No, that's *you*," Eamonn, said, still laughing. "But I have to say, I like this new Scarlet, this bright-side Scarlet." He paused. "And you forgot the bit about the flood buggering up our wedding, too. Don't forget that."

Scarlet held up her index finger. "That's one of the reasons I wanted to meet you."

"And there was me thinking it was my inherent charm."

"Ha ha," Scarlet said. "As I said in my text, I might have the answer to your reception dilemma."

"I'm all ears."

"Don't be so down on yourself, you just need them pinning."

Eamonn gave her the look that deserved.

"Anyway, it's Grasspoint, the old people's home at the top of Fairbank."

Eamonn tilted his head. "What's that got to do with my wedding?"

"They've got a brand-new function room they're planning to hire out for events, and it's available. It was only finished two weeks ago, so you'd be the first user if you want it. You'd have to clear it with Celia first, the manager, but she didn't seem to think it would be a problem." Scarlet smiled at Eamonn. "So, have I brightened up your morning?"

Eamonn gave her a puzzled look. "You have, and it's

weird. You're looking on the bright side *and* coming up with a solution to my massive problem. I could kiss you."

Scarlet held up a hand, laughing. "You could, but I wouldn't advise it," she said. "Besides, Steph would kill me and I don't want to get on her wrong side. I've seen her when she's dragging you out of the pub."

"Wise woman," Eamonn replied, as their food and drink turned up.

Eamonn scoffed his teacake in five bites before Scarlet had even picked hers up, then quickly ordered another one. "They are *so* good," he said, wiping butter from his chin. "Seriously, though, this is a lifesaver, so thank you. How did you find out about it? I thought we knew every single venue this area and beyond had to offer."

Scarlet smiled. "Don't thank me — thank Joy. Her gran lives at Grasspoint, and she took me up there to meet her. It was her gran who suggested it — she knows Steph's gran, too."

"That's a lot of grans," Eamonn said, frowning. "But hang on, rewind. You went to meet Joy's gran? Are you sure there's something you're not telling me here, because this sounds awfully like something's going on." He pursed his lips. "And you seem… different. Almost… is 'happy' the word I'm looking for?"

Scarlet's cheeks turned pink at Eamonn's words, mainly because she knew he was speaking the truth. But she wasn't about to admit it. "Shuddup," she said, eating her teacake. "You're right, these are great."

"Stop trying to change the subject," Eamonn said. "Am I right, is there something — or someone — who's putting a smile on your face?"

"No," Scarlet said, reverting to her teenage self in an instant. She wasn't ready to have this conversation, not after last night with Joy, and not after the night she'd spent tossing and turning in Joy's spare room, thinking about Joy on the other side of her bedroom wall. There had been so little to stop them taking the next step last night, but then again, so much.

"Not a certain lady mayor, perhaps?"

Scarlet threw Eamonn her best scowl. "No!"

"Yeah, well, actions speak louder than words in my opinion." Eamonn tucked into his second teacake as soon as it arrived. "And you're allowed to like someone and be happy, just so you know." He paused. "I take it what my mate Dean said was right?"

Scarlet froze: she didn't want to betray Joy's confidence, but Eamonn did kind of already know.

"Yes, Dean was right, but nothing's going on. It's just been nice to get to know her, that's all."

Eamonn smirked at Scarlet, just as he had a million times before in the pub after football. In many ways, Eamonn had taken the place of her brothers for Scarlet, filling the banter gap.

"I believe you, thousands wouldn't." Eamonn gave Scarlet a wink, then slugged back his coffee. "So when can I go and see this hall?"

Scarlet got her phone from her pocket and scrolled through to her notes app. Then she frowned. "Shit, I thought I put the number in my phone. Bugger." She glanced up at Eamonn. "You planning on going to the shop later?"

He nodded. "Yep — still loads to do down there. Never-ending to-do list."

"I'm going to try to get into my flat today if I can, so I'll be going down there. Joy's got the number, so I can call in after, or just text you, failing that."

Eamonn nodded, sympathy flooding his features. "Shit, I forgot about that. Just remember, it looks and smells terrible, and it is. But it's amazing what you can clean up in a few days. Don't get me wrong, the shop is still fucked, but I suppose you come to accept it more when you see it a few times. But the initial shock… just prepare yourself, is all."

Fear bubbled up inside Scarlet. "I will," she said.

"Do you need me to come with you? Because I absolutely can."

Scarlet shook her head. "Joy's coming with me, she's going to juggle some of her meetings."

Eamonn raised an eyebrow. "I'm saying nothing. Honestly, *nothing*."

Scarlet hit him on the arm. She didn't need Eamonn on her case about Joy, too.

She was already on her own case 24/7.

* * *

When they got to Scarlet's street, she could see the tarmac — that was a start. However, the road looked like a battlefield, with carpets strewn across pavements, sodden and sad. There were washing machines, desks, and shelving, now not fit for purpose; sofas, broken dining chairs, and clothes, never to be sat on or worn again.

The street also had a strange copper hue from all the claggy mud left behind after the flood waters had receded, which was now visible in clumps. The sun was shining bright today, making a mockery of everything that had gone before it. It was like a stage set, just waiting for the actors to enter, stage left.

Only, there was no stage left.

Literally.

Beside her, Joy sucked in a breath. "All this stuff, it's people's lives." Joy stepped over a discarded lamp and shade, then a suitcase. "So much waste, it's terrible."

And it was. Three days ago, her street had been normal, with cars buzzing up and down on their way into the centre. But now, it was eerily quiet, just the odd person appearing to bail out yet more unsalvageable belongings. A woman across the road had a box in her arms, so wet it was drooping. She leaned against her dining table, now out on the street too, and her body began to shake.

Scarlet's feet were stuck to the ground — she wanted to help the woman, but she couldn't face someone else's pain right now. She had to protect herself from what she was about to see.

Joy came to the rescue, because that was Joy's forté. She walked over to the woman and muttered something to her, and the woman just bowed her head and cradled the box. Joy gave her an awkward hug, before coming back to Scarlet.

"Family photos, ruined," Joy said with a shake of the head. "Some things can't be replaced, can they?"

They picked their way down the street until they reached Scarlet's front door, which was wide open. The hallway had a tide mark on the wall — Scarlet reckoned it reached to about her thigh. When she put her foot down, the carpet squelched beneath her feet. She recoiled, holding her breath. She wasn't sure if she could do this, but she had to face whatever was down the stairs. But right now, it felt like going down to the basement in a horror movie: what lay beneath? Scarlet conjured images of her flat before the flood, but that just made her want to weep. And she wouldn't do that; she'd promised herself.

It was just stuff, she could replace it. She had to keep remembering.

"Okay?" Joy asked.

Scarlet nodded, took a deep breath, then wished she hadn't: a mix of sewage and damp filled her lungs, taking her breath away. The bleach hadn't reached this part of the street yet. Her part of the street. Her flat.

She choked, then began to cough, which meant she had to breathe in more air. A bad move.

Joy put a hand on her arm. "You want me to go first?"

Scarlet shook her head. She was more than grateful Joy was there to support her, but this was something she had to do alone. "No, you stay here. I think I'd like to see it on my own first, to see how bad it is. That okay?"

"Whatever you need, I'll be right here."

Their conversation was interrupted by a man coming up the stairs, his every step accompanied by the splodge of water underfoot. He was wheezing as he came up, his massive stomach held in by a cheap-looking brown belt. He was wearing wellies, as was everyone around town, along with a thick red-and-grey anorak that wouldn't have looked great on anyone. His forehead furrowed when he saw them, then he looked down and consulted his clipboard, lifting up a couple of pages before clearing his throat.

"Scarlet Williams?"

Scarlet frowned. "Yes — who are you?"

The man scribbled something on a form, then tucked the clipboard under his arm and held out his hand.

"Paul Barker, Best Place Insurance."

Scarlet shook his hand — it was stone cold.

The man blew onto his hands. "Freezing down there and still very wet." He glanced at her feet. "But you've got wellies on, you've come prepared." He sniffed, got a tissue from his pocket and blew his nose. "I was just assessing the damage, seeing what you're going to need. A new flat, to be blunt, but that's what we're here for." He gave Scarlet a smile. "I know you hear a lot of scare stories about insurers, but you won't get that from us in this case. This is cut and dried." He frowned at his choice of words. "Or at least it will be dried, eventually — you're going to need dehumidifiers, heat and bleach. Lots of bleach.

"There's still a couple of inches of water, although now we've got the pumps on full blast as well as sunshine, it should be out in a couple of hours. We've got lorries coming to clear out the major items today, too. You're welcome to have a look, but you won't be able to get down there to start the clean-up proper till we've cleared the worst. Tomorrow, all being well." He paused, not quite willing to look into Scarlet's eyes. "And I have to warn you, it's a mess, as you might expect." He paused again. "And it smells." He wrinkled his nose.

"Do you have somewhere to stay?" He consulted his clipboard again. "I don't have a note of you needing any emergency accommodation?"

Scarlet shook her head, still trying to take everything in. It was a lot. "No, I'm staying with my friend, Joy," Scarlet said, nodding towards her.

"Excellent," Paul said, smiling at Joy. "Friends are just what's need in a situation like this." He paused. "I was just nipping out to my car to get my tape measure — the electronic one's not working, would you believe. Back in a minute, so I guess I'll see you down there?"

Scarlet nodded again. "Sure," she said, as Paul squeezed past them both and out onto the street.

Scarlet still hadn't moved forward.

"I thought you said you didn't have insurance?" Joy said.

"I've got buildings insurance, just no contents." She inhaled, then coughed. She wasn't going to stick around here for long, not with this smell. Paul hadn't seemed concerned with it, but Scarlet guessed he was used to it. She scrubbed insurance assessor off her list of possible jobs.

"I'm going down. Second thoughts, will you come with me?" Scarlet had thought she could do it alone, but now, after Paul's damning verdict, she needed reassurance. She needed someone to back up what she saw. But most of all, she needed someone to hold her hand.

As if reading her thoughts, Joy took Scarlet's hand in hers.

Even that simple act made Scarlet smile on the inside, if not on the outside. She couldn't move her face. It was stuck in alarm mode.

"Of course I will. But you have to walk forward in order for me to follow you."

Scarlet did as Joy asked.

The bottom of the stairs held a cold, brown well of misery, as Paul had warned. The water was still up to just over Scarlet's ankles, and judging by the smell, she didn't want to know what she might be treading on or through.

"Fucking hell," she said, covering her nose with her arm. Joy was already doing the same.

Her light fitting in the lounge, her gorgeous chandelier, was covered in brown sludge, some of which she could only assume was shit. Her sofas, too. Her once-white walls were now a curious grey-brown colour, and dripping. She breathed in, then wanted to retch.

Joy touched her back and she immediately calmed down.

Scarlet walked through to the kitchen. It was bleak. There was sewage on every surface, her once white cupboards now... not so. She didn't want to even open a cupboard; she knew what she'd find.

Scarlet turned, her face stricken. This was almost too much, but she was determined to carry on.

Joy touched her arm, her sleeve across her nose. "You sure you want to carry on today? We can come back tomorrow when the insurers are finished throwing the majority of it."

Scarlet shook her head. "I just need to see... everything." She waded through the brown waters towards the bedroom, her foot hitting something solid. She stumbled, but Joy caught her. Her heart sped up so much, it was nearly out of her mouth. She wobbled.

"Please don't fall over. I don't want to drag you out of the sewage, too," Joy said.

Scarlet laughed, despite herself. "I'll try not to."

The bedroom told the same story: sodden, ruined, bedraggled. She'd spent so long choosing that bed linen, too, and had only had it six months.

But she could get some more. That's what she needed to tell herself.

Joy's hand was on her elbow now. "You can replace all this, you know."

Joy could clearly read minds. Which must mean she was an awesome life coach.

"I know," Scarlet replied. And she did know that. But it didn't stop her mind spinning at just what needed to be done.

Everything. Absolutely everything.

There was one room left that Scarlet had been dreading the most. Her bathroom. Her pride and joy. The one she'd photographed in Milan and spent a ton of money having modelled just as she liked it. Mosaic tiles, double shower, the works. She took a deep breath as she approached it, then opened the door.

The double shower was raised, so was almost free of water. But it also had human waste sitting in its tray, along with some sodden clothing, some toiletries, and a dead bird.

She'd seen enough.

"Let's go," she said to Joy, moving faster now, the water still sloshing around her feet. She pulled her boots free and trudged up the stairs, remembering all the times she'd worried about stepping in dog poo and treading it into her carpet. Her whole flat was one giant cesspit now. How ironic.

Scarlet took the stairs fast, then almost ran out of the hallway and into the fresh air. She hadn't thought it was fresh when she'd arrived on the street, but it tasted mighty fresh now. She opened her mouth wide, doubled over, gasping for breath, trying to get rid of the stench that was clogging up her body. Scarlet retched, but nothing came out. She could hear Joy taking deep breaths behind her, too, then her soothing hand was on Scarlet's back, rubbing gently up and down.

Scarlet stared at the pavement below her, full of what she'd thought was claggy mud, but now realised was probably sewage. She retched again, this time some sick winding its way up her windpipe. She allowed it to escape, retched a second time, and then stood gulping in air, her palms on her thighs, doubled over. The world was spinning up above and below; nothing made sense.

Eventually, Joy's arms were around her, levering her slowly upwards. She let her.

Then Joy handed her a tissue to wipe her mouth, and led her away.

* * *

They walked for a while without saying anything, just concentrating on getting out of the street without tripping over people's possessions. When they'd breathed in enough fresh air to kill the smell of sewage burnt into their lungs, Joy spoke.

"So that was rough."

"Uh-huh."

"How you feeling? Apart from the nausea."

Scarlet smiled at that and stopped walking, staring up into the metallic grey sky. "That was more a reaction to the smell than anything else," she said. "Honestly? I feel detached, like that wasn't really my flat. Which essentially, *it wasn't*. My things weren't my things anymore — and they're just things, and I can replace them." She started walking again, thrusting her hands into her pockets.

"I was thinking about this before, and it's like stages of grief. I'm going through denial at the moment, pretending that flat's not really mine." She paused. "It's a coping mechanism at the end of the day, but whatever works."

"Makes sense," Joy replied. "When something's too difficult, your mind can't process it, so you shut down."

"Shutting down was definitely the best option. But not totally, just temporarily. Just so I can cope." She glanced at Joy. "Before you go into full therapist mode on me."

Joy nudged Scarlet. "I wasn't going to do that. And anyway, I'm allowed. And for your information, I wouldn't be doing it as a life coach, I'd be doing it as a friend. There's a big difference."

Scarlet smiled at Joy as they turned onto the High Street, which was a similar scene to Scarlet's road, just wider.

"Holy shit," Scarlet said as they walked in the middle of the road — the lack of cars meant they could.

Not one of the businesses were open to customers, but they were all a hive of activity. Just like on Scarlet's road, equipment and furniture was strewn across the pavement, and the stench of bleach was overwhelming as people fought to get their premises cleaned up. Joy stopped to chat to the owner of the material shop, rolls and rolls of ruined fabric lying on the street in front of them.

Scarlet drifted left and drew in breath when she saw the state of the town's bookshop. She could see the mark where the water had reached inside the shop, and on the pavement out front, there were piles upon piles of sodden books. That almost made Scarlet want to weep more than her own flat. This flood wasn't just about her: it was about the whole town. Her possessions held memories and experiences that were personal to *her*. But all these wasted books had held ideas, answers, and dreams, until a torrent of water had been poured on them. Now, those dreams would never be read and realised. It was devastating.

"What a sight." Joy joined her, staring at the books. "But they'll get it cleared up and we'll recover. I was just talking to Gayle at the material shop, and she said Steph has been making sandwiches for everyone to keep their spirits up, and the community have been bringing mops, food and drinks."

Scarlet nodded as they fell into step on the road again, heading towards Great Bakes. "That's great, but why do things like this happen?"

"To test human nature?" Joy replied. "Who the hell knows?"

When they arrived at Great Bakes, Eamonn was bleaching everything in sight and Steph was making coffee. When he saw Scarlet, he did a double-take.

"Twice in one day — people will start talking," he said, putting down his sponge and giving her a bear hug. This was Eamonn's new greeting post-flood, and Scarlet had to admit she kinda liked it.

"This is Joy — our esteemed mayor and my current landlady," she told him.

Joy shook Eamonn's hand and smiled. "Good to see you again."

"You, too. I hope you're keeping Scarlet in check. Although she walked in here sort of smiling, and I assume you've been to the flat already?"

"Unfortunately, yes."

"So why are you smiling?"

"It's either that or break down, and I've decided to give that a miss today. It's buggered, but walking around here makes me realise I'm not alone, and it helps a bit. Not that I want other people to share the misery, but it's nice to know you're not the only one."

Steph came out of the back of the shop and hugged Scarlet in greeting, shaking Joy's hand when she was introduced.

"I hear I might have you both to thank for saving our wedding this weekend — Eamonn mentioned something about a hall."

Joy clicked her fingers. "Let me make a call now and speak to Celia while I remember." She stepped out onto the street, phone in hand.

Steph watched her go, then turned to Scarlet. "So how's it going living with the mayor?"

Scarlet shrugged. "Strangely okay, considering we're strangers. But she's on her own like me, so it's sort of nice having someone to chat to, especially at a time like this. Odd, but good."

"And how was your flat?"

Scarlet exhaled. "Fucked, still under a foot of water. I can go back tomorrow and start the clean-up process. I'm really not looking forward to that. And the smell — like something from the bowels of hell."

"Some roads are more affected than others with that — luckily, we haven't found that part too bad. Still, when they clear it, it might help." Steph put an arm around her. "We can help Scarlet tomorrow, can't we?" she said to her fiancé.

Eamonn nodded. "Totally — I can don my Marigolds again, no problem."

Scarlet shook her head. "Really, you don't have to. You've got your own disaster to contend with, and the wedding, too..."

"Nonsense, we can still spare a few hours — one for all and all that. You can't do it on your own, it'd be too much. Plus, we're dab hands with bleach now, so you're getting expert help with us. It's not like we could open even if we wanted — the electricity's still not on, so I can't bake anything, and the cash registers don't work. I've brought our camping stove down for hot drinks, and the whole road has been using it." She paused. "You want a coffee?"

"I'd love one — even being in my flat was so cold."
But even though she was cold, she was warmed with their
generosity of spirit: warmed to the core. "It's going to take
months to dry it out and get it back to normal. And that's
not even imagining the cost." Her face slumped as she said
it, and Eamonn jumped to her side, her ever-present mascot.

"It's going to be fine, you'll see," he said, putting an
arm around her. "Because if all else fails, you know the
lady with the camping stove and the cakes she baked at
home. So you're already ahead of the game."

Just then, Joy came in, giving them a thumbs-up. "I've
arranged a meeting with Celia — I assumed you could get
up there any time? She says pop up tomorrow morning to
see the room, but it's fine, they've nothing booked. It's just
a matter of you saying yes."

"I could kiss you right now, Mrs Mayor," Steph said.
"Really, thanks so much."

"Thank my gran when you see her — it was her idea."

"We will," Steph said. "And you're both invited, of
course. I had a whole table plan and was stressing over
numbers, but now, those things don't seem so important,
do they? And I'd love you both to be there, if you're free?"

Joy looked at Scarlet, who gave her a smile and
a shrug.

"I was going to the evening anyway, and I don't
have any other pressing plans on Saturday, apart from
mopping my flat," Scarlet said. It wasn't lost on her this
was their first joint invitation to anything, but she said

nothing. "And we all need a reason to celebrate more than ever now, don't we?"

"That's settled then," Steph said, not even waiting for Joy's answer. "Now, coffee all round?"

Chapter Nine

Back at home, Joy and Scarlet were sat in the lounge, both on their tablets. They were the picture of domestic bliss, which made Joy smile inside. In just a few days, they already had their set stools in the kitchen and set sofas in the lounge. Plus, now, they had their first joint wedding invitation. If they ever did become a couple, they had the basis for their relationship already set in stone.

"Did you call your brother yet, by the way?" Joy looked up from her emails: it looked like she'd have to go round to George's house tonight to talk about co-ordinating the clean-up this week.

"Which one?"

"I don't mind, but perhaps the one who lives an hour or so up the road. But either of the mythical creatures." Scarlet was being evasive about it, but Joy was having none of it.

"Not yet," Scarlet said, shifting her tablet on her knee.

"Don't you think it might be time? What if he tries to contact you?"

Scarlet sighed, and Joy could just imagine her as a

teenager. Stubborn, infuriating, but immeasurably cute. Not for the first time, Joy wished she'd met her sooner.

"He probably wouldn't be surprised to find I'd moved and not told him. Hurt, sad, but not surprised."

Joy rolled her eyes. "All the more reason to call him, fill him in on the fact you're homeless and destitute." She'd been on at Scarlet to do it ever since she'd revealed she had family nearby, and having seen her flat today, Joy was convinced the more pairs of hands they had to help out, the better.

"You make it sound so glamorous."

Joy raised a cynical eyebrow at Scarlet. "If I have to see my brother, who's a prize idiot by the way, then you have to see yours, who sounds lovely. He's going to be happy you called, isn't he?" She paused. She understood Scarlet's reasoning for not calling, but this was an emergency. "Why don't you do it now? Take your cup of tea up to your room or into the kitchen or wherever you might feel most relaxed and just call him. I've got to go out in a minute anyway, so you could even do it in here in ten minutes if you don't want to move."

Scarlet sighed. "It's not that simple."

"You're over-thinking it."

Scarlet pursed her lips. "This is a brother who I've been ignoring for the past two years. A brother I've seen once and send Christmas cards to. A brother who's never been anything but lovely to me and doesn't deserve any of this."

Joy smiled at Scarlet. "So he'll forgive you — if everything you say is true, and I'm sure it is, he'll forgive. He wants you in his life. You're the one who's been blocking him out. If you call him, he'll be over the moon, trust me."

She hopped off the sofa to give Scarlet some space: she wasn't going to listen to Joy, she had to come to this on her own terms.

"I'll leave you to it," Joy said, patting Scarlet's knee as she walked by.

* * *

And so here Scarlet was, ten minutes later, phone in hand, lump in throat. Her mouth was dry, her fingers tingling.

Clark. Pain in the arse, lovely Clark.

He'd always had her back, even though he was four years younger than her. Always wanted to be her protector, even though Scarlet had never needed protecting. But that's the way Clark was, just like her dad had been. And her dad would want her to call Clark. That thought drove her finger down on the green button and sent her heart-rate through the roof.

He answered after three rings.

"Scar?" His voice sounded incredulous, like he didn't believe this really would be her.

"Hi," she replied.

"Is everything okay?" He sounded like their dad: strong and reliable. Just the sound of his voice made Scarlet wobbly.

"Everything's fine," she said, before she remembered it wasn't. "Well, not really, but I'm okay."

"Not sick or dying?"

She smiled. "Not last time I checked. Nope, all present and correct."

"Well, okay then," he said, exhaling. "Then if you're not sick or dying, can I shout at you for not returning my calls?" He tried to be serious, but she could hear the smile in his voice.

"You can try, but I'll hold the phone away from my ear."

"I'll just seethe silently," he said with a laugh. "So what's going on? Three months and now a call. You're not moving to Australia, too, are you?"

Now it was Scarlet's turn to laugh. "No, I'll leave that to Fred. You know I don't work well in hot climates." She paused. "I'm just calling to let you know I have moved, though — but not through choice. My flat was flooded on Saturday, and as you know it's in the basement, so it didn't fare well. It's totally gutted and I've lost everything. But strangely, I feel okay about it."

"Shit, I'm so sorry — that's why I texted, but you said you were okay." He paused. "But you *are* okay — at least, you sound it. You sound calm, accepting, and that's very weird. Especially for you."

"I wish everyone would stop saying that; makes me sound like the Grinch."

"You haven't exactly been a ray of sunshine over the past few years. But I blame Liv."

Scarlet rolled her eyes — there he went, trying to be her protector. He'd never liked Liv. Turned out, Clark was a rather better judge of character than she was.

"Well, anyway, I'm living with the mayor temporarily."

"The mayor?"

"Which sounds worse than it is. She's a woman for a start, really lovely, my age. Plus, she has a spare room and we get on great."

"If you need somewhere to stay, you could always come and stay with me. I don't like the thought of you living with strangers."

"And I would, of course I would, but the hour and a half commute to work might be a killer. And honestly, this is working out well. She's been nothing but welcoming, and the community has really rallied round, too. I'm fine — which is more than I can say about my flat."

"I'll come over to help when you get back in — when will that be?"

"Tomorrow I think, or perhaps Wednesday."

"Call me and I'll drive over."

"You don't need to, Clark."

"I know I don't need to, but I want to. You've cut me out of your life for way too long, but this is what families do — help each other in times of need. So call me, and I'll drive over and help you out. Is there anything else you need?"

"A bed, a sofa, coffee table, books…"

"You know what I mean — anything you need *right now*?"

"Actually, if you could bring some money, that would be great. I can pay you back, but the nearest cashpoint that's working is a half hour drive away, and my car's buggered, too."

"I can bring you cash, no problem. Just promise me you'll text or call this time, and not just forget like all the other times?"

Scarlet blushed as she thought of all the times she'd let him down. Yet here he was, ready to drop everything to come to her aid when she needed him. She really should have called him sooner.

"I promise I will text you, you have my word. Plus, you're bringing cash, so added incentive."

"You always were the more mercenary sibling."

Chapter Ten

Joy had a whole roster of clients on Tuesday, and she was glad when the end of the day finally ticked around. She shut down her Skype client, turned off her mic, and went downstairs to get a drink of water. Scarlet's guitar was sat on one of the chairs where she'd left it last night after the call with her brother, which had put a positive spring in her step.

Joy liked that Scarlet was leaving things around the house now; her tears had stopped and she was starting to feel at home. And so was Joy, finally, after nearly two years in the house. Her friend Wendy often told her she needed a life coach of her own, but Joy had steadfastly resisted so far. But looking at her life now, maybe Wendy had been right.

The front door opening signalled that Scarlet was home from work — Joy had given her a key, much to her embarrassment. Scarlet had tried to negotiate paying rent, too, but Joy had told her that could wait until they knew how long Scarlet would have to stay. For now, Scarlet was giving Joy some welcome company and friendship, and that was more than enough payment for her.

"How was your first day back?" Joy asked, as Scarlet walked in and put the kettle on. If Scarlet looked good in her casual attire, her work gear held allure, too. Her dark trouser suit was well tailored and she'd added make-up and polished loafers for added impact. An impact that wasn't lost on Joy. She loved the company Scarlet was providing her, but being around her was getting more difficult by the day.

"Strangely fine. I wasn't the only one affected but I'm probably one of the worst. Still, after today at work I've already got an offer of a bed and a coffee table, and my boss gave me the rest of the week off to sort everything out. I texted my brother and he's going to come over tomorrow to help me with the flat." Scarlet turned, gripped the kitchen counter and exhaled. "So I'm not feeling quite so daunted about it all now, which is weird." She paused. "It's nice to know people have your back."

Joy gave her a smile. "Good, that's real progress — optimism. It's contagious, and it's in the air. Especially after the council's refuge service did such a great job today clearing up the streets. It's like clutter at home — you always feel better when it's tidied up, don't you? Clearing the streets has cleared people's minds, made them see things afresh."

"It has," Scarlet said. "And I can feel the optimism. I just wish the looters shared it — they're spoiling it for the rest of us."

Joy shook her head. "There are always some." Looters

had gone into homes and businesses last night, stealing what was left to take, but Joy didn't like to dwell on those parts of humanity. "But while you're in this upbeat mood, I have a proposition for you."

A smirk tweaked Scarlet's mouth as she crossed her arms over her chest. "Really?"

"I didn't mean that exactly as it came out," Joy added, heat creeping into her cheeks.

She was only semi-lying.

"When I saw George, the council leader, last night, he asked a favour. The local news want to do a personal interest story with one of the flood victims, and he asked me for suggestions seeing as I've been more out and about with the people. I said I'd get back to him, but I was thinking you, Steph and Eamonn, to get the home owner and business angle. What do you think?"

Scarlet winced and shook her head. "It's not really me, being in front of the camera, is it?"

Joy got up off her stool. "But that was the old Scarlet, the one who hid away. The new one is strong, capable and would make a gorgeous TV interview. Just look at you," Joy said, waving a hand in front of Scarlet, not bothered how she sounded. "Come on, give them something pretty to look at on-screen. Otherwise it'll be Sue Janus spouting off again." Joy held Scarlet with her gaze. "For me?"

"Are you on a mayoral bonus if I say yes?"

"I get double cakes from Maureen Armitage if I come through," Joy said with a smile. "So is that a yes?" She didn't want to stop and analyse what she'd just said to Scarlet, because that would be too scary. She'd just told Scarlet she was gorgeous, she'd just shamelessly flirted. Nope, Joy was just going to crash through this conversation and see if she could get to the other side without falling on her face. Or perhaps, falling onto Scarlet's face with her own.

Scarlet held her gaze for a moment, then nodded. "Okay, why not? It slots in nicely to what has been the most bizarre week of my life so far."

"Awesome, I'll get back to George. And can you ask Eamonn and Steph?"

"I will, but they'll be up for it. They're way less camera-shy than me."

"That's what I thought," Joy said, getting mugs. "Cup of tea?"

"Do you need to ask?"

Chapter Eleven

Clark picked Scarlet up from Joy's house at 11am the next day in his white Audi, and Scarlet made all the right noises.

"Fancy car, little brother," she said. "You must be doing well at work."

He smiled at her. "This old thing? I may have been promoted since last we spoke and I may have treated myself to some new wheels."

"You have my blessing — very fancy."

"Glad you approve." He paused, looking over his shoulder to pull out. "Are we going to be able to get near to yours, or should I park elsewhere?"

"Not sure," Scarlet said. "The council did a big clear-up this week, but our road might be full again if people are only just getting back into their houses. Probably best to park a couple of roads away and we can walk the rest."

"Got it." He pulled up at some traffic lights and glanced across at Scarlet. "It's really great to see you, even if it's not the best circumstances. And you look better than I've seen you in ages — not like someone who's lost everything."

"I'm beginning to think that maybe I haven't," she replied. "I mean, on the surface, yes, I have. I had no insurance, I've got nothing left. So yes, I'm fucked. But I've met some amazing people, my boss was so kind yesterday, and my football friends have been amazing, too. It's just been humbling, and if I hadn't been flooded, I'd never have known it could happen." She shrugged. "Everything happens for a reason."

"I like this new Scarlet," Clark said, beaming. "And I know you said you don't want to move in with me, and I understand why, but at least come for a weekend — you haven't seen my new place yet. Give Joy some time alone." He paused, glancing sideways. "Or bring her, if you like — there are some great pubs and restaurants I could take you to."

"I will," Scarlet replied, avoiding the obvious fact he'd just invited Joy to stay at his when Scarlet had no idea whether or not she'd want to come. She might indeed want some time alone, and Scarlet couldn't blame her — her home had been invaded. Yet the thought of going away and leaving Joy behind filled her with sadness.

Now, they'd just pulled up two roads over from Scarlet's flat: she was just about to get out when she felt Clark's hand on her arm.

Scarlet turned, and he was holding out a brown envelope to her.

"Just before I forget, this is for you. And it's not a loan, it's a gift."

She peered inside: the enveloped was thick with

money. Scarlet shook her head. "I appreciate that, but I can't take your money—"

"—Yes, you can."

"I can't, Clark."

"You can. Listen, this is from my inheritance — I haven't spent it yet, been too busy working. But this is *our* money, family money. And if Mum and Dad were here, they'd give it to you, but they're not. But I am. So please, just take it. I don't want any arguments. You need it more than me, it's that simple."

Tears pricked the back of her eyes. Scarlet was overwhelmed with his love and generosity. "I don't know what to say."

"You don't have to say anything," he replied, taking her in his arms.

They stayed like that for a few seconds, until Scarlet spoke. "Clark?"

"Yep?"

"The gear stick is jammed into my ribs and it really hurts."

He laughed, letting her go.

Scarlet wiped her eyes with her sleeve, then fished a tissue out of her pocket to blow her nose. "Can I put it in the glove compartment for now? I don't want to take it into the flat in case it gets wet."

"You can do what you like, it's your money."

"You're an absolute gem, you know that?"

He cast his gaze down, then back up. "Anything for you," he replied.

She shook her head. "I don't deserve you, little brother," she said.

They got out of the car. "Ready to face the music?" Scarlet turned up her collars against the wind as she walked onto the pavement.

"By the way, I didn't say anything wrong before, did I?"

She furrowed her brow as she fell into step with Clark. "No, why?"

"You just went a bit quiet when I mentioned Joy coming, too. I picked up a vibe when you were talking about her — is something going on?" He paused. "I'm assuming you want it to."

Scarlet licked her lips. Was something going on? It was the million-dollar question. But the honest answer was, Scarlet wasn't sure. She was putting a heck of a lot of her faith in hope right now. That, and the feeling she got when she was with Joy, which she knew was 100 per cent real from her side.

"We're not together... yet, even though everyone else thinks we are," she said. "I think we're on the same page, but we've been skirting the issue. Too much else to deal with. But hopefully, we might be at some point in the future."

Clark gave her a cheesy grin. "It's about time," he said. "Liv's been over for too long, you need to start living again."

Scarlet rolled her eyes: everybody in her life was a bit too *carpe diem* at the moment for her liking.

"I wish everyone would stop saying that, too. It's getting old."

"Like you, grandma," Clark replied.

She gave him a slap, but laughed anyway. It felt good to laugh with her brother, someone who understood exactly where she came from.

"I'm so glad you're here," she said, as they turned into her road. She stopped when she saw the now-lessened piles of debris, with the familiar faces of her neighbours hauling it around. She clung to Clark's arm to steady herself. He took her hand and guided her around her nextdoor neighbour's piano, waterlogged and useless.

"We're doing this together, okay?"

Scarlet nodded.

"And not just us — Mum and Dad are watching over us, too," Clark said. "I can feel it."

Chapter Twelve

The following day, having chaired a few more meetings and met with the heads of all the agencies to get a response update, Joy met Steve at one of those out-of-town retail parks, the ones you have to drive at least half an hour to get to and everyone always looks sad. Today was no exception.

Steve had been vague on the phone as to why he wanted to meet, but Joy wanted to speak to him anyway and was happy to get out of Dulshaw, to go somewhere that wasn't flood-affected. It made a pleasant change to drive down clear roads as if nothing had happened, and she was glad the sun had made an appearance again — Scarlet needed all the help she could get today going back to her flat. She'd seemed apprehensive but determined this morning, which was as much as anyone could hope for.

Joy recognised Steve's truck as she pulled into the parking lot — it was hard to miss, being bright red, with his company's building logo down the side. Steve had started The Builder Man just after they got together, and from being a one-man band, he now employed a crew of workers. Joy tugged on the handbrake of her Mini Cooper — her pride and joy, but not a car that was useful for ferrying much around apart from her and some shopping — and got out, wincing as the sunshine caught her unaware. She ducked back into her car and grabbed her sunglasses; the weather this week was so different to five days ago, it was astounding.

Steve jumped out of his cab and gave Joy a hug, before they started walking towards the shops. He was dressed in jeans and a hoodie, along with some new black boots she hadn't seen before. He hadn't washed his fair hair today yet, either — she could tell from the way it was still matted on one side. Steve reserved his shower for the end of his workday, when it was more needed.

"So why are we here? And if you say to buy tiles, you know my answer." Joy had a tile phobia, the origins of which she could never explain.

Steve laughed. "I'm well aware you think tiles are the devil, I was married to you for quite some time, remember?" Steve gave her a grin. "No, I need to buy some bedside lamps and I wanted your opinion."

Joy stopped walking, taking off her sunglasses. "Bedside lamps? With your ex-wife? Really, Steve?"

He raised both eyebrows and gave an exaggerated shrug of his shoulders. "What? I want a woman's opinion, as Sharon told me I need some. And you were always good at interior design, whereas me, I'm more your house builder than your house decorator."

"That is true," Joy replied. "Just don't tell Sharon, okay? There are some things a woman never wants to hear, and her boyfriend calling up his ex for style advice is one of them."

"Women are weird. But you're going to find out all about that soon, aren't you?"

Joy gave him a look as he pushed open the door to the homeware store and stepped aside for Joy. "With any luck, yes," she replied.

"Talking of which, how are things going with your new lodger?"

"There's nothing going on. I'm just being a good Samaritan in her time of need, that's all." She wasn't sure he bought it, but she kept her poker face anyway. Besides, strictly speaking, nothing *had* happened. They hadn't had sex or even *kissed* yet. But Joy could feel it every time she looked at Scarlet, kept wondering when it would happen. She believed it was a case of *when* and not *if* now, but she was prepared to wait till Scarlet's life began to resemble some kind of normality first.

"Sure you are," Steve said, as he skirted round some sofas near the door and led the way, following the signs to the bedroom department.

"How are things going with Sharon?" Joy asked, changing the subject.

Steve dug his hands into his pockets — his defensive

gesture. "Things are good," he said, not sounding too sure. "She's lovely, and we get on great, so you know." He paused, glancing sideways at Joy as they arrived at the bedroom department. "I'm a lucky man. Not as lucky as I used to be, but still." He busied himself consulting the price of a lamp with a pink shade.

"You're not buying a pink lampshade, just FYI."

Steve turned. "No?"

"Nope." Joy paused. "And you're better off with Sharon, believe me."

Steve said nothing, walking round to the side of one of the beds to look at another lamp.

"You know, we really should try the lighting department — this is more bedroom furniture." Joy began craning her neck to look at the signs hanging from the ceiling. In the meantime, Steve lay down on the bed, patting the space beside him.

"Test this one out for me. I need a woman's opinion on a new bed, too."

She gave him a withering look.

"Come on!" he said with a smile. "I really do need a new bed, you know that," he said. "Our old one is... well, old."

"You've still got our bed?" she said, making a face. "I thought you were buying a new one." It was the first thing Joy would have got rid of: too many memories, and not all of them good as far as she was concerned.

Steve looked embarrassed. "I never quite got around to it, but there's no time like the present." He patted the bed again. "Come on, tell me what you think. I'm hardly going to jump on you in public, promise."

Joy stood firm for a few moments, before shaking her head and laying down beside Steve. "If someone comes in with a camera now and we're suddenly on Facebook on a bed together, you're dead meat, okay?"

"I think the paparazzi are too busy chasing other celebs, lucky for us. The mayor of Dulshaw isn't high on their list."

They both laughed at that. Then there was a pause.

"You know, I miss this — I miss us," Steve said. "And yes, I know, before you say it, I know it's done. I know we're over. But I'm still allowed to miss you. You can't stop that."

He looked so sad, Joy reached down and squeezed his hand, before turning her face to him, the plastic underneath her head squeaking as she did. "I miss you, too. But we have to move on. And we're still friends, aren't we?"

He nodded. "We are — we're so modern," he said. "But Scarlet — you like her, don't you?"

Joy paused, turning her face skywards, pondering whether or not to lie to Steve and tell him no. But what was the point of that? The whole reason she broke up their marriage was to be who she really was, so why try to hide it now? She nodded her head slowly.

"I do," she said, turning her head to him. "I really do, but I don't know if she likes me. I *think* she does, but until you say it or act on it, how do you know for sure?"

She exhaled. "All of which means, I'm keeping everything under wraps for now, till we know each other a bit better. But what if she just thinks we're friends? Then I'm going to make a right tit of myself, and we'll never be friends again. And that would be awful." She turned her head. "Maybe you're right — maybe going out with women was a mistake if they're going to be this complicated."

If Scarlet *did* turn down her advances, Joy would probably go into hiding for the rest of the year.

Steve smiled at that. "Welcome to my world," he said. "But I don't think you've got anything to worry about. I saw the way she looked at you when I turned up the other Sunday, and believe me, there was nothing platonic about that. She wants you, too, but she's probably worried about overstepping her boundaries. It's your house, after all, she doesn't want to mess up her homelife when she doesn't have anything else to go to." He paused, squeezing Joy's hand right back. "But I'd say one of you should overstep the boundary at some point, because even if you didn't feel the sexual tension in that room, I did."

"Oh, I felt it alright. And you turning up was completely the wrong time, but maybe in a way, a good thing." Joy felt it all over again, all over her body just thinking about it. "It's just… scary, the thought of getting into something real. Something 3D, rather than 2D."

Steve's face fell. "I was 2D?"

Joy shook her head. "Not you — the other women I've been with. We were real, Steve. Just not *right*."

Steve's face hadn't perked up. "There were other women?" His voice was choked.

"Yes — but only after we split up, never before. But they were never going to be long-term. Whereas Scarlet…" She didn't finish her sentence.

"Scarlet might be?"

Joy swallowed down hard, then nodded. "She might."

They lay on the bed together, holding hands, lost in a moment.

"Did you ever think we'd end up here, laying on a bed in public, holding hands and discussing women like this?"

Joy let out a strangled laugh. "I never did."

"Funny how life turns out, isn't it?" Steve said, squeezing Joy's hand again.

She squeezed it right back. "It is."

Joy remembered the day they got married, remembered the hope, but also the distinct lack of *oomph* she thought she should have been feeling. And now she knew why.

Then Steve dropped her hand and started rolling around on the bed, trying it out. "So what do you think?" he asked. "Is this the type of bed for a man about town?"

"It might be — if you meet him, tell him it's a go."

Chapter Thirteen

Scarlet had decided to go with an all-black suit and shirt for the news interview, and Steph had approved. According to her, it lent Scarlet an air of authority you didn't tend to get when these news crews just interviewed someone on the street, still shell-shocked by what had happened. Scarlet cast her mind back to earlier, retching on the pavement in front of her flat. Yep, she was glad the news crews hadn't been there to catch that particular moment.

She'd spent the past hour at Steph's getting made up; Steph had insisted.

"We're going to be broadcast across the county, we have to look our best."

Scarlet hadn't liked to object. Only now, looking in the mirror Steph had just given her, she was pretty sure she could give a circus clown a run for their money. Scarlet normally favoured the subtler make-up approach, whereas Steph favoured the 'caked-on' look.

"You don't think the blusher's overkill?" Scarlet asked, twisting her face to the left.

Steph shook her head. "You need more make-up on camera, so overkill is good — think of it as a performance."

Scarlet screwed up her face. "I'm just telling them about what happened."

"It's a performance! Remember, you were the star of your very own cliffhanger: will Scarlet get out in time or drown as the flood waters rise?" Steph painted the scene with her hand above her head.

"I always told her she should be in the movies," Eamonn said, lifting his head from his phone. The mobile networks were all back up now, and he'd been glued to his device ever since Scarlet arrived. "She's wasted in a cake shop," Eamonn added.

"Artisan bakery," Steph corrected, smudging some eye shadow above Scarlet's right eye.

Scarlet winced as she did it.

"Although right now, it's more like a sad, wet statement of industrial art. God knows when we'll be up and running again. At least the insurers look like they won't be an issue, fingers crossed." Steph's shoulders sagged as she spoke.

Scarlet checked her watch, then raised an eyebrow at Steph. "Save your sad looks for the camera, remember — way more effective if you haven't just had the same thought five minutes previous."

"Good point."

"It's a performance," Scarlet added.

Steph shot her a grin. "Glad to hear you were listening."

"Should we be going soon, by the way?" Eamonn asked, leaning over to grab a biscuit from the tin on the counter.

"We should," Steph replied. "Ready?"

Scarlet nodded. "Face on. I'm ready." And she was.

* * *

The street was strangely quiet as the camera crew set up, with Scarlet standing behind the camera, her heart racing. The news anchor, Kay, was chatting to one of her colleagues, and she'd just finished briefing Scarlet on the questions she was going to ask her, telling her to relax. Easy for her to say. If nothing else, Scarlet was going to concentrate on Kay's fabulous hair and just-so make-up. Mind you, her own hair was looking none too shabby tonight, a shock of dark gloss all held in place with a gallon of hairspray — Steph had seen to that.

Steph and Eamonn were standing behind her now, their piece to camera already done. Joy was on her way, and Scarlet wished she was here now to squeeze her hand and give her reassurance. Somehow, in only a week, Scarlet had come to count on Joy's support in her daily life, even welcomed it.

Someone tapped on her arm: it was Kay. "Ready?"

Scarlet nodded. She was used to giving presentations at work, she could do this. Piece of cake.

"Hello and welcome to Valley News, this is Kay Wright reporting from Dulshaw, which was hit badly by last week's devastating floods. And I have with me Scarlet

Williams, who was one of the worst affected residents. Scarlet was given half an hour to evacuate her basement flat before it was completely flooded due to the flood barrier failure." The camera swung from Kay, and Scarlet squinted as the bright lights shone in her eyes.

"Scarlet, tell us, what was it like getting that knock on your door?"

Scarlet licked her lips: her heart-rate was strangely normal, her breathing steady. Not at all how she'd expected to feel. "Surreal — like it wasn't really happening to me."

"I bet. And what did you take in those brief moments you had?"

"Laptop, phone, guitar, clothes. But there wasn't much time to decide."

Kay nodded, fake concern on her face. "And then you just shut the door and left?"

"Pretty much, yes."

"What a feeling that must have been," Kay added, gravely.

Scarlet nodded. "It was the start of what I thought was going to be the worst week of my life. And believe me, I've had some rival weeks in my time." She smiled, replaying them in her head: Dad, Mum, Liv. "But actually, it turned out to be one of the best weeks."

Kay's face registered surprise. "Really?" She glanced over at the camera crew and indicated towards Scarlet.

Scarlet guessed they were going in for a close-up. She tried to block it out.

"My flat was flooded and I lost everything I own,

more or less. I was there today, trying to get stuff out, and it's still a total mess. And I wasn't insured for contents, so that's pretty bad, right?"

"I would say so."

"But it hasn't been. One thing, I'm not the worst affected. Dulshaw FC lost its brand-new gym, facilities, and stadium — that affects many jobs and lives. Businesses have been sunk, like Great Bakes, and next to them the bookshop was shovelling out piles of ruined books — that's a tragedy. And the cinema's shut, with livelihoods affected, too. I'm one, tiny story — just one of many."

"That's a great way of looking at it, if you don't mind me saying so."

Scarlet shrugged. "It's the only way to look at it. It's going to take a while for me to get back on my feet and replace everything I lost, but I will. I have a job, I have friends, I have family." She paused, then beamed. Yes, she really did have family. It felt so good to say that sentence and really mean it. It meant the world.

"And I have the support of my job and my community, who've all rallied round to help. The emergency services have been terrific, the council on top of things, and thanks to our wonderful mayor, Joy Hudson, I have a roof over my head. She kindly took me in on the morning of the flood and now it looks like she's stuck with me." Scarlet glanced around and saw Joy standing behind the camera — she'd missed her arriving. She smiled a grateful smile at her, and got one in return.

"And how is your flat?" Kay asked.

Scarlet smiled. "Buggered," she said, before clamping a hand over her mouth. "Sorry, am I allowed to say that?"

Kay laughed, shaking her head. "It's okay — let's go again." She turned to the crew. "You getting all this?" Her voice held urgency.

The crew nodded.

Kay counted Scarlet in and asked the question again.

"It's going to take weeks, maybe months for it to dry out — basement flats have a harder time recovering than most. All my stuff has had to be thrown away having been submerged for a few days, and we're back to bare walls, no plaster. It's a damp shell and it needs to be dried before any rebuilding work can start."

"But you seem — almost *upbeat* about it." Kay sounded like she didn't believe the words that were coming out of her mouth, let alone Scarlet's.

Scarlet nodded. "I am. The flood's restored my faith in people and pulled me back to life. In a weird way, I'm grateful. I'd never have met the wonderful people of this town and known their generosity without it."

"Your attitude is commendable."

"If you'd asked me at the beginning of the week, it might have been a different story, but now…" Scarlet paused, then looked directly into the camera. "But there are still loads of people and businesses who really need your help, so please give whatever you can — time, food, money, whatever. It all adds up to us all rebuilding our town together."

Kay waited to see if Scarlet had finished, then brought the camera back over to her. "There you have it, I couldn't have said it better myself — let me know if you ever need a job," she told Scarlet, smiling. "The rebuilding effort needs your donations — the number and website are on the screen now, or just go to the website for more information. Thanks to Scarlet for speaking to us."

"You're welcome," Scarlet replied.

The cameras stopped rolling and Kay tapped Scarlet on the arm, just as she took the few steps towards Joy. "Can we get some footage in your flat, too, just so people can see the damage?" Kay asked.

"Sure." Scarlet was pumped, jigging from foot to foot: she was so glad she'd agreed to do this. Making Dulshaw's plight visible to as many people as possible was the plan, and if Scarlet could be part of that, she was thrilled.

She turned to Joy and Kay and her camera crew readied themselves. "Was I okay?"

She couldn't quite read the look on Joy's face, but she was smiling.

"You were glorious."

Scarlet grinned at her. "Give me ten minutes to show Kay around the flat?"

"I'll be waiting," Joy replied.

* * *

"You were brilliant, a natural on camera." Joy was sitting beside Scarlet in the pub, a look in her eye that Scarlet still couldn't quite pin down. "And I loved the look you gave that woman when she asked you how you felt about having to evacuate your house at four in the morning."

"They ask stupid questions, that's why I tend to avoid the local news. How does she think I felt? I wanted to say thrilled, but I thought that might make me public enemy number one."

"Probably a good move."

"You were just… incredible," Steph said. "I can't put it any other way. I thought you were going to tell them a sob story!" The interview was due to be broadcast any moment now on BBC local news. The pub already had the TV set on, ready to roll.

"I was," Scarlet said, running a finger up and down her fresh pint of Peroni. "And then all this stuff just came out of my mouth. Did I sound like a twat?" She was pretty sure she had, and the crackle of doubt was still crunching through her veins. She hated looking at photos of herself, never mind watching herself on the telly.

Joy shook her head. "Far from it — you sounded like a compassionate, caring person."

"Which is what threw me, to be fair," Eamonn added, grinning. "Invasion of the bodysnatchers. You've definitely been taken over — bring back moany Scarlet. I miss her."

"She's still here, she's just sulking," Scarlet said, putting her elbows on the table, her jaw cradled in her palms. "So I didn't come across as a twat?"

"If Mother Teresa is a twat, then yes," Eamonn replied. "You're going to be a local celebrity and saint after this, mark my words. People are going to come up to you in the street and thank you." He glanced at Joy. "You might have a queue of people outside your door, waiting for advice on how to be more giving like Saint Scarlet." He paused. "And frankly, I blame you."

"Me?" Joy said. "Why am I to blame?"

"Because you're the one thing that's changed. Scarlet used to be reliably miserable and pessimistic, then she goes to live with you for a week and *boom!* She's spouting self-help and heal-thyself bollocks down a TV screen."

Scarlet rolled her eyes. "Okay, we get your point, Irish boy."

Eamonn grinned, pointing a finger. "You see — casual xenophobia! That's the Scarlet I know and love. Not this airbrushed flood poster child."

"I think you did brilliantly," Joy said, ignoring Eamonn. "You spoke from the heart, and that's what people will respond to — on that point, Eamonn is right. You're saying what many of us are thinking: yes, we'd rather there wasn't a flood, but look what it's done for the community spirit and pride in our town."

"I didn't sound preachy?" Scarlet pouted. She was still worried, but she'd find out soon enough.

"You made me sound like a right wally, if anything, going on about my plight," Steph said. "There's us two, going on about our business and our wedding, and then there's you, pushing away the spotlight and turning it on those in need. I really might start calling you Saint Scarlet."

Ten minutes later, and it looked like Steph was right. The interview had been aired, and they'd all come out of it well, but Scarlet in particular. The pub erupted in applause when it finished, and Scarlet was now installed in a circle of locals, all wanting to hug her, offer her furniture, or buy her a drink. Like the whole of the past week, it was all too surreal.

Scarlet's phone lit up with a text from Clark. *'Proud of you sis — you were amazing. X'*

She'd just said what came naturally — she didn't see what the fuss was about. Like Joy said, she'd just told the truth.

"What did I tell you?" Eamonn said, as they eventually sat down an hour or so later.

"I have never in my life had so many people give me their email address and phone number. I think I have a bed, two wardrobes, an armchair, and a coat that didn't fit Amy over there, but she thinks would look great on me. Unbelievable."

"That's the power of TV."

Scarlet shook her head as her phone buzzed again. She clicked, read the message, then her mouth dropped open.

"That was Kay," she said. "Apparently since it aired, they've been deluged with calls of help and support. The flood fund has been swamped and she's had calls from people who want to help *us* specifically," she said to Steph and Eamonn. "Your shop and me." Scarlet shook her head. "It's crazy."

"You can say that again," Steph said. "But crazy good — that's amazing!" She gave Eamonn a kiss on the lips and he grinned back at his fiancée.

"You're amazing," Eamonn told Steph.

"Maybe your prophecy was right," Joy said, covering Scarlet's hand with her own.

Scarlet felt it right the way down to her toes. Eamonn had just kissed Steph, and she really wanted to kiss Joy right now. *Right at this very moment.* Suddenly, Scarlet couldn't remember the reason why she hadn't done it before. Because she was stupid? What exactly had she been waiting for? This was a victorious moment, one to be celebrated. And she couldn't think of a better way to do it than that.

"My prophecy?" she asked, tuning out the rest of the pub. In this moment, it was just her and Joy.

"The one about it not being the worst week of your life, but rather, one of your best."

A fuzzy haze ran down her and she was suddenly drenched with desire. It wasn't the best week of her life *yet*, but she knew how to make it happen.

Scarlet reached over and took Joy's hand under the table, holding Joy's gaze with her own. Scarlet's grip was firm, belying the weakness in her knees and the thundering in her chest. This was it — the push they'd needed. There was no going back now. Scarlet had opened the door and they were both about to step through.

"You want to go home soon?" She hoped that sentence communicated everything it was laced with: her voice had dropped an octave, which spoke volumes. She dropped her gaze to Joy's lips, back up to Joy's eyes, then back to her lips.

Joy's gaze never left hers, her eyes pooling with unmistakable desire.

"I would love to," she replied.

Chapter Fourteen

They got a cab home, at Scarlet's insistence, and held hands all the way home, without talking. Joy's heart was beating hard, and her palms were beginning to sweat, too, but she tried not to think about it. Keep calm, that was her motto. But it was hard to keep calm when she cast her mind forward and almost wilted with yearning. She'd visualised this moment so many times in her mind, and now here they were, Scarlet smiling nervously at her, on their way home.

Scarlet paid the driver and unlocked the front door, moving aside for Joy to go in first. She closed the door gently and turned to look at Joy.

Joy hadn't moved. She was just standing, staring, her breathing sketchy. She couldn't take her eyes from Scarlet, who suddenly seemed larger in her vision, almost pulsing. Joy's mouth was gluey, and when Scarlet spoke, the words felt like they were coming from a speaker in the wall and not from her at all.

"You want to go through to the lounge?"

Joy nodded, wordless, shrugging off her coat. When Scarlet took her hand to lead her through, it trembled with want. Joy had to get a grip, or she was going to pass out before anything happened. And she seriously didn't want to do that. Not after this lifetime of wait.

Not now.

Joy sat on the sofa, taking her usual seat, staring at the magazine on the coffee table. It was Scarlet's magazine, one on guitars. She liked that Scarlet was feeling comfortable enough to leave her magazines around the house now. Joy's insides glowed at the thought that Scarlet was beginning to relax here.

Joy's gaze settled on Scarlet, who was on her haunches, filling the log burner with wood and firelighters. When it was done, she closed the tiny door and glanced over at her sofa.

Scarlet's seat.

Scarlet hesitated as she stood, but then veered left and sat next to Joy.

Joy held her breath. The logs began to smoke and glow, a bit like her. Joy was the kindling, and Scarlet was the firelighter.

Scarlet took Joy's hand. "I don't quite know where to start," she said. Scarlet was shaking. "You've been so amazing to me since I arrived, and you've been by my side through this exhausting week." She exhaled. "And after the interview, after seeing Eamonn kiss Steph, all I wanted to do was kiss you." Scarlet licked her lips, her gaze caressing Joy's face. "It's still all I want to do. But I don't want to do anything you don't want to do. We can do this however you want, slow as you like; you're in control."

Scarlet swiped her thumb over Joy's knuckles.

Joy's body trembled from head to toe: Scarlet was causing mini-earthquakes with a minimal touch.

"That's the thing," Joy replied, leaning in so their faces were within touching distance. Up close, Scarlet was even more beautiful, and Joy stroked her cheek with the back of her hand.

Scarlet closed her eyes on contact.

Joy continued: "I don't think I've been in much control since the moment you walked through my door. I've kept a lid on it, but that's about it. I've been wanting to kiss you since you swept into my life almost a week ago, and that's *a lot* of waiting. So going slow wasn't on my mind today." Joy paused. She seemed to have turned into a character from a film, one with gumption and sass. "This is what's been on my mind today."

Joy leaned forward and pressed her lips to Scarlet's, leaning in for dear life. When they finally made contact, the impact was instant, their lips crashing together with a hunger that had been building for days. Scarlet's lips were warm and wet, and they tasted of glittering potential. Joy was transfixed: now she'd finally kissed them, she only wanted more. Finally, after days of flirting, and nights of longing, she was kissing Scarlet Williams and it was divine. It was as if this was what Joy had been born to do, and really, what the hell had taken her so long?

She moved closer to Scarlet just as Scarlet moved to her, their breasts brushing against each other as their lips locked. Joy drew in a breath and her clit stood to attention. She clung to Scarlet as pent up need overwhelmed her. The longing wasn't just for Scarlet; the longing was for the last 38 years she'd wasted. *So much time.* But she couldn't dwell on that: now was the time to look to the future. But mainly towards getting to know Scarlet better.

So much better.

Joy ran a hand up Scarlet's back, and Scarlet kissed her harder. Raw energy and passion collided as they raced through her, and when Scarlet's tongue glided into her mouth, Joy swelled with passion. Scarlet was everything Joy had dreamed about and more. And the way she'd been on camera today? Joy didn't think she'd ever been more attracted to anyone. *Ever.*

Until Scarlet began to nibble the side of her neck. That was when Joy had a feeling this attraction was only going to go one way: skywards, to the moon.

Scarlet's breathing was heavy as her tongue flicked over Joy's neck, before settling near her ear. "I've been wanting to do this all week, too," she whispered, placing a hand on Joy's breast. "And you feel incredible."

The words rolled down Joy's body like a thunderclap, sending shuddering sparks of electricity through her.

Scarlet had felt it, too: a small chorus of rejoice began in Joy's mind. She smiled, before tilting her neck, giving herself over to Scarlet.

Scarlet didn't need a second invitation, setting to work, her tongue and mind working in perfect harmony.

Within minutes, she was tugging at Joy's top, her nimble fingers pulling it over Joy's head. And then Scarlet stopped to admire Joy.

"You're even more beautiful than I imagined," Scarlet said, before enveloping Joy in her arms, running her hands up and down Joy's back.

A smile creased Joy's face as she breathed in Scarlet's sweet scent. "I'm glad you approve," she said.

Scarlet's eyes were dark pools of want as she stared at her. "One hundred per cent."

And then Scarlet pushed the fabric of Joy's bra to one side, wrapping her mouth around one of her dark nipples.

The sensation almost wiped Joy out. Looking down at Scarlet like this, Scarlet's mouth on her breast, it was almost too much to handle. Joy couldn't rip her eyes from Scarlet as she reached round and unclipped her bra, releasing Joy's breasts. Scarlet cupped them both, nibbling left then right, her focus laserlike.

Joy, for her part, was now pulsing inside and out. Her knickers were already drenched; she couldn't wait for what was to come.

And yet, she also wanted to. She wanted to lie in the moment, revel in it, savour it. Because even though there was nothing she wanted more right now than Scarlet's touch, there was also only ever going to be one first time and she wanted it to be as perfect as it could be. Because she'd never wanted anything so much in her life.

Scarlet tugged Joy up and led her to the rug in front of

the fire, easing her onto her back. Then her mouth was on Joy's stomach, then her breasts, then her neck.

Joy didn't know what to concentrate on or what to think: Scarlet kissing her did so many things to her, she was almost floored. Everything she'd ever known before had been wiped away, Scarlet had made sure of that. The room went fuzzy around her as Scarlet's tongue worked its magic.

Then Scarlet straddled Joy and slowly undid her own black shirt above her, a slight smile playing on her lips.

Joy's blood was rushing so fast, it was almost deafening.

When Scarlet slipped off her shirt, Joy couldn't take it anymore — she was too far away from Scarlet, she wanted to be closer to the action. She wanted to touch Scarlet, so Joy got to her knees, facing her, then placed her tongue on Scarlet's breasts, drawing back the material of the white bra and claiming them for her own.

Scarlet moaned as Joy sucked, licking and teasing Scarlet, who was lost to her touch just as Joy had been to hers. Seeing the effect was mesmerising, and only made Joy want to do more. To go further. To take Scarlet to places they'd never been before, together as one.

It only took a couple of minutes for Scarlet's bra to be removed and then they were kneeling together, breast to breast, lips locked, hands over backs.

Kissing Scarlet naked, bare flesh to bare flesh was *so* much more erotic than with clothes on. Exquisite tingles rippled up and down Joy's body as Scarlet trailed her tongue along Joy's bottom lip, before sliding it into her mouth, at once rough but also gentle. Scarlet's kisses were scrambling Joy's senses and she could think of nothing else but the here and now. Of making love to Scarlet. Her mind was a blank page, and Scarlet's tongue was writing a new story with every second that passed. Joy was in heightened emotional territory, somewhere she'd never been before. But she wasn't scared — not one bit.

She wanted to open her arms, then her heart, then her legs. She didn't think she'd be able to open them wide enough. She wanted to open up, and offer Scarlet whatever she wanted. Joy was ready — *so ready.*

Then Scarlet was easing off Joy's trousers, then her own, all the while her heated gaze never leaving Joy's face.

Joy's blood was still rushing around her entire being, her head in the zone. When Scarlet placed a hand on her butt cheek and squeezed, Joy gushed. When she then lowered her to the floor and poured her naked body on top of her, Joy sagged with longing. Scarlet's hands were all over Joy, branding her body like no other ever had before.

Nobody else in the whole wide world.

"If you don't touch me soon, I might die," Joy said, the words sounding odd, like they were in a different language.

Scarlet smiled on top of her, nibbling her way around Joy's earlobe, settling a thigh between Joy's legs. "I wouldn't want that," she said, pressing down between Joy's legs.

Joy closed her eyes as her clit pulsed.

And then Scarlet was travelling south, licking and kissing her body as she went, before she arrived between Joy's legs, her breath hot over Joy's centre. When Scarlet ran her wet tongue under the edges of Joy's knickers, Joy trembled. She reached out to hold onto something, but there was nothing to hand, only the white rug, so she clung to that. She doubted it was going to be enough, however. Not when Scarlet eventually reached her destination.

Scarlet's mouth was pressing through the cloth of her knickers, her mouth hot over Joy. Joy was woozy with desire, she'd been waiting *so long* — but with Scarlet's tongue on her body, she didn't need anything else. Scarlet on Joy was seamless, like they were already moulded into one.

When Scarlet discarded her own knickers and gently pulled down Joy's, Joy finally spread herself fully, opening herself up to new possibilities, to new experiences. But she wanted to do it *with* Scarlet, not have it *done* to her. She wanted to feel Scarlet, taste Scarlet, to love her all at the same time. So she told her so.

Scarlet's face registered genuine surprise, but also distinct pleasure.

"You're in charge, we can do whatever you want to do," she whispered, slipping a tongue inside Joy's mouth and pressing her lips onto Joy's, claiming her rapidly.

Joy whimpered, then nodded. "I want this to be us: *both of us*." And then she gushed again. Joy was so wet. So ready.

With that, Scarlet reversed her body so that Joy

could reach her, her knees planted on either side of Joy's shoulders, before parting Joy's legs and lowering her head.

Joy tensed as Scarlet's breath was hot and heavy over her pussy. Seconds later, Scarlet guided her tongue into Joy, easing through her slick folds. Then she trailed her tongue slowly, deliberately from top to bottom, swirling around Joy's clit. Joy's brain almost short-circuited such was the intensity of pleasure. There was nowhere to hide, but she didn't want to. Joy let out a piercing moan which dripped with desire, much like Joy herself.

"Oh, yes!" she said, panting, pushing up her hips to let Scarlet know exactly what she wanted, just in case there was any doubt. Joy wanted her: all of her. When Scarlet responded to Joy's encouragement by slipping two fingers inside Joy and sucking her clit gently into her mouth, Joy almost came on the spot.

Holy fucking hell.

But then she remembered: this was a two-way street. So as Scarlet slid her tongue up Joy and moved inside her, Joy took a deep breath and did the same to Scarlet: sucking her gently into her mouth and pulling her close, revelling in her scent and her very womanliness.

Scarlet stopped what she was doing and moaned into Joy, the exquisite vibrations exploding all over Joy as she did. This was off-the-scale insane, but Joy was determined to concentrate — she owed them both that. Scarlet tasted delicious: she tasted of Joy's dreams.

As Joy dove into Scarlet and greedily sucked her in,

she knew this was a life-changing moment. She would never be the same again. She wanted to tell Scarlet that she'd dreamed about this moment, but she'd never dared to think it might be this good.

She was inside Scarlet and Scarlet was inside her. She was making love with Scarlet, to Scarlet, and the women that had come before were instantly erased. This was it. This was what Joy had waited for.

Joy's world would never be the same again.

* * *

Being inside Joy was beyond glorious: it felt like a homecoming. Scarlet had pictured it throughout the week, but now, here she was, full of Joy.

Literally.

Because if being inside Joy was beyond glorious, having Joy inside her at the same time was too much for words. With every flick of her tongue, Joy drew Scarlet into her web; with every thrust of her finger, Scarlet fell deeper and deeper. And Joy wasn't holding back or being shy. Far from it, which only made Scarlet warm to her all the more. Who could resist, when Joy had her exactly where she wanted her?

And having sex with another woman again? Scarlet had been worried she might be a little rusty, but while she hadn't done this in a while, it was like riding a bike: she still remembered how to pedal and change gears. She could almost feel herself coming back to life with every move, every kiss. It was as if, for the past two years, she'd been in a love coma, refusing all efforts to bring her back to life. But Joy had broken through: she'd taken the time to listen and unlocked the real Scarlet. And now it was time to show Joy how much she appreciated it.

"Oh my god, Scarlet," Joy said, as Scarlet trailed her tongue into Joy, then over Joy, exploring every fold and ridge. Scarlet fitted Joy perfectly, like two halves of a magnet being drawn together. And as she sunk into Joy, fucking and sucking her slowly, Joy returned the favour, till the point where Scarlet had no idea what to focus on, and frankly, she didn't really care. She was in the moment, rocking and rolling to Joy's glorious rhythm, reflecting it right back. They were orbiting each other perfectly, on a stellar collision course.

If Scarlet's intention was to overwhelm Joy, it also had the desired effect on Scarlet, too. She'd been absent from life and from love for too long, but now, she was beginning to colour outside the lines again. Emotion bubbled up inside Scarlet as Joy increased her speed, moving inside her, enveloping her whole.

"You feel so good," Joy whispered into Scarlet, her tongue writing the words on Scarlet, her fingers pushing the words right inside her. The effect made Scarlet clamp down around Joy's long fingers.

She was on the edge.

Joy ran her tongue hungrily around Scarlet, before circling her clit expertly. Then, with her fingers thrusting deep inside, giving Scarlet all she had, Joy sucked Scarlet into her mouth once again. And that was all it took to send Scarlet over the edge, her body shuddering as she came on top of Joy, Joy fucking her hard and fast and never letting up. Scarlet was flying high, and the feeling she had? You couldn't bottle it, but if you did, you'd be a rich woman. It was a five-star moment, off the menu, a unique moment that could never be recreated.

And as Scarlet came, as she soared high into clouds of ecstasy, Scarlet's scrambled brain still remembered Joy: so she gave Joy what she needed, too. As Scarlet's orgasm played out, Joy's erupted through her, shaking her to the core, encouraging Scarlet on from the sidelines. And Scarlet was ready and waiting, her arms wide open, ready to take Joy with her, to love her fully.

Neither of them would let up, both wanting to please the other. Seconds later, they came again, in a blur of tongues and fingers slipping and sliding, heads thrown, glorious moans filling the air. Once more, with feeling, and then they slumped onto each other, still inside each other, twitching, lazy smiles, flushed faces. Eventually, they both withdrew and Scarlet crawled around so her face was level with Joy's. She kissed her lips, her face, her eyelids.

And when Joy's eyes fluttered open, Scarlet gave her the widest smile possible.

Sometimes this week, Scarlet had wondered if she was going to make it through, but Joy had always been on her side, been there for her. It was Joy who'd made the difference, Joy who'd told her to buck up when she was at her lowest.

And look at her now: lying in Joy's arms. She hadn't thought it often over the past few years, but maybe life did have something to offer her, after all. Scarlet was coming back to life and Joy was piecing her back together, piece by piece.

* * *

Nobody had ever made Joy come like that, or *feel* like that. How did she know what to do? She was so on Joy's wavelength, it made Joy want to weep hot, salty tears of euphoria. Nobody had ever deciphered her code with such aplomb, such ease. It was as if Scarlet had just turned up with a key that spelled 'Joy', and started her ignition. And now, Joy's body was on overdrive, going so fast, everything was vibrating. Her heart, her soul, her everything. Joy let the moment wash over her again and again, never wanting it to end.

Scarlet covered her now, stroking her, whispering in her ear. She kissed her neck, her face, her shoulders, and Joy was only vaguely aware of it. She was floating away on a cloud of bliss, the only thing holding her down was Scarlet, the woman responsible, so she didn't mind. If she floated away, she might never come back, and she wanted to.

Oh, how she wanted to.

Because the story unfolding had only just begun in so many ways, and Joy didn't want to miss a thing. And she never wanted to be parted from Scarlet — not if this was what happened every time. She had so much lost time to make up for and she was hungry to make up for it.

Joy was ravenous.

She latched onto Scarlet, hoping her kiss told Scarlet just how much that had meant, how much Joy had hungered for her touch all her life. *All of her goddamn life.*

When Joy finally opened her eyes, letting the world back in again, Scarlet's eyes were on her, a smile tweaking the corners of her mouth. Joy had never seen anything so refined, so sexy, so delectable.

"Hey," Scarlet said.

"Hey."

"I've got to tell you, you are magnificent." Scarlet pressed her lips to Joy's once more.

Another hot flush of want rolled through Joy.

She smiled weakly. "I think I should be telling you that after what just happened."

Scarlet shook her head. "It's still fresh in my mind, and you are." She paused, her eyes trailing down Joy's body, then back up to her face. "I can't believe this has finally happened."

"In a good way?" Joy was pretty sure, but she just wanted to double-check.

Scarlet smiled deliciously.

"Of course," Scarlet said, cocking her head to one side and kissing Joy again. "Do you really think this is how it goes when things don't work out?"

Joy grinned. "I hope not."

"Stop trying to deflect compliments. Because I promise you this: you really were magnificent."

"Thank you," Joy replied, reversing their positions, rolling on top of Scarlet and kissing her hard.

She couldn't help it. Scarlet had ignited a fire inside her, and she was going to burn from the inside out if she didn't act on it now. She was sure Scarlet would understand. Joy bit Scarlet's lip, trailed her tongue along her swollen lips, licked the length of her neck.

When she drew back, surprise was painted on Scarlet's face, along with pure desire.

"Let's see if I can up my magnificence level a notch further, shall we?" Joy said, slipping two fingers inside Scarlet.

"I'd like that very much," Scarlet replied, followed by a sharp intake of breath.

Chapter Fifteen

Scarlet was frying bacon in the pan — she had the eggs on standby, but couldn't decide whether she should go with fried, poached or scrambled. After some consideration, she decided on fried. She wasn't worried about calorie intake today: she'd been up half the night having sex with Joy, and she was damn sure that whatever calories she put in her body now, she'd still be playing catch-up. Their first night together had been a riot of sex and emotion, and she was hoping they could do it all over again.

Very soon indeed.

She moved the bacon around the pan, and some fat shot up from the pan and hit her hand. "Fucking hell," she said, just as she heard the slap of Joy's slippers on the tiles behind her.

"Good morning to you, too," Joy said, walking over to Scarlet, putting her arms around her waist and kissing the side of her neck.

Scarlet's body fizzed all over, her clit waking up once more — or else, it'd never gone to sleep.

"Mmm," she replied, now a little unsteady on her feet. "I could get used to mornings like this."

"And I could get used to you making me breakfast like this, too, so we're both happy." Joy kissed her neck a final time, then let her go, filling the kettle and retying her dressing gown which had fallen open.

Scarlet's eyes were now resting around Joy's breasts. "Were you trying to have a *Carol* moment there with your dressing gown?"

Joy frowned. "A *Carol* moment?"

"You know, the bit in the movie where she stands behind Rooney Mara with her dressing gown invitingly open. Just before they have sex for the first time."

Joy smiled. "I think that horse has bolted, but I'm happy to roleplay if you like."

Scarlet blushed. "Roleplay on day two? We haven't even had a date yet."

Joy let out a laugh as the kettle boiled and she grabbed two mugs to make the tea. "What can I say? And if it makes you feel better, I've never offered to do roleplay with anyone else in my life before. You're the first."

"I'm flattered," Scarlet said with a smile.

Joy placed a tea beside Scarlet on the counter, then sat down on her stool, swinging round one way, then the other.

Scarlet could feel her gaze boring into her. She turned and grinned. "So this is a bit different to yesterday morning."

"It is," Joy replied. "For a start, I'm aching in places

I'd forgotten *could* ache." She paused. "In fact, I think I'm aching in places I've never ached before — *never ever*. And I've got you to blame for that." She sighed contentedly. "And I'm hoping I'll have you to blame for more of the same later on."

"I'm sure it could be arranged." Scarlet took the bacon out of the pan, then carefully cracked the eggs in. "Fried eggs okay?"

"Whatever you're cooking, I'm famished."

"Sex is hungry work."

"Apparently when it's done right, yes."

Scarlet put a lid on the pan to let the eggs set. "So you're alright this morning? No regrets? No, 'what have I done, shagging that Scarlet woman'?" She smiled at her own joke. She hadn't had a chance to use it for a while. It used to be a favourite of hers back in the day.

Joy laughed. "Now I know you really *are* a scarlet woman," she said. "But no, no regrets." Joy scratched her nose. "Actually, scrap that, I do have regrets. Regrets that we didn't meet sooner and do *that* sooner. But I *know*, everything happens for a reason. I'm just glad it happened at all." She took a sip of her tea.

Scarlet studied Joy for a moment. "How old are you, by the way? I just realised I don't know for sure. You know I'm 39, but you could be any age."

Joy grinned at her. "How old do you think I am?"

"Oh no, I'm not playing that game, that game only goes wrong."

"Spoilsport." Joy paused pushing a stray hair behind her ear. "I'm 38, which makes you a cradle snatcher."

"Excellent, I've always wanted to be one of those. One off the bucketlist."

Joy's phone beeped in her pocket, and she got it out. "It's from Gran, asking if I'm coming in to see her on Saturday and telling me to bring you." She glanced up at Scarlet. "You think she has a sixth sense? Like she knows something happened?"

"I wouldn't put it past her."

"She's going to be overjoyed — there's nothing my grandma likes more than people getting together. She's an incurable romantic, as well as being a rampant ho."

Scarlet spluttered. "Your cute, sweet grandma is a rampant ho?"

"Don't be deceived by the looks — she's been through the men in that home like you wouldn't believe."

Scarlet laughed as she turned off the eggs. "She won't be the only one who's pleased. After initially questioning my decision to move in here, Eamonn is now wholeheartedly behind the 'Scarlet & Joy' campaign. He's dropped so many hints and unsubtle winks, I was thinking he was going to get T-shirts printed and start to campaign around the town. I think he might have, too, but the print shop was flooded."

Scarlet walked over to Joy. She needed to kiss her, she hadn't done it in at least five minutes. "I think you'd look gorgeous on a T-shirt, by the way," she said, before planting her lips where they belonged.

Before she knew it, the kiss had escalated, and now Scarlet's hand were inside Joy's dressing gown, kneading her breasts, sweeping down in between her legs. Their kissing was haphazard, ragged, intense: Scarlet knew where this was going. She pulled Joy off her stool and tugged off her knickers, then guided her back onto the stool, holding her gaze, telling her what was going to happen.

Desire clouded Joy's eyes. "Fuck me," she panted.

Scarlet grinned, kissing Joy and pulling her close. The room around her melted to liquid as she parted Joy's legs as far as she could, then slid two fingers inside her. Joy was *so* wet already.

Joy bit Scarlet's lip and clung onto her shoulder as Scarlet began to fuck her, thrusting deep inside her, curling her fingers and making Joy moan.

If last night had been about connection and emotion, this morning was about reconnection and pure lust, wild and unleashed. Scarlet steadied Joy on the stool as their movements made it swing left and right, which made them both laugh. Then she pushed Joy's legs wider, fucking her with everything she had. If Joy had been in the driving seat last night, this morning, it was definitely Scarlet at the wheel.

Joy was thrusting forward to meet Scarlet's rhythm, head tilted back, gripping Scarlet's arms. When Scarlet's thumb connected with Joy's clit, she stiffened; when Scarlet increased her pressure and speed, Joy moaned loudly again.

But that was nothing compared to Joy's guttural roar as she came all over Scarlet's fingers seconds later, mouth wide open, head back, wanting all that Scarlet could give.

Scarlet looked into her eyes and saw such raw emotion, such openness, that tears threatened again, but she wasn't going to give in to that this morning. Right now, her only intention was to fuck Joy till she could take no more. And so she did.

Moments later, Joy turned the tables, showing Scarlet that anything she could, Joy could do better. Stumbling off the stool like a drunk, she tugged down Scarlet's shorts, then pushed her into a dining chair, before dropping to her knees.

"Seeing as I can't stand properly, getting on my knees would seem to be the sensible option," Joy told Scarlet, with a languid smile.

And then Joy's head was between Scarlet's legs, pushing them wide.

As Scarlet put her hands in Joy's golden hair, Joy sucked Scarlet into her mouth, teasing her with her teeth, swirling her tongue with panache.

Scarlet's mind went blank as she let her head fall back and allowed herself to relax into the moment. Joy's head between her legs was immeasurably beautiful, and her tongue was exquisite. When she entered her, time stood still, Scarlet pushing forward to give Joy the best angle. Joy's tongue was inquisitive and persistent, everything Scarlet wanted it to be.

With such relentless persistence, it didn't take long for Scarlet to topple over the edge, which she did seconds later, clinging to Joy with her feet and hands, fireworks exploding inside her body. As Joy sucked and fucked her simultaneously, Scarlet was woozy with lust.

She could so get used to mornings like this.

As she came again with Joy applying the killer pressure with her tongue, Scarlet was suckerpunched, reeling. She had no idea where she was or who she was. All she could feel was Joy, reverberating in her head and in her heart.

When Joy stopped, the room was silent for a moment, nobody moving, just the smell of cooked breakfast enveloping them.

Joy exhaled, placing her wet chin on Scarlet's thigh, before looking up at Scarlet.

"Fuck me," Scarlet said.

"I think I just did."

Chapter Sixteen

Friday afternoon, and the rain was coming down in sheets so thick, they might as well have been made of steel. This was not the weather anybody wanted for Eamonn and Steph's wedding day, but Joy just hoped it bucked up by tomorrow and they wouldn't have to row to the ceremony.

She was checking the weather app on her phone when Scarlet walked in.

Seeing her, Scarlet gave her a wide smile, followed by a lingering kiss, before taking her place on her stool.

Joy felt the effects *everywhere*.

"Can you believe the rain?" Scarlet asked, glancing up at the skylight.

"They reckon it's going to clear up by tonight. I hope they're right — more rain is the last thing we need."

"Amen to that." Scarlet paused. "Are you coming with me to Grasspoint to help Eamonn and Steph set up in a bit?"

Scarlet had agreed to it when Eamonn texted earlier.

"I'll try — but I told you, I've got this meeting later, so whatever time that runs till. Plus, I said I'd go for coffee with George afterwards, too, so I'll play it by ear."

"George at the council?"

Joy nodded. "I'm just glad I'm not in charge of this whole disaster effort — being the actual leader would have been a real challenge. Plus, I wouldn't have had time to get to know you, either."

"Then I'm glad, too," Scarlet replied. "Plus, I don't fancy George half as much as I fancy you."

Joy let out a bark of laughter. "Glad to hear it."

Scarlet got up off her stool and walked back to Joy. She cupped her butt cheek with one hand, before lowering her lips to Joy's exposed collar bone and kissing along it.

Joy sighed with pleasure.

"You smell so good." Scarlet paused, raising her head to Joy. "So about us — are we telling everyone tomorrow at the wedding? Going public as a couple?" As she spoke, Scarlet took Joy's hand and kissed it. "I can't wait to tell everyone, by the way."

Joy shrunk back.

That was taking things a giant step forward in an instant. She was only just getting used to Scarlet kissing her; she wasn't sure she was ready for the whole world to see it, too.

"I haven't really thought that far ahead," she replied. "Plus, I don't want to take the limelight off Eamonn and Steph — it's their wedding day." She also hadn't had time to process everything in her head. Sure, this felt like the most natural and right thing to her, but Joy was still nervous of telling the rest of the world. To them, she was the mayor: the straight, divorced mayor.

Scarlet stiffened, her face creased with concern. "I wasn't meaning to announce it mid-ceremony. I just want to know if I can hold your hand, maybe grab a dance with you later?"

Joy took a deep breath, avoiding Scarlet's gaze. Her insides were churning; she wasn't sure she was quite ready for the next step just yet, but how could she tell Scarlet it didn't mean anything more than that? That she *absolutely* wanted to be with her, but going public was a separate issue?

Her own issue.

One she hadn't pushed forward herself in two years, yet Scarlet wanted her to do it *overnight?*

"I don't know," Joy said eventually. Which wasn't the most useful answer, she had to admit. Why couldn't she just blurt out what was in her head?

Scarlet's face hardened. Her eyes narrowed and she dropped Joy's hand.

The drop of contact was like a kick in the guts to Joy. Scarlet had her arms folded across her chest and she was looking at Joy with confusion painted across her features. Confusion and hurt. "What do you mean, you don't know?"

Joy desperately wanted to wipe away the hurt. She never wanted to cause Scarlet any pain at all.

"I just mean I haven't really thought about it yet." She paused. "And I might need a little more time to get used to it myself, you know? I just... I'm a public figure, it's not so easy for me to just turn up to a wedding with another woman when I used to be married to a man."

Scarlet blinked, then took one step back, then two. She opened her mouth to speak, then swiftly closed it. "I can't quite believe what I'm hearing," she said. "Did we not share the same experience last night? This morning? But you're still worrying about what people might think? I told you before, you coming out is not going to change people's opinion of you. We're living in the 21st century." Scarlet shook her head. "Are you really going to hide this? Because I can't hide this — being a lesbian is who I am. It's like me supporting Dulshaw, like me hating Marmite. I can't change it, it's just part of me. And I thought you were ready to live your life, too. But maybe I was wrong."

Panic rose in Joy as she saw Scarlet recalculating their relationship, like a jigsaw puzzle that suddenly made no sense. Scarlet couldn't find the corners, had no idea where she was meant to put all the pieces, yet last night, it had all made sense. Joy flicked back through last night and this morning, but the images were fuzzy, one of the wires not quite connected. She frowned and stroked Scarlet's arm.

Scarlet flinched like Joy had just slapped her.

"I am ready... or at least *I will be*. But tomorrow might be too soon to tell everyone we know. I might just need a little time to sit with it, to get used to it myself. Can you understand that?"

Scarlet didn't even blink. "The trouble is, I've been here before. Got together with people who said they were one thing, but actually didn't have the guts to be themselves. And frankly, I'm too old for this shit. Far too fucking old." She stared at Joy, as if taking a mental snapshot. As if it was going to be the last time she ever saw her.

Joy's cheeks flushed red as alarm spread through her. Scarlet was going to leave. She didn't want Scarlet to leave. Why couldn't she explain it better? Why didn't Scarlet understand? She wanted to be part of a couple, but this was all new to her. She was a novice.

"I think I'd better leave," Scarlet said, giving Joy a pained look. "I'm going to help Eamonn and Steph, I'll be back later, don't wait up." Scarlet paused. "And don't worry, I'll keep my distance."

Joy went to say something as Scarlet walked past her, but nothing came out. Her body and her voice had locked up, and even though she desperately wanted to change what had just happened, she couldn't. Not right now. She just wasn't there yet. She gripped the kitchen counter and stared out to the garden. The rain was still hammering down, aptly reflecting her mood.

Ten minutes later, the front door slammed shut.

Only then did Joy dissolve in tears, her body sliding down the kitchen cupboards, heaving with great, guttural sobs. What had she done? Had she just ruined the best thing that had ever happened to her almost before it had begun?

Chapter Seventeen

Scarlet was drenched by the time she got to Grasspoint, but not in the same way she had been last night or this morning. But last night and this morning were a world away right now. She still couldn't quite believe this had happened, but it had. What was the first rule of lesbianism? Don't get involved with sex tourists. And if you are going to get involved with them, certainly don't fall for them.

Definitely don't fall for them.

Lesbian 101.

But Scarlet had fallen for Joy, and now Joy wasn't sure she was ready to come out, when all along, she'd told Scarlet she was. *She'd left her husband*, for goodness sakes, and Scarlet had just blindly assumed that was enough. Enough to back up Joy's assumption she was ready to truly be herself. And after what had happened between them? The sex? The connection? Was Joy really denying everything that had gone before?

Scarlet shook her head as she let herself into the function room at the old people's home. She needed a towel, she was dripping wet. The room was set up with round tables and a top table at the head, but nothing apart from that. This evening had been ear-marked for decorating and table setting, but Scarlet really wasn't in the mood. She checked her watch: 4pm. Her body still felt alive and raw from sex, yet her spirits didn't match. Her spirit had been punched and kicked, and all Scarlet wanted to do was go home and retreat into her sanctuary. But she didn't have it anymore. She didn't have a home. And for a while there, she'd entertained the idea she might have found a new home with Joy. But now, she wasn't so sure.

She got her phone out of her bag and texted Eamonn, sitting down in one of the chairs, sighing heavily. He texted back immediately, telling Scarlet he was tied up at work and would be late, not there for another hour.

Great. If it were up to her, she'd go home, but as she didn't have one, she'd have to wait it out. The reality of having nowhere to go hadn't hit her until now, when she needed her own space. Up until now, she'd been happy sharing Joy's home. But today she saw how hopeless her life was again. Without Joy to hold her up, she was in danger of sinking again. Perhaps she'd have to take her brother up on the option of living with him for a while. Scarlet put her head in her hands, just as the door to the function room opened. When she looked up, she saw Celia, the home manager. Celia was probably around Scarlet's age, but had clearly been named after some far older relative. Scarlet didn't know anybody else her age called Celia — it was a name about due for a revival, like Ethel and Mabel.

"It's you," Celia said, walking over to her. "I saw someone come in and just wondered if Eamonn or Steph were here already and needed anything." She paused, taking Scarlet in. "Are you okay?"

Scarlet gave her a fake smile and nodded her head. She had to hold it together, she didn't want this to come out.

"Fine, just a bit tired, what with the week we've had."

Celia placed a concerned hand on her arm. "Totally understandable — you haven't had it easy." She paused. "I just made tea and served up some cake — you want to come through and have some? Joy's gran and a few others you know are in there."

Scarlet bit her lip. She didn't really want to see Clementine right now, but she might seem rude if she said no. After all, what was she going to do in an empty hall all on her own instead?

"That'd be lovely," she said, easing herself to a standing position.

"And I can get you a towel once we're there, too, so you can dry off a bit."

"Thanks," Scarlet said, following Celia out the door and across the lawn to the main building.

Once inside, Clementine waved her over and Scarlet pulled up a chair, getting smiles from all the residents. Celia brought her over a cuppa and some cake, along with the promised towel, then disappeared down the corridor.

Clementine gave Scarlet a smile as she dried off.

"Here on your own? What's that granddaughter of mine up to today?"

Scarlet cast her eyes to the ground, then around the room. "She had council business, stuff to do," she muttered.

Stuff to do that wasn't Scarlet. Stuff to do that wasn't them. Stuff that was duty, whereas Joy clearly found emotion far less easy to deal with because it wasn't cut and dried. Even though she was a life coach. But weren't they meant to be the worst at taking their own advice, Scarlet had heard somewhere?

Scarlet was suddenly overwhelmed. What the hell was she doing here and with her life? Here she was, nearly 40, and she was sitting in an old people's home because her girlfriend — or she'd dared to dream she might be her girlfriend — wouldn't come out fully. Wasn't this kind of drama meant to have stopped by the time you were nearly 40?

And then, there they were again: the tears. Tracking their way slowly down Scarlet's cheeks, giving the game away.

Clementine looked alarmed, but she took a moment to manoeuvre herself out of her armchair, before guiding Scarlet over to two empty chairs on the other side of the room, away from the TV, overlooking the grounds. Whoever looked after the grounds did a very good job, Scarlet thought.

Once Scarlet was seated, Clementine stroked her arm.

"What's the trouble?" she asked, looking into Scarlet's eyes with concern. But all Scarlet saw was Joy looking at her; she hadn't noticed that before, that her and her granddaughter shared the same deep blue eyes. Looking at Clementine now, she saw she was looking at Joy in 40-odd years' time. Not that it mattered. She probably wouldn't even know Joy then. She'd just be a passing acquaintance from a bygone era, an era when Scarlet had dared to almost love again.

But how could that possibly be after the night they'd had? The week they'd had? The connection they'd made? Scarlet refused to believe it, but the facts were irrefutable. She shook her head to try to stop more tears coming. It didn't work.

"This isn't to do with the flood, is it?"

Scarlet shook her head, still avoiding Clementine's gaze.

"Is it to do with my granddaughter?"

Scarlet nodded her head slowly.

"I thought it might be." Clementine paused. "What's gone on?"

Scarlet took a deep breath, finally looking at Clementine. "We... we got together last night... after the broadcast."

Clementine squeezed Scarlet's arm.

"And everything was fine... great, even. Until this afternoon when I brought up being together at the wedding tomorrow. Joy's not happy about that, says she's not ready to be out to everyone yet, but I can't live like that. I am who I am and I can't be with someone who wants to hide."

Clementine nodded. "I understand. I really do — but Joy will come round. She just needs some time to adjust, that's all. She knows who she is, but letting the whole world know is a different matter."

Scarlet exhaled a long breath. "She told you."

Clementine smiled. "She knows nothing she ever said could change how I feel about her — she's my special girl. But everyone else in the town, it's a big step. Telling her parents, her brother. Only Steve and I know the real reason they split. Joy didn't tell anyone else. So this is still a big step and if you want to be with her, you have to be patient with her."

Scarlet nodded. Had she overreacted? But then again, she didn't want to be with someone who wasn't out and happy with themselves. She simply couldn't be: her life was so far removed from that, she couldn't even contemplate it.

"I get that, but I can't ignore her tomorrow. I want her to be happy, and I'm happiest with her. And I thought she was with me, too. But clearly, I was wrong." Scarlet hung her head.

Clementine patted her knee. "I don't think you were, and I bet you a million pounds that Joy's fretting far more than you right now. She's an honourable woman, and she wants to do the right thing by you. And if the right thing is giving it a bit more time, then so be it. You've had far more time to come to terms with this. Joy has been dealing with an abstract notion of her identity since she split with

Steve. Now that it might be real, she's flummoxed, that's all." Clementine paused. "Promise me you'll let her sort her head out before you give up hope?"

Scarlet rolled Clementine's words around in her head before she nodded. "I will, but I thought we had something. And if Joy's not prepared to acknowledge that, too, then we might have a problem."

That was the understatement of the year.

***

Joy got in that night around 9pm, frazzled after never-ending meetings that hadn't really needed her input. However, as the impartial referee at council meetings, she had to be there, it was all part of the job. But she didn't think her mind had ever been as absent at a meeting as it had tonight. Not when everything she'd ever hoped for and dreamed about had fallen into her lap, but then she'd thrown it all away. She was stuck fast and she didn't know how to change her situation.

She was just shrugging off her coat when there was a knock at the door. She sighed — Joy really didn't want to talk to anyone tonight about anything much. She just wanted to crawl into bed and pretend today hadn't happened. Well, not all of today. Everything after 2pm. Everything that happened before she still remembered vividly, as did her body. Her body was still hyped and ultra-aware. She thought about not answering the door, but what if it was Scarlet?

That thought made her grab the handle and yank the door open. When she saw Steve on the doorstep, her face fell. His short fair hair looked darker from where he'd got caught in the earlier rain.

"Oh, it's you."

Steve's face fell at her greeting. "Lovely to see you, too," he said. "Can I come in?"

Joy stepped aside, on auto-pilot, as Steve stepped past her, wiping his feet on the mat. The rain had stopped and the forecast tomorrow was for less, but it was still a possibility.

Joy followed Steve through to the kitchen, where he was already putting the kettle on.

"To what do I owe this pleasure?" Joy's voice was deadpan, telling Steve she didn't think it was much of a pleasure at all.

"I've got news." He paused, looking nervous.

Joy waited, folding her arms across her chest. She wasn't in the mood for guessing games tonight.

Steve cleared his throat. "I wanted you to hear it from me and nobody else," he said, wincing. "Sharon and I are engaged," he said eventually. And then he leaned back on her counter, waiting for a reply.

"Engaged?" Joy hadn't been expecting that. "You never said anything the other day when we were out buying bedside lamps."

Steve shrugged. "It wasn't planned." He paused. "She asked me, actually. I told her she might have waited till

February 29th, but apparently, women ask men all the time these days."

Joy licked her lips. Even though that should be true, she was pretty sure it wasn't: marriage between a man and a woman was still very much steeped in tradition. She briefly wondered who asked in lesbian relationships, but then put that thought to the back of her mind — it wasn't something she was going to have to worry about any time soon, was it?

Joy took over making the tea, while Steve sat down on a stool, looking dazed.

"Well, congratulations, I guess." Joy turned to Steve. "You are happy about it, I take it?"

He looked down, before nodding almost imperceptibly.

Joy was no detective, but she knew Steve well enough to know that didn't count as enthusiasm.

"I am. I mean, Sharon's great. I just never thought I'd be getting married again. It almost feels like I'm being unfaithful to you, which I know is stupid. But that's how it feels."

Joy shook her head and flicked the kettle off. Then she went to her fridge and pulled out two bottles of Heineken.

"You want a beer instead of tea?"

Steve nodded his head and took the offered bottle from Joy.

Joy sighed. "We're a right pair, you know that? You're hesitating marrying someone else because of me, and I'm hesitating taking things further with Scarlet because of me. I'm the common denominator here. Maybe I should just leave town and let everyone else get on with their lives. It would make things a whole lot easier, wouldn't it?"

Steve frowned. "I don't think that at all. And what's going on with Scarlet?"

Joy sighed again. "I shouldn't really be discussing this with you, you're my ex. Doesn't that make me unfaithful, too?"

Steve laughed. "And I shouldn't really be coming round here telling you what I just did, but I have." He paused. "We were always friends first and foremost, don't forget that."

"I know." Joy took a long swig from her beer, as if using it to fuel her next sentence. "Scarlet and I slept together last night." She didn't look at Steve, just in case he was wincing. But if he really wanted to be friends, he had to take the rough with the smooth.

"So what's the problem?"

However, when Joy looked up, all she saw in her ex's eyes was concern, so maybe she sold him short. There must have been a reason he was so easy to be married to for all those years, after all.

"We've been invited to Scarlet's friend's wedding tomorrow and she wants to go as a couple. But I just don't know if I'm ready to come out to the whole world: I only just met a woman I care about. Is it too much to want to keep it to myself for a little bit?"

Steve laughed. "You slept with her last night, right?"

Joy blushed, but nodded. Hell yeah, she slept

with Scarlet. Although there really hadn't been much sleeping involved.

"This morning, too?"

More blushing.

"Then she asks to take you to her friend's wedding as her date, and you tell her you don't want to go with her? Did you just use her for sex?"

"No! It's not like that at all! I just… I'm not out to everyone else. I'm barely out to myself. Only you and Gran know."

"Not out to yourself? I hope you are; you ended our marriage because of it." Steve shook his head, sighing. "And anyway, I think you might be surprised."

"What does that mean?"

"It means you haven't had a partner for two years. It means that people don't really care who you're with, so long as you're happy. I've been asked about you before."

Joy stood there, her mouth hanging open. "Who's asked about me?" People already knew she was a lesbian? *This was news.*

Steve waved a hand, batting the question away. "That doesn't matter. What matters here is you. And the other day, you told me that Scarlet could be important. She could be the one. Am I right?"

Joy looked at the ground as she nodded this time.

"So why are you dragging your heels? I don't get it. You're the only one standing in the way of your happiness."

Steve shook his head. "You life coaches are all the same: you can give it out, but you don't like to listen."

A wry smile crossed Joy's face: this was an argument they'd had many times in their married life. "Am I being stubborn?"

"A little. Look at it from Scarlet's point of view. You slept together, everything's great, but then you rejected her. I can see how that would hurt, like you're embarrassed to be with her."

"I'm not embarrassed! God, the last thing I am is embarrassed. She's absolutely amazing, it's me I'm doubting." And it was true. She'd never been a proper lesbian before: not a full-time, in-a-proper-relationship lesbian. She'd only ever been a theoretical lesbian. What if she was no good at it? What then?

Steve smiled. "But that's not how it looks to her. To Scarlet, you slept together and then you pushed her away. You might have done it for your own reasons, but you still did it." Steve took a swig of his beer and Joy did the same.

"I fucked up, didn't I?" She wouldn't blame Scarlet if she hated her. This was a disaster.

He smiled. "Kinda." He took another swig of his beer. "What do you think about me and Sharon?"

Joy saw the worry painted on Steve's face. It wasn't the face of a man who was thrilled to be getting married. "Is it what you want?"

He paused. "I don't know."

"If you're not 100 per cent sure, then you can't go through with it. It's not fair to her."

Steve nodded. "I thought you might say that." He drained the rest of his beer in one. "And Scarlet?"

Joy frowned. "What about her?"

"Is she what you want?"

Joy nodded. "One thousand per cent." And there it was, just like that. She hadn't known it until she'd had time to process, had time to think. And then it just slipped out of her mouth, the glittering truth.

One thousand per cent. Joy was even breaking maths rules when it came to Scarlet.

"Then I think you know what you need to do, too."

Joy exhaled, smiling broadly at Steve. No matter what, he had her back, she was sure of that.

"And you're going to be okay, when I tell everyone? I know it's tough on you."

Steve shrugged. "Losing you was the tough part, not the reason — and I can take care of myself. Anybody badmouths you, they've got me to answer to."

Joy walked over to him and put her arms around his solid waist, placing her head against his chest. She'd always felt safe with Steve, always loved. That hadn't changed. Sure, they'd had their share of tears and heartache when she'd first told him, but now they were back to where they'd begun. Friends. Where they always should have stayed.

She looked up at him. "And are you going to be okay about Sharon?"

He nodded. "I think, deep down, I kinda knew Sharon and I weren't right. And when she proposed the other night, I didn't know what to say. It was scary. I'll remember that for next time, if I ever do it again. Sharon and I got together a little too soon. I might take some time on my own for a bit."

"That sounds like a good idea," Joy said, kissing Steve on the cheek and pulling away from him.

The sound of someone clearing their throat startled Joy, and when she looked over, Scarlet was standing in the doorway, a puzzled look on her face.

"Scarlet," Joy said, stepping back from Steve. Joy hadn't heard her key in the door, and her heart began to leap around in her chest once more. Scarlet walking into a room made life exciting. Unpredictable, nervy and exciting.

Steve looked from Scarlet, to Joy, then pulled himself upright. "Anyway, I should get going — thanks for the pep talk."

He walked out of the kitchen, giving Scarlet a sharp smile as he did. "See you round."

When the door slammed shut, Scarlet folded her arms across her chest.

"I didn't hear you come in," Joy said, fiddling with her hair. Scarlet was still angry with her, she could tell that. Joy tried to focus on the 1,000 per cent feeling she'd just been talking to Steve about, but it seemed to have faded into the distance.

She didn't want Scarlet angry with her. She wanted Scarlet to love her.

"Evidently."

Joy sighed. "Don't be pissed off with him, it's not his fault. He was actually just telling me I should go to the wedding with you. And I really want to, honestly I do. I just… it's hard, that's all."

Scarlet shook her head. "It's only hard if you make it hard. I'm just asking you to come as my date. There'll be plenty of other people there doing exactly the same thing. Laughing, dancing, drinking, smiling. That's all you have to do. It's no big deal."

Joy's breath caught in her throat. She knew Scarlet was right. She knew Steve was right. But her voice had dried up again. And the brief moment of positivity she'd embraced? It'd just scuttled out the door with Steve.

Joy wanted to tell Scarlet she'd come, that there was nothing she'd rather do tomorrow, that being her date to Eamonn and Steph's wedding was all she'd ever really wanted. To be happy, be in a relationship that felt *right*.

But when Joy opened her mouth, no sound came out. Nothing at all. And just like that, that moment ebbed away like a slow tide.

"But I can see you don't want to come with me, so I have to assume it's for some other reason. Perhaps it's Steve, perhaps it's me; I've no idea because you won't tell me." Scarlet studied her shoes, and when she looked back up, her eyes were glistening. "I can't believe this is happening tonight, not when this time last night was so very different."

Joy nodded, still silent.

Scarlet's face spelt disappointment. "Anyway, I'm going to bed, big day tomorrow."

And with that, she turned and left.

Joy watched her go. She wanted to run after her and tell her she'd come, but her legs wouldn't move.

Somehow, Joy was in a prison of her own making.

Chapter Eighteen

Scarlet hadn't slept well at all, not that she was surprised. She'd considered packing up and going to Eamonn's house, but the night before his wedding, it didn't seem to be the done thing. She'd considered calling Clark to come and get her — and while she had no doubt he would, she was a little old to be calling her brother to come and rescue her late at night.

So in the end, Scarlet had just got into bed, waited for the knock on her door from Joy that never came, and had eventually fallen into a fitful sleep, wondering where she was going to live once this weekend was over.

Because one thing was for sure, she couldn't possibly stay here. And that thought made her sadder than she ever thought it was possible to feel. This week had brought excitement and life back to her world, but she knew from experience they could be fleeting. They were slipping from her grasp already.

And because she hadn't slept well, she was up late, grateful that Joy was either still asleep or out: she didn't need histrionics today. Her plan was to get to Grasspoint to see what else Eamonn might need, then head over to the town hall. The timing might also mean she had to hang out at Grasspoint for a while, or maybe even head to the community hall for somewhere to be until it was time for the wedding. But she couldn't stay here too long, it was too risky.

Her home situation had become untenable.

Twice in just over a week: quite an achievement.

* * *

Grasspoint was a hive of activity when Scarlet arrived — and amazingly, the sun was shining.

When Eamonn saw her, he did a double-take, then wolf-whistled.

"Don't you scrub up well!" he said, giving her the once over, and Scarlet had to admit she did. She had on a gold dress and black jacket, teamed with low black heels. She'd added a gold necklace and earrings, and employed make-up techniques stolen straight from Steph. All of which meant Scarlet had grudgingly admitted she looked okay this morning, despite her mood.

"Thanks," she replied. "Anything I can do to help?"

Eamonn, still in jeans and a T-shirt, gave her a face. "In that outfit? I'd be scared to muck you up."

"I can do the non-dirty work."

He pointed a finger at her. "Flower-arranging? It's not really my forté."

Scarlet laughed. "And you think it's mine?"

"You've got heels, doesn't it come with the territory?"

She rolled her eyes. "I won't let Steph know you said that till *after* the ceremony."

"I think we can manage from here — it's all nearly done and my family are all in there helping. I need to get home and change soon, time's ticking on!"

"It is." Scarlet smiled at him. "See you at the town hall, then, Mr Nearly Married Man."

Eamonn stepped forward and gave her a brief hug. "See you there."

Eamonn turned to walk back into the function hall, and out of the corner of her eye, Scarlet saw Clementine waving from the lounge of the main building.

She waved back, then the old lady began to beckon her over.

Scarlet hesitated. She liked Clementine, but she didn't really want to talk about her and Joy. Not after last night when Joy had made it clear she didn't want to be with her. It was just about the last thing she wanted to talk about. But then again, she couldn't be rude. Plus, she liked Clementine, admired her spirit. It was just a shame her granddaughter didn't inherit it, too. A real, crying shame.

So despite her better judgment, Scarlet walked over and opened the door, stepping inside and giving Clementine a hug. She kept her eyes on the old lady, not wanting to have to work the room. A quick hello, then she'd be off.

"My, don't you look a picture," Clementine said, sweeping her eyes over Scarlet. "I hope my granddaughter knows what she's doing. You think she does?"

Scarlet smiled. That was the thing with old people: no messing around. They jumped straight to the point.

"I think she's doing what's right for her." Scarlet's shoulders sagged as she spoke. "But it's not right for me, and for what it's worth, it's not right for her either. She needs to stand up for herself, be who she really is, otherwise, she's not truly living. I'm sad she doesn't want to be the person she is, but what can I do?"

Clementine nodded. "I understand," she said. "And I told her that, too."

Scarlet's ears pricked up. "She's been here?" She was scouring the room, checking for signs of Joy, the scent of Joy. How she missed her already. She couldn't fathom not being with her, and they'd only lasted 24 hours. But what a 24 hours they'd been. They'd contained every emotion under the sun, packaged up and ready to go.

Clementine nodded again.

"And I do want to be the person I am."

Scarlet's eyes shot wide open and she whipped her shoulders back. That wasn't Clementine's voice. That was Joy's voice, coming from behind her gran.

Scarlet had been played, but she didn't mind one bit.

Within seconds Joy walked around to stand beside her grandmother, and two pairs of the same velvety blue eyes were staring back at Scarlet.

"I'm sorry," Joy said, biting her lip, barely able to look at Scarlet. "I know everything I said hurt you, but can we start again? I really want to. And if you'll still have me, I'd love to be your date to the wedding." Joy paused. "Be your girlfriend for the wedding." Joy's eyes searched Scarlet's face. "It's taken me so long to find you, and I don't want to lose you so early. So I hope you can find it in your heart to forgive me?"

Scarlet's stomach lurched and her vision went fuzzy. This was the last thing she'd expected to happen this morning. But it was happening, right before her eyes. She glanced at her watch, then at Joy and Clementine.

"You're sure?"

Joy smiled. "Never been surer of anything in my life, and you can thank Steve for that. Steve and this wise old bird." Joy placed a kiss on Clementine's cheek.

"Steve? I was thinking about slapping him when I saw you in his arms last night."

Clementine turned to Joy, alarmed.

Joy shook her head. "That was nothing — that was just two friends hugging. He's splitting up with Sharon because he's not sure about her. And he asked me if I was sure about you — and that's when I realised I've never been surer about anything in my life."

Scarlet glanced from a teary Joy to a beaming Clementine, then back to Joy.

Joy had changed her mind. Joy wanted to come to the wedding with her, as her girlfriend. Scarlet couldn't help the grin that broke out on her face. Then she glanced at her watch one more time.

"Well, if you've never been surer of anything in your

life, I can hardly say no, can I? Only, it's 12.15 and you're not even dressed yet, so we better get a move on if we're getting you home, changed, and then to the town hall in time for the wedding."

Joy stepped forward and took Scarlet's hand in hers, then planted a gentle kiss on her lips.

For Scarlet, it was a kiss of reconnection. A kiss with a promise of far more to come, coupled with a rush of relief. She hadn't wanted to face life without Joy, didn't even want to consider it — and now she didn't have to.

Now, Joy was back in her arms, where she belonged.

"Thank you for giving me another chance," Joy said, her eyes searching Scarlet's.

"How could I not?" Scarlet replied, her lips burning onto Joy's again.

"And you look absolutely ravishing," Joy whispered in her ear.

"Don't make me cry again," Scarlet replied, holding Joy as close as she possibly could.

Scarlet never wanted to let go, ever.

Chapter Nineteen

Scarlet would never put herself down as the romantic type, but after everything that had happened this week, her emotions were like a leaky tap, overtaking her at every turn. Seeing Steph walk in resplendent in her delicate white dress and Eamonn all dapper in his blue suit, she wasn't embarrassed to admit she'd shed a tear, and even glanced at Joy, wondering if she was also entertaining the idea this might be them one day.

Scarlet didn't want to ask — seeing as they'd only just reconciled, it seemed a little forward to be talking about marriage. But this wedding couldn't have been better timed for making her want to proclaim how she was feeling, too. Because since Thursday, and despite all the obstacles, Scarlet was as sure as she could be: she was falling for Joy, hook, line, and sinker. Which made it all the more glorious that Joy had decided to come back to her.

And now they were back at Grasspoint, saying hi to Joy's gran before heading into the reception. Clementine was chatting with her friend Carol when they approached, and when she saw them, her eyes lit up.

"How are you two doing?"

Scarlet grinned shyly at Joy. "So far, so good," she replied.

"My favourite granddaughter and Scarlet, the town hero — you make a lovely couple." Clementine gave them both a hug. When she let Scarlet go, Clementine held her at arm's length. "You were splendid on the news, you know — I forgot to say earlier. You brought a tear to my eye." She turned to Joy. "And you," she said. "I love you in a dress, even though they're not your favourite things."

"I said the same," Scarlet told Clementine, smiling at Joy. "She looks gorgeous, doesn't she?" Joy's dress was a flowery number and she'd paired it with some tan shoes, with matching handbag and jacket.

Clementine eyed Scarlet, smiling. "She does indeed, as do you." She paused. "And how was the ceremony?"

"It went really well, Steph looked radiant," Joy said. "You're coming later, aren't you?"

Eamonn and Steph had invited a fair smattering of the home's guests to the evening as a thank you.

"Just try and stop us — we've been planning our outfits all week, haven't we?"

Carol nodded. "I don't get to dress up in my finery that often anymore, and it's not far to walk to get home either, is it?"

Scarlet laughed. "Sounds perfect," she said, taking Joy's hand. But once she did, she froze: Joy had said she was fine with everything, but was she really? Scarlet had no idea and it was still such early days.

However, as if reading her mind, Joy brought Scarlet's hand up to her mouth and kissed it.

Scarlet was so touched, she had to hold in a gasp. If she'd been in any doubt, she wasn't now: Joy had meant it fully, just like she said.

"So we'll see you later — just thought we'd pop in to say hi before the meal," Joy said.

"See you at seven," Clementine replied, taking Joy's hand. "Have a love-filled afternoon," she added, looking from Joy to Scarlet.

They gave Clementine a hug goodbye, then hurried nextdoor, stopping en route for a brief kiss in the empty corridor that linked the venues. The weight of Joy in Scarlet's arms was divine.

"Was that okay, holding your hand?" Scarlet asked. She didn't want to push Joy harder than she was ready for, despite what Joy had said.

But Joy just nodded her head. "You can hold my hand all night if you like." She paused. "Although that might be a little overkill."

Scarlet smiled, giving Joy a kiss. "I totally can if you want me to."

"You know, I never used to hold Steve's hand much, if that makes any difference. I'm just not a hand-holder." She paused, pulling back slightly. "Or perhaps it's more, *in the past, I wasn't a hand-holder*. But then again, I wasn't much of a corridor-kisser, either, and look at me now, so who knows?" Joy kissed her again. "The fact that every time you hold my hand, I go weak at the knees makes the deal sweeter."

"I make you weak at the knees?" A 100-watt grin split Scarlet's face. Knee-weakening at such an early stage of a relationship was a good sign. *A very good sign.*

"Apparently, you do."

"Glad to hear it," Scarlet said, easing Joy backwards. "And I know we talked a little back at the house, but are we okay? You sure this is all good with you?"

Joy took a deep breath and nodded firmly. "You know what, we're better than okay: we're amazing. Nothing felt right yesterday with you gone, nothing's felt right at any moment when I haven't been with you. This past week has been a blur, but it's righted my life. *You* right my life, *you* make it make sense." Joy exhaled. "I'm just so glad you wanted me back after me being so stupid."

Scarlet shook her head. "I didn't have a choice in the matter. My heart had already chosen you." Scarlet was shocked those words had tripped out of her mouth, but she wasn't scared by them, and the way Joy's face softened, it looked like she wasn't either. Scarlet was done pussy-footing around and she didn't want any more misunderstandings when it came to her and Joy: she wanted to be clear, concise, and understood.

"Is it too soon to be saying stuff like that?" Scarlet asked. She really hoped it wasn't.

Joy shook her head. "Nothing about us is too soon. We can't come soon enough for me."

"I'll hold you to that later," Scarlet replied with a wink. "But no more soppy talk in this corridor because I don't have waterproof mascara on. I think we should make an appearance at the wedding, seeing as that's what we're here for. Ready to drink free bubbles and eat substandard, mass-catered food?"

Joy laughed. "When you put it like that..."

* * *

The reception went off without a hitch, which was all anyone could ask for after the week the town had endured. The sun shone so the happy couple could have some photos taken in the grounds outside, and the dessert was the highlight of the meal: Joy never could resist the lure of profiteroles.

Both Eamonn and Steph gave speeches, thanking everyone for rallying round to save their day, including Celia for providing the hall for free, and Maureen Armitage for stepping in at the last minute to make the delicious Victoria Sponge wedding cake.

And now the tables had been pushed back to turn the hall into a dancefloor, a local band were playing classic covers, and the home's residents were pouring in, congratulating the couple of the moment.

Scarlet and Joy were standing by the bar, chatting to Scarlet's other football buddy Matt and his wife Viv.

And after all her hesitation, Joy was going with her heart: she and Scarlet were now officially out, standing hand in hand.

"So is this new, or have you been holding out on us at the football?" Matt asked, pointing to their clasped hands.

Heat crept onto Joy's cheeks: yes, they were out, but it was still going to take some getting used to. However, far from feeling nervous, every sinew of Joy's being finally relaxed: and after 38 years of clenching, that was both freeing and exhilarating. Despite what she'd thought, the world hadn't stopped turning as people found out, and Joy wasn't as fazed as she thought she might be. Rather, she was proud of being with Scarlet. Who wouldn't be? She was drop-dead gorgeous.

Scarlet nodded. "It's new — it's our debut as a couple today."

"Congratulations," Matt said, holding up his glass. "It's been quite a week. First, you get flooded, then you become the poster girl for flood optimism, and now you've bagged yourself the mayor as your girlfriend."

Scarlet laughed. "When you put it like that, I guess it has been a pretty good week." She clinked her glass to Matt's. "But the poster girl for flood optimism? I'm not sure I'm happy about that."

"Believe it, that's exactly what you are. From hard-boiled pessimist to flood superstar, all in the blink of an eye. You might have to stop swearing so much at football now, seeing as you are a public figure and shagging the mayor."

Scarlet roared with laughter at that. "Shagging the mayor? I'm sure we can come up with a more elegant way of saying it, can't we?"

"It is what it is," Joy replied, with a smile that butter couldn't melt.

Matt grinned. "Eamonn's married, you're loved up — now we just need Dulshaw to win the league and it'll be the best year ever."

"They have to get somewhere to play first that isn't waterlogged."

"Minor detail," Matt replied.

Their conversation was interrupted by Clementine and Robert walking up to them, Clementine eyeing Joy and Scarlet, a wide smile on her face.

"Hello, lovely ladies," she said, giving them both a kiss once more, beaming.

"Hello, you," Joy said, returning the greeting and also hugging Robert.

"Have you had a good afternoon?" Clementine asked.

"It was fabulous, wasn't it?" Joy said, giving Scarlet a heated glance. And it had been. Just having Scarlet by her side and being *with* Scarlet had been the best reward of all.

"Today's been a day where love wins," Matt added.

"Love should always win," Clementine replied with a shrug. "I've been on this earth long enough to know that it really is all you need." She paused. "Well, that and money," she added with a grin.

"Love failed to win earlier when that wedding singer

was belting out *Up Where We Belong*," Scarlet said. "I almost died laughing she was so out of tune."

"Me, too," Matt said, laughing all over again. "But you couldn't say anything seeing as the singer was Eamonn's aunt. So if anyone asks, it was grand. I just hope they didn't catch me laughing on video."

Matt and Viv saw someone they knew, so excused themselves, which left Scarlet and Joy, Clementine and Robert.

"Talking of love winning the day — I've also got news." Clementine took Robert's hand in hers and all of a sudden looked bashful. "Seeing as you're announcing your relationship today, we're going to announce ours. Robert and I are officially together."

Robert buffed up his chest and stroked his shiny head. "And I'm thrilled to have her," he said.

"You're a sly fox," Joy said, hugging Clementine. "And you're a brave man," she told Robert.

"Oh, I know," he replied. "But also a lucky one."

"And how do you think Michael will take all of this?" Clementine asked Joy. "Or Christopher, come to that?"

Joy rolled her eyes when she thought about her brother and her dad. "I'm sure Michael will have loads to say, possibly along the lines of 'Robert's after your money', and 'have you really thought through this idea of being a lesbian, Joy'? But he can lump it — it's our lives after all, isn't it? As for dad, he won't care, so long as it doesn't interfere with his sun-splashed lifestyle."

"True enough. Anyway, I say *carpe diem*. Isn't that right?" Clementine said to Robert.

He gave her a nod. "Every day, Clem. Every day."

Clementine looked over at the band, a smile on her lips. "So lovely to have live music, too. I used to love going dancing and seeing bands when I was younger, and it's something I really miss. You forget what you like to do after a while, once you get out of the habit."

Joy could definitely relate to that. She'd forgotten she liked to be wooed, be kissed, be loved liked she'd never been loved before. And she'd also forgotten the luxury and comfort of companionship — especially with the right person.

"You're so right," Joy said. "Scarlet's a terrific guitar player, she's been giving me special concerts for one at home."

Clementine's face perked up. "We used to have someone come over and play piano for us, but she had to stop. It was a real shame." She paused. "Would you consider coming over and playing for us sometime, dear? I know the residents would love it. And you wouldn't have to just play old songs — we like modern music, too."

Surprise crossed Scarlet's face, but within seconds, she was nodding. "If you'd have asked me last week, I might have said no. But this week, having lost everything, I'm beginning to agree with your *carpe diem* statement. So, why not? I need to play more and you need entertaining. I'm sure we could marry the two needs up."

"Splendid!" Clementine said, squeezing Scarlet's arm. "I'm liking you more and more every time I see you."

"The feeling's mutual," Scarlet replied.

The band began to play a version of Andy Williams' *Can't Take My Eyes Off Of You*, and Clementine spun round to Robert, holding out a hand. "Now this is one of my favourites," she said. "Shall we?"

"We shall," Robert said, leading her slowly onto the dancefloor.

"And I'm expecting you two up here in a minute," Clementine shouted over her shoulder.

Joy laughed, before turning to Scarlet, rolling her eyes. "Sorry," she said. "She can be a bit bossy when she wants to be."

Scarlet shook her head. "She's great, I like her. I hope I can be just like her when I'm her age."

"I don't know about the 'just like her' bit," Joy said. "We can't have both of us being quite that feisty, can we?"

Joy followed up her comment with a laugh, but it stuck in her throat when she realised she'd just committed to her and Scarlet being together for the next 40 years. Were they even a couple yet? Joy had no idea; she hadn't dated anyone in 15 years.

She risked a glance at Scarlet, wondering what she was going to find. But all that was there was Scarlet smirking at Joy, a shocking grin on her face.

"So you're expecting us to be in this home together, or

were you picturing us elsewhere?" Scarlet asked, putting a hand on Joy's back.

Want rippled through Joy's body at her touch.

"I don't know. I wasn't really looking that far ahead. It was just a figure of speech." Joy doubted the make-up she'd applied so carefully was doing much to protect her flushed cheeks.

Scarlet leaned in and kissed Joy lightly on the lips. "I don't mind. It's kind of cute picturing us your gran's age, still together. Makes me feel all warm inside. So long as we're still having sex as hot as we did the other night."

Joy let out a bark of laughter. "Of course we will be, goes without saying." Her gaze drifted onto the dancefloor. "But if you make one mention of *my grandma* having sex, I'll slap you."

Scarlet laughed. "I promise I won't say a word." She held out her hand. "Now, may I have this dance?"

Joy hesitated for a moment, but it was a brief one. This morning, she hadn't been sure how it'd feel being out with Scarlet, being a couple for the whole world to see — but now she had her answer.

It felt natural. It felt exactly right. It felt like all the moments leading up to this one had been slightly skewed, off-centre. But walking onto the dancefloor with Scarlet, and allowing herself to be held in her arms — Joy simply didn't care what anyone thought.

Joy was finally comfortable in her own skin; it was like

she'd stopped running. Scarlet was her chequered flag, her gold medal. Dancing with Steve had never felt like this: he'd always trodden on her toes and made jokes in her ear. Kissing Steve had never felt like kissing Scarlet. And making love with Steve: well, there was no comparison.

Standing in Scarlet's arms, breathing in her scent, touching her soft shoulders, Joy was 100 per cent Joy, something she'd never been with a partner before.

"Okay?" Scarlet asked, understandable concern lingering on her face.

Joy nodded her head. "More than okay." And she finally was: Joy saw it now more clearly than she ever had in her whole life. This is where she always should have been, and it'd taken Scarlet to show her. After the flood, Joy thought she'd rescued Scarlet by giving her somewhere to stay, but it was actually Scarlet who'd rescued her from a life stuck in a rut. A life unlived. In Scarlet's arms, Joy was finally who she was meant to be.

When Scarlet gazed into Joy's eyes, before pressing her lips to hers, Joy worried the floor around her was shaking, such was the magnitude. The band faded out, the room went blurry, and Joy responded with gusto, clinging to Scarlet, kissing her as if she'd just been told she had moments left to live. If Scarlet was surprised, she didn't show it. If anybody else was surprised, they said nothing.

In that moment, it was just Joy and Scarlet, on the dancefloor, lost in the glory of their burning kiss.

Chapter Twenty

They didn't make it home till after 1am from the wedding, and then Scarlet and Joy were up even later, making good on the promise of that dancefloor kiss. So Sunday morning wasn't a hurried affair. In fact, it was a downright sleepy affair, right up until someone started banging on Joy's front door.

Joy opened her eyes, whereas Scarlet sat up straight in bed, a worried look on her face.

Joy reached out a hand and stroked her back.

"Someone's at the door," Scarlet said, shaking her head. "The last time someone woke me up from my sleep banging on the door, I lost everything." She paused, turning to Joy. "You don't think we're being flooded again, do you?"

Joy yawned, sitting up and kissing Scarlet's flushed cheek. "I don't. This house won't be flooded, take my word for it." She looked at her clock. "Plus, it's Sunday morning, so I have an idea of who it might be."

Joy jumped up from her bed, grabbed her dressing gown and left the room.

Scarlet flopped back down, her pulse racing. She concentrated on breathing in through her nose, out through her mouth, and crossed her fingers everything was okay. Whatever it was, it couldn't be for her: the worst had already happened. But then she jumped out of bed: what if it was bad news for Joy?

Scarlet got up, gathering up her wedding attire which had been thrown on the floor in the throes of passion last night. She grinned as she recalled — she wasn't going to look at Joy in quite the same light ever again. Joy was capable of things Scarlet hadn't even imagined, especially considering this was a woman who didn't like to swear — but Scarlet wasn't complaining. Far from it. She walked through to Joy's spare room where her case still was, grabbing some jeans and a T-shirt, before taking the stairs two at a time.

When she got to the kitchen, she almost laughed out loud. She needn't have worried.

It was Steve. *Of course it was Steve.*

Scarlet had only lived at the house for nine days, but she already knew Steve's routine, and this was his Sunday morning call, regular as clockwork. They might have to have words with him to alter that now Scarlet was on the scene. Still, Steve wasn't going anywhere and Scarlet imagined he was always going to be in Joy's life, so she'd better make an effort with him.

When Scarlet walked in, Steve looked up, smiling.

"Hi," he said, as Joy turned around.

Scarlet saw panic in her face, followed by something else she couldn't quite place. She held back on her natural instinct, which was to kiss Joy before sitting down. Joy had to take control of this one, she couldn't do anything to help her. The ball was in her court.

"Hi," Scarlet told Steve, who was sitting on her breakfast bar stool. She let it slide: this morning was about bigger things than that. This morning was about righting their life just that little bit further.

"Not running this morning?"

Steve looked down at his jeans and shirt. "Not today," he said. "But I was in the neighbourhood, so I thought I'd call in. How's your flat? I saw you on the news — you're quite the hero."

Scarlet shrugged, blushing. She'd heard that a few times over the past few days, but she still wasn't buying it. She'd just said what was in her heart, the truth. "It's still buggered, but I've had so many offers of furniture, I could probably make a fortune on eBay." She smiled. "We're going over there in a bit — never in my life did I think I'd get through so much bleach in one go."

"You and half the town," Steve replied.

Joy had been watching this exchange with interest, Scarlet noted. She still wasn't committing to where she was sitting or what she was doing next. It was as if the situation was too surreal: her ex and her lover perched in her kitchen in a tableau of Sunday domesticity.

"So, Steve," Joy said, eventually.

Steve turned his head to her.

"I know we talked the other night, but I just wanted you to know that Scarlet and I have worked things out and we're together." Joy flicked her gaze from her ex, to Scarlet, looking for reassurance.

Seeing as they hadn't really had a chance to discuss anything yet, Scarlet nodded her support.

"We're out in the open, just so you know." Joy exhaled, as if that little speech had taken it out of her. She fiddled with the tea towel in her hand, then turned back to the sink.

Seeing as Joy had run off mentally at this juncture, Steve gave Scarlet a smile in response. "That's great news," he said. "Congratulations."

"We're not getting married," Scarlet replied, smiling uncertainly.

"I know," Steve said with a shrug. "It just feels like the right thing to say."

If Steve held any resentment, Scarlet couldn't detect it. In fact, he looked like he wanted to reach over and shake Scarlet's hand, as if conceding defeat. Scarlet was glad he didn't.

Joy turned back to them, a brittle smile on her face.

Steve shifted on his stool. "I mean it though, for both of you." He paused, glancing from one to the other. "Whatever happens, I want you to be happy, Joy. And you look happy, you really do." He sighed. "So I'm pleased for you — and I hope we can still be friends."

"Of course we can," Joy said. "In fact, when we get a bit more settled and everything has calmed down a bit, you should come over for dinner, then Scarlet can get to know you better, too."

Scarlet coughed. Nope, they hadn't discussed this one at all.

Joy looked up. "Right?"

Scarlet nodded. "Absolutely — and then I can tick off the box in my head that says, 'have dinner with my girlfriend's ex-husband'. It's been one I've been meaning to tick for years."

Steve narrowed his eyes. "You're kidding, right?"

Scarlet laughed. "I am. But not the part about you coming for dinner."

Steve smiled. "Good."

"So now that's out of the way and the awkward tension has dissipated somewhat — cup of coffee?" Joy asked, pouring out the hot, black liquid from her cafetière.

"Wouldn't say no to some breakfast either, if you're doing some," Steve replied.

Yep, Scarlet could tell he was feeling more relaxed by the minute.

"I'm sure I can rustle something up," Joy said, bringing their drinks over, and placing a brief kiss on Scarlet's lips.

That gesture wasn't lost on Scarlet, who rested a hand on Joy's waist, pulling her close. It was a natural action, but Scarlet was also doing it to mark out her territory. She couldn't help it.

Steve clocked it, but said nothing.

"Bacon sandwiches okay?" Joy asked, kissing the top of Scarlet's head before heading for the fridge.

"Perfect," Steve and Scarlet replied in unison.

Then they both raised an eyebrow at each other, before bursting out laughing.

* * *

After Steve left, Scarlet and Joy had a full day planned. First up, they were headed to Scarlet's flat to do another bleach clean, then take delivery of some dehumidifiers that were being bulk supplied by the insurance company. Then this evening, they were headed to Scarlet's brother's house for dinner.

This was the second full bleach clean they'd done this week after clearing the flat of debris with the help of Clark, Eammon, and Steph. It hadn't been fun or pretty, but Scarlet had been amazed at the speed of the operation. It was true what they said: many hands really did make light work.

And now, when Scarlet turned into her street, it looked like it always had: like nothing had ever happened. The last bits of rubbish had been cleaned up by the council and the fire service, and all the flats had been pumped of water. Now, it was just a case of staying on top of the cleaning and waiting for her flat to dry out.

Walking into it again, Scarlet was struck by the cold and the damp, which wormed its way under your skin within minutes. She couldn't imagine a time when it wouldn't, when her flat would be dry and habitable again.

"It really is going to take months, isn't it?" Scarlet said.

Joy rubbed her back. "It is, I'm afraid. But you can stay at mine. Even if your flat was ready to move back into, I'd still want you to stay at mine."

"I know," Scarlet said. "I just wish you could have seen it before. Before it was so bleak and dead. That's what it feels like, doesn't it? It feels like the building has died."

Joy shook her head. "It's been knocked out. Concussed. But the spirit is still there, and you can coax it back to life, given time. Just not right now." Joy gave Scarlet a smile. "But you'll get there. *We'll* get there."

Scarlet offered a weak smile. She appreciated Joy's optimism: it balanced her out when hers was drained.

"I hope so. But what if it happens again? Will I even be able to get insurance after all of this?" Scarlet's shoulders slumped as she gazed around at the empty shell of a flat, with its bare brick walls and stone cold floors. "Even though I know it's my flat, it doesn't *feel* like my home anymore. It's just a load of bricks and I'm scared to put my hopes into it again."

Joy walked over and pulled Scarlet into her arms.

Scarlet let her: it was always good to be held by Joy, it took away her fears for the moment. It was good to know that whatever else, she always had that to return to.

"You know, that's the same argument you could have used for your entire life, and I seem to remember you did, for quite some time. Have you forgotten you're meant to be this newly reformed optimist?" Joy said, easing herself away from Scarlet.

Scarlet laughed. "Sometimes, I slip back into my old ways." And given everything that had happened, she reckoned she was allowed.

"Putting all your hopes and dreams into something is scary, but we do it every day, because what other choice is there? And yes, things go wrong, but you have to keep trying, otherwise you really would give up." Joy paused. "I've put all my hopes into you, for instance," she added, taking Scarlet's hand. "Well, you and the lottery."

Scarlet chuckled. "You've got to be in it to win it."

"Still waiting on the lottery. Have I won you?" Joy asked, one eyebrow raised.

"You've made a very good start."

"Pleased to hear it." Joy pressed her lips onto Scarlet's before continuing. "And same rules apply to this, too. Yes, the river might flood again, there's *always* that possibility. But they're fixing the flood barrier, so the likelihood is that it won't. And if it does? Then you just clean up, dry it out, and start all over again. It'd be better if that didn't happen, of course, but it's not going to be the end of you, is it?"

Scarlet shook her head. Joy was right, as usual. She had a very annoying habit of being right.

"I guess not."

Joy smiled. "Good. Now, let's get going: the sooner we get this done and get the dehumidifiers on, the quicker we can drive over to your brother's for dinner. What time is he expecting us?"

"Any time after six."

"Let's get a move on, then."

Chapter Twenty-One

The following Saturday, Scarlet accompanied Joy to see Clementine at Grasspoint, carrying her guitar case on her back.

"Ready to face the music?" Joy asked as they climbed the stairs to the home.

"I'm not facing the music, I'm *embracing* the music," Scarlet replied.

Joy chuckled. "Whatever you say."

Scarlet had been practising her guitar all week, even learning some old classics with Joy's guidance as to what her grandma might like, as well as polishing up some older favourites of her own. Joy wasn't sure if the Indigo Girls or Bruce Springsteen were going to be Grasspoint favourites, but you never knew until you tried.

Clementine was sitting with Carol and Robert when they walked in, and she got up to greet them, beaming broadly when Scarlet put the guitar case down.

"Let me round up the troops, I've been telling everyone you're coming!" she said to Scarlet.

"Maybe let her have a cup of tea first," Joy replied, as Scarlet got the guitar out of its case.

"Of course, of course," Clementine said. "I'm just excited, you'll have to forgive an old lady. We don't have much to get excited about round here, do we?"

Scarlet flashed Clementine a smile. "I don't mind. Tell you the truth, I'm excited, too."

"See?" Clementine told Joy.

Joy threw up her arms and went in search of Celia. What did she know?

When she returned ten minutes later, Scarlet was sat on a chair with a gaggle of around 30 pensioners around her, strumming her guitar and singing Tracey Chapman's *Fast Car*. Honest-to-goodness singing, out loud, eyes closed, in touch with the song. And she sounded heart-breakingly beautiful.

Joy wasn't surprised: she'd heard it at home all week, and Scarlet had even serenaded her in bed. But her heart filled with pride watching Scarlet playing with such genuine feeling — it just went to prove how much had changed in the few weeks since the flood. She doubted Scarlet would have entertained the idea of playing and singing a month ago, yet look at her now.

Things had changed for Joy, too. In the space of a month, she'd met a woman who met all her criteria: criteria Joy wasn't even aware she had until Scarlet showed up. All along, it turned out she'd longed to meet a woman who was brave, strong, and knew with certainty exactly who she was. And in turn, who allowed Joy to be exactly who she was. And Joy was finding out new things about who she actually was every single day, most of them good.

A round of applause broke Joy's train of thought, and she joined in, giving Scarlet a thumbs-up from across the room.

In response, Scarlet beamed at her. "Thanks very much, you're all very kind." She paused, glancing up at Joy. "I'd like to dedicate this next song to a someone who's come into my life recently and made a world of difference, made me see the sunshine. Joy, this is for you."

Scarlet began strumming her guitar strings, her fingers beautiful, and Joy grinned: she couldn't help it. She was used to Scarlet singing songs for her at home, but out in public? This really was something else. And then Joy recognised the song: *Kiss Me*, by Sixpence None The Richer. And then she blushed beetroot red.

Scarlet was singing a song about kissing her in front of her *grandma*.

Joy was going to kill Scarlet later.

Right after she got over the fact she'd just had a song dedicated to her in front of an audience for the first time in her life. The way it made Joy swell up inside, Scarlet might as well have been playing Wembley stadium to an audience of 60,000, rather than an old people's home lounge to an audience of 30.

When she'd finished, Scarlet got a round of applause, and promised to be back in ten minutes. She walked over to Joy with a massive grin on her face.

"So, do I get a kiss after that?" Scarlet asked, coming to a standstill in front of Joy and putting her arms around her waist as Joy stood up.

"Do you deserve one after embarrassing me in front of my gran?"

"You loved it," Scarlet replied, kissing Joy anyway.

Joy gave her a mock scowl, but still kissed her back. "Maybe I liked it a little," she said with a knowing smile. "Are you enjoying it? You look like you are."

Scarlet nodded. "I'm loving it. I feel like a rock star, I can't imagine what it must feel like playing an *actual* gig," she said. "But this will do me. I've got some requests, so I thought I'd take a break and look them up on my phone while they have a cup of tea."

"Good plan," Joy replied.

Scarlet sat down on a chair nearby and got out her phone, just as Clementine walked over to them.

"You were wonderful," Clementine told Scarlet. "And you told me you weren't any good. From where I'm sitting, you're not too bad at all." She flicked her gaze over to Joy. "She's a keeper, this one, you know."

Joy smiled at her gran. "I know."

"Not only for her guitar-playing, but also for putting a smile back on my granddaughter's face. It's been missing a while, but now it's back with bells on." Clementine reached down and cupped Joy's cheek. "It's beautiful to see, my darling."

* * *

Back at home later that day, Joy was sat on her couch with her iPad on her lap when Scarlet walked in, carrying a present wrapped in red tissue paper and tied with white string. She walked over and put it on the sofa next to Joy, then sat down opposite her.

Joy glanced down at it, then back over to Scarlet.

"What's this?"

"Open it and find out."

"But it's not my birthday."

"No shit," Scarlet said. "I bought you a present, just because."

"Because what?"

"Open it and find out. Are you this difficult with all your presents?"

Joy grinned, swung her legs onto the floor and ripped open the present. And then she started laughing. "How did you know?"

Scarlet grinned. "Just a wildly random guess. That, and the fact that every time we have a drink in here, you nearly smash the coffee table. So I decided to take charge. Do you like them?"

Joy got the coasters out of their box and stood up, putting them on the table. "I love them: coasters with images of Wonder Woman and Catwoman on them. What's not to like?" She walked over and sat next to Scarlet, before pressing her lips to hers. "You are the absolute best girlfriend," she said, as she pulled back. "We're calling each other girlfriend now, right?"

"Girlfriend, live-in lover, sex slave, whatever you like."

Joy laughed. "I'll introduce you as my sex slave at Grasspoint next time someone asks."

"They'd probably love it," Scarlet replied. "They don't hold back up there, do they? Audrey asked if I'd ever had sex with a man and when did I know I was a lesbian for sure. I think Audrey might be having some issues of her own."

"And I thought I was a late bloomer," Joy spluttered. "When did she ask this?"

"Just after I finished — she'd clearly been stewing on it while I was playing."

"Serves you right for dedicating a song about kissing to me. Stands to reason they're going to start thinking about us kissing, or worse."

Scarlet recoiled. "But not all of them wanted to know about our sex lives. Robert was asking me about my flat, and when I was likely to get back in. I told him it was looking more like months, than weeks."

Joy rubbed Scarlet's back. "Have you heard anything from the insurance people yet?"

"This week they reckoned."

"Good job you're not in a hurry then, isn't it?"

Scarlet smiled. "Good job." She paused. "And I really am grateful you letting me stay here. I will be giving you some money towards the bills and mortgage, so don't try to fight it."

"You know I will."

Scarlet wrestled Joy onto her back on the sofa. "Stop trying," she said, tickling her. "You're only going to lose."

Then she went for the jugular: Joy's sides, tickling her until she shrieked in submission. Then Scarlet was lying on top of Joy, her weight on her elbows, and she leaned down to kiss her. Doing so still made Scarlet tingle all over, every single time.

"You're amazing, you know that?"

Joy looked bashful. "So says you."

"So says everyone. You do so much for this town, and you've done so much for me. Am I your favourite subject, Mrs Mayor?"

Joy reached a hand around and squeezed Scarlet's butt cheek. "You definitely qualify as having my favourite bum in the town, if that helps?"

Scarlet chuckled at that. "It'll have to do, I guess." She paused, wrinkling her forehead. There was so much she wanted to say to Joy, but the old Scarlet was still lingering, and she was still a little tongue-tied when it came to emotions. "I don't know what I'd do without you."

Joy kissed her lips. "You don't have to worry about that — we're stuck together, like it or not."

"I like it."

"Good," Joy replied. "I kinda like it, too."

"And you're really okay with me staying here?"

Joy rolled her eyes. "How many times do I have to say? You are welcome to stay as long as you like. I *want* you here, Scarlet. I hope you know that."

Scarlet nodded.

"I don't want to freak you out, but you've made the difference. I've lived here two years, but it's only since you've moved in that it's felt like a home. It's taken you to make me start living again, and turn this house into a home. So you've got no choice, you have to stay."

"Well, when you put it like that," Scarlet replied.

"In fact, I'm kinda dreading you moving out when your flat's ready." Joy's face fell at the thought.

Scarlet kissed her lips again. She'd been putting off thinking about that at all, as it seemed such an abstract notion when her flat was still the shell it once was. Besides, this felt like home now, not there. But that conversation was for another day. "That's a few months off yet, so you're stuck with me for now."

"Good," Joy replied. "And I've been thinking — we should go on a date. A proper date, with cutlery, drinks in sparkly glasses, the works. And I'd like to go on a gay date, too."

Scarlet grinned. "A gay date? Do we have to wear feather boas and sing Kylie?"

Joy rolled her eyes. "That's a gay man date. I mean a lesbian date, where we shave our heads and get tattoos." She let out a laugh. "Seriously, I mean go to a gay bar, then for dinner. I've never been out on the scene with a girlfriend before, so it'll be fun."

Scarlet smiled. "We can do that," she said. "I'd be honoured to be your first official gay date. We can snog in a corner of the bar if you like, too."

"I would love that," Joy replied.

"Me, too."

Chapter Twenty-Two

Two weeks later, and the town was almost back to working order, even if it was going to take many months for some businesses and homes to recover. The school was running out of the village nextdoor and Dulshaw FC were set to play the next few home games at their local rivals until the stands could be fixed.

Bucking the trend, the local cinema had just reopened its doors thanks to the hard work of the staff and volunteers, and many residents were installed back in their homes, the scent of bleach fading. However, for some properties, including Scarlet's, the road to dryness and total rebuilding was still some way off.

But tonight, that wasn't at the forefront of Joy's mind, as today was date night in Manchester, and Joy was tingling with excitement. She'd never been out on the gay scene in Manchester, but she'd seen it on TV. Now, finally at the age of 38, she was getting to explore it.

A train and a cab took them to the gay village, and then Scarlet was guiding her down some steps and into a bar with low lighting, a long, chrome bar, and bartenders wearing black shirts and slick hair.

"It looks like a bar," Joy said, sitting down on a black leather couch by the far wall with her rum and coke. She'd stopped trying to keep up with Scarlet's pints now they knew each other a little better.

Scarlet gave her a look. "What were you expecting?"

Joy shrugged. "I don't know. I just expected it to be more *gay*, I suppose."

"We're starting off easy — this is more of a cocktail bar. It used to be different, but times have changed. You wouldn't have wanted to come in here a decade ago."

"It might have been better than what I was actually doing. You know, being married to a man."

Scarlet laughed. "Don't be so sure. You could have been gay and miserable, too."

"Not if I was having sex with you," Joy said, before kissing Scarlet.

Joy glanced around, taking in groups of friends and couples, both gay and straight, enjoying the evening. Then she sucked on the inside of her cheek.

Scarlet narrowed her eyes. "What is it?"

"Nothing."

"Don't 'nothing' me," Scarlet said. "We may be new, but I know stuff about you already. And that face says you're thinking something but you're not quite sure if it's okay to say it out loud or not."

Joy opened her mouth to speak, then shut it. How did

Scarlet know that? It wasn't the first time in their brief time together Scarlet had read her thoughts, and honestly, it was a little off-putting. "I was just thinking, do I fit in here? I mean, am I a lesbian? What does it take to qualify as a lesbian? I've only ever slept with three women. I've slept with more men than I have women, so does that make me still straight? Bisexual? It's a bit confusing."

Scarlet smiled at her. "Are you happy?"

Joy smiled. "More than I've ever been in my life." She'd never uttered a truer sentence.

"Then don't worry about it. It doesn't matter what you are. I'm happy with you, you're happy with me. That's all that matters, isn't it?" Scarlet's gaze was loving, warm.

Joy took it all in, before nodding. "I suppose so. It doesn't matter if I'm a lesbian, as long as I'm a Scarlet-lover?"

Scarlet nodded. "Works for me," she said. "But just as a test: who's the best looking person in here?" She paused. "Apart from me, of course."

Joy swept her gaze around the bar, before settling it back on Scarlet. "You win by a country mile," she told her. "But if pushed, either the redhead woman in the corner, or the blonde at the bar."

Scarlet grinned at her. "If you're worried about whether or not you qualify as being a lesbian, I don't think you need to be."

Joy grinned widely. "I suppose not."

Scarlet gave her a kiss before continuing. "Anyway, lesbian, I have some news."

Joy sat up. "Me, too. You want to go first?"

"Sure," Scarlet replied, putting her martini down on the table. "Mine is *unbelievable:* I got the money from Dan — the guy with terminal cancer? It actually hit my bank account this morning. Ten thousand pounds to help with my flat. Can you believe it?"

Joy whistled, shaking her head. "I honestly can't. That's *so* generous."

"It really is. And Eamonn texted me earlier to say they got their money, too. Dan is paying for them to go on honeymoon, so they can start looking to book now." Scarlet shook her head. "Plus, he's giving the flood fund 50 grand and helping the bookshop get back on its feet as well. There was me thinking everyone was out for themselves, but it turns out, I was wrong. Human nature can be very kind, too."

Joy nodded. "It can." She put a hand on Scarlet's knee. "And I'm thrilled for you. If anyone deserves it, you do. And if you don't think that yet, we might have to book you a couple of hours on my life coach couch till you do."

"Anything that involves lying down with you, I'm up for."

Joy smiled. "Wanna hear my news?"

"So long as it's good — I don't want any bad news blighting our day."

"It's more than good. In fact, you're going to be thrilled."

Scarlet leaned back on the couch, never taking her gaze from Joy. "Go on, then."

"The developers have pulled out of the stadium deal: they decided they can't take the risk of developing on grounds that are so susceptible to floods. So it looks like Dulshaw FC live to fight another day."

Scarlet's face lit up, then she gathered Joy in her arms. "That is incredible!" she said. "When did you hear?"

"There was some talk about it last week in the council, and I got wind of it. But I didn't want to tell you till it was all confirmed and rubberstamped." She paused. "That's not all, though — the council have decided to put a stop on anybody building there for now, so you're saved for the foreseeable future. So once the stands are back in order, the club can start planning its long-term future."

Scarlet shook her head, a grin covering her features. "You don't know what a relief that is. I was wondering if I was going to have to start supporting Milton FC, or worse, Cranbridge." She shivered. "This is the best news ever." Scarlet paused. "And just another way the flood has managed to be a positive influence on my life. Who knew that a load of shitty water would lead to such a turnaround? And I wouldn't have thought so when that police officer knocked on my door at four in the morning."

"Or when you turned up at my front door looking so forlorn."

A bashful look crossed Scarlet's face and Joy narrowed her eyes.

"What's that look for?"

Scarlet blushed, then shook her head. "It's nothing."

Joy lowered her head to one side. "Come on, Williams, out with it."

Scarlet began to laugh. "It's just… I never told you, but on the morning of the flood, I wasn't *actually* allocated to your house. I just overheard some people talking about it, and the thought of staying in the hall was too much to bear. So I thought I'd blag it, turn up anyway and hope you let me in." Scarlet grinned. "Worked out okay in the end, all things considered."

Joy let out a bark of laughter. "So our whole relationship is based on a lie?"

"Looks like it."

She smiled. "Who said honesty is the best policy? I'd say this is one lie I can live with." Joy paused. "Before you came along, I was just existing, not living. I was covering up the cracks in my life by running around being mayor and being the best businesswoman I could be. To tell you the truth, I was getting a bit scared about where I'd end up when my mayoral duties ran out. But now, I'm not so worried."

"I'm glad," Scarlet replied. "I'd say we've both come into each other's lives at the best possible moment, wouldn't you?"

"I would," Joy said, running a hand up and down Scarlet's thigh, thrilled she could do it in public as well as in the house. In public, it felt that little bit more daring. And when their eyes met, Joy knew Scarlet understood. She just did. It was something about them she'd known from the start. Scarlet and her were on the same wavelength, no explanation needed.

A woman behind them knocking over her glass of wine shook Joy out of her daydream, and she did a double-take, before taking a sip of her rum again and refocusing on Scarlet.

"And talking of Eamonn and Steph — we should invite them over. Our first dinner party as a couple and celebrate with them before they jet off to sunnier climes. What do you think?"

Scarlet gazed at Joy, her eyes filling up. "I'd love that," she said. "And I'd love to get Clark over, too — repay his hospitality from the other week."

"We can absolutely do that."

Scarlet sat up straight as she continued. "And I was also thinking, I might do a fundraiser for the flood fund — get some local celebs to come along and give things away, offer people experiences they can't buy. Raise a bit more money — what do you think?"

"I think that would be very noble and community-minded of you, but nothing more than I'd expect from you these days. I might start calling you Scarlet AF — After Flood."

Scarlet frowned. "I hate to tell you, but that's not very catchy."

Joy laughed. "You're not loving my ideas already? Is my allure wearing off?"

Scarlet kissed Joy on the lips. "On the contrary, I'd say I'm falling more and more under your spell every day."

Epilogue

Six Months Later

Nothing prepares you for the shock of losing everything you own — nothing at all. And Scarlet still had nightmares, waking up covered in sweat, but then the relief would wash over her like a cold breeze and she'd collapse back in the bed. And then turn to her girlfriend, her lover, her everything. And then she'd wonder: what had she done to deserve Joy?

Because, while nothing would ever prepare Scarlet for the shock of losing everything, nothing had prepared her for the shock of what her life had become. And since the flood, it'd filled up with love, riches beyond wealth, family, and friends. In fact, all of the things that, if another flood were to arrive that very night, it wouldn't touch.

She laughed as she dipped her paintbrush into the can to touch up the final wall in the living room, hearing Clark admonishing her for not stirring it properly first. ("Your colours will be all uneven!") Clark had been there every week after the flood, and had been a huge help getting the flat decorated over the last month, too. The kitchen, bathroom, and bedroom were done, and Clark had finished the hallway this week on his day off — he had a set of keys to her flat now, he'd been there so much.

Thinking about it all, Scarlet knew again one key fact: she'd got lucky. Lucky to have been flooded, lucky to have been a disaster victim, lucky to have had her life washed away, but then so miraculously resurrected. Five streets away, and she might still have been where she was this time last year. But the fates were having none of it, and she couldn't thank them enough.

Footsteps coming down the stairs startled her from her thoughts, and she looked up to see Eamonn, coffee and cakes fresh from Great Bakes in hand.

"Knock, knock," he said, stepping into her flat without waiting to be invited. He popped in every day, so an invite wasn't necessary. "Steph sent me round with these, with instructions to invite you and Joy for dinner on Saturday. Are you free?"

Scarlet nodded. "I think so, but let me check with the boss. Or you might be able to ask her yourself — she's due any minute."

"I won't stick around for that, don't want to get in the way of you two lovebirds."

Scarlet gave him a look, resting her brush on the lip of the can. "I think we're beyond that stage after six months."

"Not what I witnessed when I came round the other day." He covered his eyes. "Some things I can never unsee.

It's a good job she's not the mayor anymore, so I don't have to see her face in the local paper every week, reminding me."

Eamonn was referring to two weeks ago, when he'd come round to Joy's house on Sunday morning to pick up a ladder. Joy hadn't realised he was in the kitchen with Scarlet, and had walked in naked to tempt Scarlet back to bed. Scarlet wasn't sure who'd been more embarrassed: Eamonn, Joy, or her. Eamonn had even forgotten the ladder that morning, such was his haste, and had to return two hours later to get it, still red-faced.

"I'll leave these for you both, I have to get back to work anyway. But I'll see you tomorrow for the game?"

"You will," Scarlet replied. "Tell Steph thanks, and I'll text you on the dinner invite."

"Will do!" Eamonn shouted from the stairwell.

Five minutes later, more footsteps on the stairs signalled Joy's arrival, so Scarlet put down her paintbrush and took the lids off the coffee as her girlfriend appeared in the lounge.

Joy whistled when she saw the colour on the wall. "Very daring," she said, kissing Scarlet, before giving the lounge an appraisal. "I wasn't sure about the darker colour, but I think it might work."

"It better, because I really don't fancy doing this all over again."

Joy patted Scarlet's bum. "It's gonna look great." Her gaze fell on the goods on the counter. "Has a certain Irishman been visiting again?"

"He has. And when he heard you were turning up, he scarpered sharpish."

Joy laughed. "Jeez, is me naked that offensive? He's going to have to get over it. You'd think he'd never seen a naked woman before. I'm sure Steph doesn't look that much different to me."

"You know what men are like, big babies," Scarlet said. "Anyway, maybe we can have a compare and contrast evening next week when we go over there for dinner."

Joy laughed some more. "We can all gang up on Eamonn again. It'll be hilarious." She kissed Scarlet again. "But honestly, this is looking good, babe. You're doing a great job."

Scarlet looked around and had to agree, she was. The walls had taken three months to dry out, then they'd had to rebuild the walls and floors, doors, and skirtings. Now she was at the final hurdle: decorating. She had a ton of donated furniture in storage at Grasspoint waiting to be moved in next week, and then it'd be home sweet home again. Well, a home for someone, at the very least: Joy and her hadn't really addressed the issue as yet.

Joy held up a present bag. "I bought you a gift, too. For your new place."

"You didn't need to buy me a gift, you wally."

"I did," Joy said. "Open it."

Scarlet reached into the bag and pulled out a bottle of Glendronach, along with two crystal tumblers. Her heart almost burst with love.

"You remembered."

"I promised you I'd bring you these, and I don't like to break my promises."

"They're beautiful, thank you." Scarlet leaned over and kissed Joy. "I've come a long way since I was sitting on your sofa sobbing about my whisky glasses, haven't I?"

Joy nodded. "You have. And maybe we can try them out next week when we've got something to sit on."

"I would love that." Scarlet paused. "Are you coming to the game tomorrow, too?"

"Of course, I wouldn't miss it for the world. First game back in the sparkly new stadium, no true fan would miss that."

Scarlet smirked, pulling Joy towards her. "And you're a true fan now, are you? Seven games is all it takes?"

Joy nodded. "It's not the length of time, it's the quality of support. It's like being a lesbian: I'm fully invested. Besides, like I told you, matches are a good anthropological experiment, watching football tribes in their raw state. Interesting from a psychological perspective, too."

Scarlet wound her arms around Joy's waist, their faces now just centimetres apart. "Promise me one thing?"

"What?"

"Never say anything like that in front of Eamonn or Matt, I'd never hear the end of it."

Joy laughed. "I promise."

* * *

"I cannot believe your brother gave you his old car — it's so incredibly kind. I can never imagine my brother doing the same." Joy was sat on Scarlet's new-to-her sofa, in her freshly painted lounge. The flat was shaping up nicely, and today they'd taken delivery of a bed, sofa, wardrobe, and dining table. They'd also taken a trip to Ikea in Clark's old car — now Scarlet's — to buy kitchen and bathroom essentials, and the flat was now somewhere Scarlet could live again, officially.

And while Joy was thrilled with that for her sake, it was also tinged with sadness. She'd waited so long to find Scarlet, she didn't want to be without her now.

"I know, he's so giving. I'm so pleased he's back in my life. And Fred is flying over next month, too, and I can't wait to meet my niece. She's going to be one spoilt baby."

Joy relaxed back onto the sofa, springing up and down. "This is not half bad, you know, for a hand-me-down."

"It's more comfortable than the one I had before, that's all I know."

"Result," Joy said. "Talking of families flying in, my parents are here next month as well, so we're going to be overloaded with guests. You ready to meet them?"

"I am — I can't wait. Your gran has told me so many stories, though, I'm going to have to be careful not to blurt them all out."

"She's a terror, that woman."

"A marvellous terror," Scarlet replied, putting an arm

around Joy. "You fancy a whisky in my new glasses to toast the flat?"

"I would love that."

Scarlet grabbed the single malt from the kitchen, along with the glasses, stopping to admire her new units on the way. "You know, I'm actually happier with the new kitchen than I was with the old one. It's a bit like my life, isn't it?" she said, handing Joy her glass of whisky.

"It is," Joy replied. She glanced at Scarlet as she sipped her drink, then put it down on the brand new beige carpet. "And have you thought about what you might do with the flat now it's done? Are you moving back in?"

Scarlet put down her drink too, then turned to Joy. "I was thinking about that when I was painting it this week. I know we kinda talked about it, but we didn't come to any hard conclusion."

Joy nodded, her heart racing. "I know." She didn't want Scarlet to move out, but she also knew she had to let her come to the decision on her own, no pressure. But that wasn't easy at all, when what she *wanted* to do was throw herself on the floor and wail at the injustice of Scarlet's flat being ready to live in again. No, Joy had to keep calm, measured. She was normally pretty good at that, but apparently not when it came to Scarlet.

"I was painting the walls, and thinking about the colours I'd chosen, and the furniture that was coming," Scarlet began, glancing at Joy, pulling her mouth one way, then the other. "But when I tried to picture myself here, I drew a blank: a complete blank. It's almost like this isn't my home anymore. I don't belong here."

Scarlet took Joy's hand in hers, and kissed it. "I guess what I'm trying to say is, would it be okay if I didn't move out from yours?" She paused, her cheeks flushing red. Then she cleared her throat and put her focus back on Joy. "Because I don't want to. Because I love you. And because it just doesn't feel right being here anymore. I belong with you, not here."

Joy's mouth turned upwards as she heard the words fall from Scarlet's mouth — a love letter just to her. These were the words she'd been waiting to hear for *such* a long time. Not pushing Scarlet to reveal her feelings had been so hard, but now she was glad she'd done it, because hearing Scarlet say this of her own accord meant so much more.

Joy had been pretty sure Scarlet loved her: she acted as though she did in day to day life, and she'd got better at revealing her feelings, but she still wasn't comfortable with it like Joy.

But telling Joy she loved her? That was a huge step. So as well as being thrilled, Joy also felt proud.

Joy took Scarlet's face in her hands and kissed her lips, hoping she was conveying everything she was feeling in that single kiss.

Scarlet loved her. And she loved Scarlet.

It really had been as simple as that all along.

"Oh sweetheart, I belong with you, too. And I don't

want you to move out, either." She paused. "I love you, too, you must know that."

Scarlet nodded, a weird noise escaping her lips. "I hoped so," she croaked. "I had my fingers and toes crossed."

Joy let out a strangled laugh. "Well, I do. And I don't want you to move out."

Scarlet grinned. "Good," she said, exhaling. "I was thinking I might rent it out for a bit, as I don't think anyone's going to want to buy it at the moment. Not after everything."

"Good call." Joy's breathing was all over the place: Scarlet's announcement had floored her. "And you really love me?"

Scarlet trailed a thumb down Joy's cheek, nodding her head. "I really do. I'm sorry I haven't said it before, but I plan on saying it again quite a lot in our future. It might just take a little while for me to get used to it, okay? Love and me don't have a good track record."

Joy smiled. "Okay." She paused. "You know what this means though, don't you?"

Scarlet shook her head. "Tell me."

"It means your whisky and whisky glasses are going to have to come and live with mine."

Scarlet smiled. "Not such a hardship. I'm sure they could get used to living at yours."

Joy shook her head. "It's not mine, it's ours. Our place, okay?"

Scarlet nodded her head. "Give me a few months, I might learn to start saying it. No promises, though."

"No promises?"

"Only to keep loving you."

"I like the sound of that," Joy replied.

THE END

Are you sad? Do you not want this to be the end? It doesn't have to be! Sign up to my mailing list to get a free bonus chapter & find out what happened when Joy & Scarlet got home after the wedding. On top of that, there are three other bonuses, too!

HEAD HERE NOW & SIGN UP: www.clarelydon.co.uk/ newsletter-sign-up

A Note From Clare

I wrote this book after reading the story of one man's plight following the devastating 2015 floods in northern England. I decided to use it as a premise for my own tale of love and redemption, and it was an emotional book to write - I hope that came over in the storytelling. I did wonder if releasing this book in the summer was the right thing, but it turns out flooding is getting worryingly more common, and in the week I published, London and the south-east had flash floods. In June. Welcome to global warming!

I hope you enjoyed this book, and if you did, I would love it if you told your friends and shared it on social media. Better yet, buy them a copy for their birthday!

And please let me know what you liked the most - you can get in touch via social media or email, details below.

Twitter: @clarelydon
Facebook: www.facebook.com/clare.lydon
Instagram: @clarefic
Find out more at : www.clarelydon.co.uk
Email: mail@clarelydon.co.uk

AND FINALLY, THANK YOU FOR READING!

Also by Clare Lydon

The London Series

London Calling (Book 1)

This London Love (Book 2)

The All I Want Series

All I Want For Christmas (Book 1)

All I Want For Valentine's (Book 2)

All I Want For Spring (Book 3)

All I Want Series Boxset, Books 1-3

Other novels

The Long Weekend

Coming in 2016

All I Want For Summer (July)

All I Want For Autumn (October)

New book in the **London** Series

8235031R00180

Printed in Germany
by Amazon Distribution
GmbH, Leipzig